Praise for THE BEATLES COME TOGETHER AGAIN

"*The Beatles Come Together Again* is a John Lennon Double Fantasy. Every fan's ultimate wish: He lives AND They Play! A well-written and realistic read."

— Joe Johnson, Host of Beatle Brunch

"A delicious piece of fan fiction from a true Beatles fan. What if John had not died? More music, tours, MTV Unplugged (if only!) Ed David delivers a wish list complete with fictional album listings and chart listings to get us all to play along. Real life rock stars and celebrities all play a role as well in the Fab Four's reunion, sometimes romantically — surprise! *The Beatles Come Together Again* will have you reaching for your albums to relive it all."

— Anne Carlini, Rock D.J.

"I genuinely like this book and got a little choked up at the ending, which was beautifully done. Not only does this book fulfill our desire to see Lennon's life play out, and our fantasy of The Beatles getting back together, the character development is exceptional. It's like getting together with friends whom you haven't seen in 20 years and getting to know them in a meaningful way all over again."

— David Aretha, editor of *The Beatles: Fifty Fabulous Years*

"A delightful dive into what should have been. This imaginative story comes complete with set lists, venues, and new songs! I find myself drawn into the dynamics of the Fab Four and rooting for their comeback success. The only bittersweet moment is found when the last page is turned, and you realize that it can never be ... So I will read it again just to take the journey once more. A wonderful read capable of transporting you to an amazing place where John, Paul, George and Ringo take center stage, right where they belong."

— Dawn Prior, Band Agent

"The story is entertaining with the familiar cast of characters in action. It's the Beatles as you would have liked it to be!"

— John Christy, bassist and lifelong Beatles fan

"*The Beatles Come Together Again* is an uplifting, albeit fictional, reminiscence of times during our joyful and overall carefree years. It is a great read and an excellent reminder of what used to be for which we can now only imagine."

— David Kouri, Music Enthusiast

THE BEATLES COME TOGETHER AGAIN

THE BEATLES COME TOGETHER AGAIN

A NOVEL

ED DAVID

Published by Deja View Press

ISBN (paperback): 978-1-7356946-0-3
ISBN (e-book): 978-1-7356946-1-0

Cover and interior design: Christy Collins, Constellation Book Services

Author photograph: Scott Scala, Scala Photography

Printed in the United States of America

I dedicate this book to my three children
— Eddie, Josh and Alexa.
You are my world.

Acknowledgments

First, I want to thank my kids, Eddie, Josh and Alexa, for their love and support and for inspiring me to be the best I can be at all times. I also want to thank them for their input to some of my stories as I bounced ideas off of them (they actually spared Paul's life in the book!) Thank you to my mom and dad, who were the epitome of loving parents. I was lucky to have their unconditional love and support. Also, thank you to them for enduring my countless hours of guitar practicing while still supporting my playing.

Thank you to my sisters (Judy, Vicki and Sharon), my nephew, Chris (and his daughter, Mallory and son, Adam), and nieces, Nikki (and her sons Zach and Shaun) and Natalie for their assistance in brainstorming for the book title. It was Judy's suggestion that made the final cut! Also, thanks to my elder sisters for bringing home The Beatles' records that rocked me to the core. If it were not for them, I probably wouldn't have been sitting on the floor as a two year old watching The Beatles on The Ed Sullivan Show.

When I was seven years old, two of my cousins were in a local band named Ellie Pop and their LP was played at my home on a regular rotation along with The Beatles' LPs. At that young age, I could not tell the difference between the two bands. To this day, I can hear the influence The Beatles had on my cousins' band.

I need to thank my cousin, George David, who gave me my first guitar when I was eleven years old. It was a Teisco electric and he warned me that if I didn't learn how to play, he would take it back. The terror of him taking back the guitar I had pestered him about for years forced me to learn Smoke on the Water (as most young guitarists of my time would learn first.) Thank you, cousin!

Thank you to David Kouri for his support, his great review and for allowing me to use that review as a Foreword to the book. Much love.

Thank you to my copy editor for being so good at his job. Thank you to Martha Bullen from Bullen Publishing Services for her assistance throughout the entire publication process. Her experience, knowledge and guidance helped me more than I could have ever imagined. I'd also like to thank Martha's husband, Martin, for offering assistance along the way. His input for the book title and cover design helped immensely.

Thank you to Christy Collins at Constellation Book Services for the wonderful cover design; Jeremy Avenarius at Real Avenue Designs for the awesome websites; and Scott Scala from Scala Photography for my author photos.

I'd like to send a big thank you to Joe Johnson, host of the Beatle Brunch program for giving his endorsement and being an overall cool guy.

Thanks to David Aretha, Anne Carlini, John Christy and Dawn Prior for reading the book and giving it fabulous endorsements.

To all the musicians along the way that I jammed with or watched from afar, thank you for helping mold my musical tastes and for inspiring me to keep trying to get better.

In loving memory of cousins Nick and Gary. Two nicer men I have not met, and they are dearly missed.

Foreword

Imagine. Imagine what our lives would have been like over recent years having the world's most famous and influential band continuing to produce music and perform. *The Beatles Come Together Again* book resurrects the excitement and reliving of youth for so many!

Imagine reading about the intricate details of the Fab Four's personalities and relationships. This novel brings one to have a closer relationship to how they worked and played together. While listening to my Beatles playlist or music station now, I have a renewed excitement for their music and wonder about the song's background story and imagine how it was written and produced.

There were plenty of other surprises with the addition of other musical super stars within the storyline. The reader gets caught up in the excitement of The Beatles performances and recording sessions through the author's detailed descriptions of events. The story described the challenges and stresses that came with stardom. I empathized with the toll it must have taken on the personal lives and family relationships of these talented musicians.

The Beatles Come Together Again is an uplifting, albeit fictional, reminiscence of times during our joyful and overall carefree years. It is a great read and an excellent reminder of what used to be for which we can now only imagine.

— David Kouri, Music Enthusiast

Preface

In this alternate reality novel, John Lennon lives after being shot in New York. The Beatles embark on their second journey as a band and make music history ... again.

On May 27, 2019, I took my two sons (fourteen and twelve, at the time) to see Paul McCartney at the PNC Arena in Raleigh, North Carolina. The show was phenomenal! He played for three hours! Even musicians much younger struggle to play that long each night. I had previously seen Sir Paul two other times, but what struck me this time was his candidness and warmth I felt through his interactions with the audience.

One particular moment resounded with me. Before his version of "Being for the Benefit of Mr. Kite," he made a comment I had never heard him mention. He stated that while he had very few regrets in life, the one true regret he felt was never telling John Lennon that he loved him. It was a memorable moment in the show, as McCartney became emotional. He went on to say that this was something they never thought to say during those times, especially because they both had grown up on the tough streets of Liverpool.

This story made me wonder "What if John had lived?" So, that was the driving force that inspired me to write *The Beatles Come Together Again*.

What if John Lennon had not died? What if the Beatles reunited to make more music? What if their legacy didn't end in 1970? This is the story of what might have happened if that were the case.

Chapter 1

December 8, 1980—It was cold and rainy on that dreary December night in New York City. A mist was in the air as the rain occasionally gave way to the evening clouds. The Dakota Apartments were draped in the folds of the gloomy New York night, as travelers and residents scurried along the outskirts of Central Park. The streetlights that shone onto the park were glazed with a halo of fog as they struggled to provide adequate security.

A small crowd gathered outside of the Dakota apartments that night, hoping for a glimpse...maybe even more...from the most decorated Beatle. It was nearing 11 p.m. as the limo carrying John Lennon and his wife, Yoko Ono, pulled up. The doors opened and out came John, who began to walk briskly through the mist to the apartments. Yoko soon followed. *Pop! Pop! Pop!* The noise from the .38 caliber pistol was almost deafening as the bullets entered John's body. At that moment, an autograph seeker threw his body on top of the shooter to try to stop the massacre. John lay face down on the ground as apartment employees rushed out onto 72nd Avenue to assist. All hell had broken loose. The attacker had been subdued by the courageous bystander and was now being swarmed by others who had witnessed the shooting.

As he was being whisked away toward the front doors of the apartments, Jose Perdomo, the Dakota doorman, said to John, "Mr. Lennon, can you talk to me?" John was unresponsive. The police arrived before an ambulance and the officers immediately recognized the severity of the wounds. One officer, James Moran, requested assistance to help get the victim into the patrol unit to transfer him to the emergency room at Roosevelt Hospital. A frantic Yoko threw herself into the police car to be with her husband. On the way, another officer, Peter Cullen, cared for John and tried to contain the wounds. It was seemingly impossible for Cullen to stop the bleeding, but he continued to apply pressure to the wounds with the towels provided by Perdomo prior to departure for the emergency room. When they arrived at the hospital, some seven minutes later, John was rushed into the operating room, where they immediately began resuscitation procedures. Three doctors and five nurses presided over the victim for the next four hours of surgery.

Finally, at 2:37 a.m. Eastern standard time, Dr. Stephan Lynn entered the hospital waiting room to inform Yoko of the news. "Mrs. Lennon," Lynn began, "John is in serious condition, but he's going to make it."

Yoko burst into tears as Elliot Mintz was there to hold and comfort her. Lynn continued, "Three bullets hit John. One in the shoulder, one entered his back and then exited the stomach area, and one right at the top of his left leg. The bullet that pierced John's leg took part of the bone. They are trying to save his leg as we speak." Yoko was hysterical. The thought of her husband losing a leg and/or the possibility of him never walking again was overwhelming.

That night, during a *Monday Night Football* telecast on ABC, Howard Cosell had announced to the viewers that "John Lennon has been shot!" Word spread like wildfire as the entire music world waited with bated breath about the condition of their beloved Beatle. Most of America had heard this news prior to going to bed that night. As the news spread, rumors quickly began that Lennon had died and there were already seeds of a cover-up. There was hope he would live, but no one knew except Lennon's close circle of family and friends.

The next days and weeks were blanketed with newspaper and television stories of how the famous John Lennon had barely been spared his life at the hands of a crazed individual. The other three Beatles were seen entering and exiting the hospital, but none would speak to the press. It became apparent that they had taken this extremely hard. They knew this could have happened to any of them throughout their illustrious careers.

December 24, 1980—Christmas in 1980 was approaching fast. Snow had fallen again for the third time this week, blanketing the vehicles on Broadway. Christmas Eve and the weather didn't stop the throng of people who descended on Roosevelt Hospital. Yoko, son Sean Lennon, and Elliot Mintz appeared in front of the blinding lights of the dozens of photographers, reporters from all over the world, and almost a hundred spectators. Yoko looked tired and pale dressed in her black suit with a black beret hat.

Networks all over America and Britain wanted to be part of this news conference. Yoko started off by saying, "Thank you all for your kind support and prayers during this difficult time. I spoke with John just a few minutes ago and he wanted me to pass along his sincere gratitude for all of the well-wishes. He is in good spirits and wants everyone to know he is doing fine. Again, thank you from us all." Yoko paused, looked over at Mintz, and said, "I think Elliot now has something to say."

The thirty-five-year-old Elliot Mintz was not much taller than Yoko. He was handsome, dressed in a light grey suit, clean shaven with no single hair on his head out of place. Mintz approached the many microphones and calmly said, "Good afternoon. First, we want to say we are devastated at what has happened to John. As Yoko said, thank you for the outpouring of support and kindness we've received in the past two weeks. This has been very difficult for all of us who care about John. Our hopes are that he will return to a normal life within a short period of time. We do want to ask of you to please allow John and Yoko some time and space to continue to work through all of this. From what we've heard, there will be a lengthy recovery period with some physical therapy to help regain strength. We want to thank everyone and we hope to meet again under better circumstances."

There was a spattering of applause from the spectators and newspeople in the room, and with that, the news conference ended. But not before the reporters began yelling questions:

"Are John's injuries life-threatening?"

"Word is going around that he'll never walk again. Is that true?"

"Will the Beatles get back together now after John's brush with death?"

Every reporter in the room knew this was a huge news story but respected the family during this difficult time. So the Lennons would be left alone during the long recovery process.

Just before they exited the room, Elliot turned to the group of reporters and spectators to say, "Oh, we would also like to thank Mike Sampson. He was the gentleman who tried to stop this shooting and prevented the shooter from further damage to John. We all want to thank him for that!" They then disappeared into the cold, Christmas Eve night.

January 12, 1981—John Lennon left Roosevelt Hospital as a crowd gathered once again to get pictures, maybe an autograph or even a glimpse of the music icon. John was escorted out of the hospital by a nurse, Yoko, and Sean. The limo swallowed up the Lennons and swooped them off toward their destination—The Dakota...where the tragedy had unfolded more than a month earlier. Inside the limo, John immediately turned on the radio, seeking something upbeat to mirror the unbridled joy he had felt that moment to be able to walk (or...more or less, limp) out of the hospital. It was a new chapter to his life, and while the trepidation of having to still recuperate and face the daily challenges of recovery was daunting, he was alive and internally acknowledged his brush with death.

The classic rock station John decided upon was in the first verse of "Bye, Bye Love" by the Everly Brothers. "How fitting!" thought John as the limo gradually made its way toward The Dakota. "You know, Mother, these were the two guys Paul and I tried to be most like," John said to Yoko as she seemed to daydream out of the tinted limo window. It was a sunny day, cold and crisp, with the sort of winter freshness that would soon give way to the blossoming scents of spring. Sensing an uneasiness in his spouse, John leaned over and asked, "What is it, Mother? You have a look about you."

Sean had been fidgeting constantly, as would most five-year-olds in the back of a luxurious limousine. "John, David Geffen called and said they were dropping you from their label. He said that this decision had been made even before the shooting happened." Yoko expected her husband's temper to surface after this news but was pleasantly surprised at the chuckle she received instead.

"David never was that bright, was he?" John calmly replied.

"I think he is looking for younger acts; newer and more poppy music," said Yoko.

"Well, he's lost his fucking mind. *Double Fantasy* went to number one on the charts! If he thinks he'll find that from his lot of poor sods, he is sadly mistaken."

John's life had definitely taken a turn, in both good and bad ways. He no longer felt the safety that had once accompanied him throughout his frequent walks and many escapades he had undertaken in the heart of this town that never slept. But he also felt a renewed sense of being and an awareness that sometimes is only gained through an incident that brings one so close to death. That is one thing he was certain of—he had cheated death and was as mortal as his paralegal neighbor or the mailman he had befriended over the years. He may have been more popular than the average being, but he now realized the fragility that life boldly displayed.

April 29, 1981—The Lennons had been planning this move for months, but it still didn't feel right. John knew that leaving New York City for London would be running away from one danger right into the arms of another. London was equally as large and dangerous as NYC, but John and Yoko believed the move was going to benefit Sean as they were eager to explore a better world for their young son.

News of their imminent move made its way around the world, and sure enough, reporters and fans gathered again outside of the now famous Dakota Apartments. The moving trucks had gotten there at 7:30 a.m. and the movers were almost finished loading. It was now early afternoon and the Lennons would only be seen momentarily as they were shuffled into their limousine. The always outgoing John asked the limo driver to stop just past the scrum of reporters. He wanted to say a few words to the small group of fans who had been pushed back by the story-hungry reporters. He rolled down the window to sing, *"If I can make it here, I'll make it anywhere...."* The fans cheered and laughed. John then said, "I love New York City and always will! I'll miss all of you and will see you on the flip side!" He waved as he rolled the window up. Yoko seemed to enjoy their last moment in this city while looking forward to what their future might bring in London. The limo scurried away and the Lennons were officially out of NYC.

Chapter 2

August 4, 1981—Having been out of the public view for quite some time, John decided to succumb to the persistent phone calls he had received from *The David Frost Show*. So, on this date, close to eight months after his brush with death, John appeared in the homes of every viewer in the metropolitan London area. As John limped out onto the studio set arm in arm with Yoko, the crowd stood in an uproar of applause. Even David Frost refused to sit for almost a minute after John had. John looked slight and somewhat pale. But besides the limp, he looked relatively healthy. When the crowd finally cooled to a grumbling simmer, David started.

"John, how are you, my friend?" It was impossible to contain the swelling excitement from the audience as they cheered not only each response from Lennon, but every question from Frost.

"I'm just peachy, Dan," he replied with typical Lennon sarcasm.

David chuckled and continued. "So, what is new in your life? How is the family?"

"Oh, we're wooberful," announced John. "We had a close one, didn't we?"

"I'd say so!" responded David.

The interview lasted twenty-five minutes as John spoke on topics from gun control to mental health and even touched on football (English soccer). When asked about the other Beatles, John replied, "Oh they're all great, ya know. They came 'round quite often during my recovery."

"So...any chance you might record with them again?" the host cautiously coerced.

"Haha...well, there aren't plans, Dave, but if there are, you'll be the first to know!"

As David profusely thanked John and Yoko for this exclusive interview, John stood, did a little dance, and waved goodbye as he and Yoko exited the studio stage. The excitement in the crowd was electric and would carry onto the streets of Walton Avenue even after the show ended.

May 14, 1982—Almost a year and a half had passed since the Dakota incident, and John had been completely out of sight to the public. He felt quite uncomfortable in their new apartment in Soho. The lighting was poor, and the noises of the busy street could be heard clearly and regularly throughout each night. There wasn't the "warmth" he had so treasured when living at The Dakota. He decided to have the whole place remodeled (in typical Lennon fashion, without the consent of apartment managers). The newly painted bright white living room was adorned with paintings, personal sketches, and two large pictures of Sean. The white piano John had used in his "Imagine" video was the heart piece of this grand room. John now found himself drawn yet again to those ivories. He sat up straight and tall on the piano bench on that spring morning.

Blang! Bing! Bloon! His hands fell upon the keys, automatically striking a C chord directly into an F chord. John smiled as the chords were the same as the ones from his masterpiece, "Imagine." He finally felt, for the first time since he'd started work on *Double Fantasy*, that it was now time to purge the backlog of melodies and words that had been floating through the inner depths of his mind.

Writing music had been the last thing on his mind, as the incident had not only taken a physical toll but had also left him emotionally disconnected. It was as though the idea of being in the same position of fame would come back to haunt him once again. On this morning, something was different. Was it that he had finally come to terms with what had transpired on that December night in New York? Or was it the positive vibe he felt in his new locale that also used to be his old stomping grounds? Or maybe it was that he felt a certain responsibility to Sean to lead by example and clear the ghosts crowding his mental closet?

Whatever the reason, chords started flowing. Lyrics that had been bouncing around in his dreams were now being put to paper. C—C—C—F—G... *"How can I prepare for what I've yet to understand?..."* The lyrics to a song he had haphazardly named "Fly Away" began appearing before him as if he had no control over what was being written. Within twenty minutes, the song was complete. John hadn't noticed that Yoko was lying on the white couch close by the whole time. She didn't say a word; she just smiled at John with approval. She knew this was a huge moment, not only for him, but possibly the music world.

Riiiing, riiing, ring.... "Hello," said Paul McCartney as he picked up the wall phone in his kitchen.

"What are you doing?" said the familiar voice on the other end.

"John?" asked Paul.

"Yeah, it's me, ya turd. What'cha doing?" he reiterated.

Paul hesitated a moment as he was not certain what his ex-partner's motives were to contact him this morning. "Well, I just returned from holiday with Linder and the kids." There was another slight pause.

"Can you get over here?" asked John.

"Is everything okay, John? I can drop what I'm doing and be there in an hour if you need."

"Settle the fuck down now!" said John. "Everything is fine. I just have some ideas I want to talk with you about."

"Okay, mate. Be there before noon."

After they hung up, a big smile came to Paul's face. He had an overwhelming sensation that they were about to make history once again. He sat back and felt his heart pounding...hard. He felt as though it would burst through his chest from the excitement.

When Paul arrived at John's London flat, John was in his robe and slippers, sipping tea.

"Like some tea, mate?"

"Sure!" Paul said with an extra bounce in his voice.

"I've written something I want you to hear."

As Paul sat back and sipped his tea, his eyes grew as wide as saucers at the opening chords, and the first verse to John's new song, "Given to Fly." Like in the old days when John would bring a song to Paul, he was chomping at the bit to get his hands on it and add one of his signature bass melodies to it. The song started off a bit melancholy but slowly evolved into a rocker...the type of song that defined Lennon's style while with the most famous group to ever grace this planet. Paul could not contain himself any longer and almost blurted out, "Let's call George and Ringo!" Instead, he internally composed himself and told John, "That is absolutely wonderful!" As always, John was seeking Paul's approval without really letting on that this was the case.

John replied, "You like it, do ya?"

"I think it reminds me of a mix of 'Strawberry Fields' and 'Imagine.' And yes, I think it's great. What's it called?"

"Given to Fly" was his response.

So many questions had now been almost bursting out of Paul's mouth, but again, he gathered his thoughts to say, "Is this something you'd like to record?"

"Yeah, I was thinking you and I could sneak down to the studio to see if we can make this thing a song." Paul knew how volatile it would be at this point to bring up a Beatles reunion, so instead he happily agreed to lend a hand in any way he could.

There were some definite hurdles that had to be cleared prior to going to the studio. As the two discussed the plan, they first called old friend and engineer Geoff Emerick.

"Hello?" answered Geoff as he picked up his phone.

"Geoff, old buddy! How's it going, mate?"

Their time apart had taken the Beatles off his radar, so Geoff was not certain of the voice on the other end.

"Who is this, please?" said Geoff.

"It's me, John, ya goof!"

"John Lennon?!"

"No, John Coltrane, you silly sod. Yes, it's Lennon."

Emerick's heart sank to his stomach. *What could he want? Does he want me to gather some old material for his listening pleasure again? Was he going to go on one of his famous tirades if I didn't respond to him correctly?*

"Oh, hey John, how are you doing? It's been years and I was devastated, like us all, to hear about what happened in New York. Are you doing better now?"

"Yeah, yeah, yeah...that's not why I called. I've got a song that I want to record, and I need an engineer. Do you know any?" he said, tongue firmly planted in cheek. At least Lennon hadn't lost his sense of humor.

"I might be able to find one. Hold on. Yeah, I've got one right here for you!"

"Good! Where can we record?"

"Well, I've been working with CBS Records and they have a really nice studio that was built last year and has state-of-the art equipment," replied Geoff.

"Perfect. Get us in," John told him.

"Okay, let me make a call and schedule it. Would next week work for you?"

"No mate. It has to be today...actually now!"

"What?" replied the shaky voice on the other end.

"Hey, Geoff, it's Paul!" said Paul as he grabbed the phone from Lennon.

"Paul? What the hell are you doing there?" said Emerick. He knew the Fab Two better than anyone in the business besides George Martin. He had a wonderful relationship with Paul, who was always kind, supportive, and open to any suggestion Geoff might make. John, on the other hand, was a loose cannon in his eyes—one minute as charming a fellow as one could meet, and the next, a raving lunatic ready to verbally bash anyone who happened to be in his line of fire. But the mere sound of Paul's voice put Geoff at ease. He knew that if Paul was involved, Lennon would most likely stay in line. McCartney had that effect on him. John would push the buttons of every individual that would succumb to his fury, but Paul would not allow certain buttons to be pushed.

Then Geoff's mind swirled around again to what this could possibly mean. He had been the engineer on some of the Beatles' most popular albums—*Revolver*, *Sgt. Pepper*, and *Abbey Road*. So, he knew how to carve a great sound and how to please these two sometimes difficult chaps. He kept thinking that if John and Paul were to record a new song, possibly a new album, that this would be history in the making.

"I'm just visiting. But we're really excited about this new song and want to track it."

"I'll make a call and call you right back," replied the excited Emerick.

"Oh, and Geoff, I think you know not to let on to the studio folks exactly who is coming in to record, right?"

"You got it, Paul," and they hung up.

Ten minutes later, the white, Georgian-style phone in Lennon's living room rang. "Yeah?" asked John.

"Hey, it's Geoff. I called down to CBS Records and the studio manager said they were booked solid today and that nothing could be done. But after some intense persuasion, I got him to free up Studio 2 for the afternoon."

"Great! Thank you, my honorary brother! We'll see you at 2 p.m."

This day in May was relatively warm, almost unusually so. It was overcast and the threat of rain emanated from above as John and Paul arrived at the studio just after 2. Geoff had informed them where they could sneak into the back of the studio without notice.

As Paul drove them toward the back lot, they noticed some people having a smoke outside the back of the studio. "Musicians!" exclaimed John, almost annoyed.

"We'll park over on the side and wait there," said Paul as he perused the area.

They sat in wait for only a few minutes when they saw Geoff Emerick appear from the back door. They watched as Emerick said a few words to the smokers and off the group went back into the studio. Geoff had noticed John and Paul in their car and waved them in.

"Here we go!" said John. They jumped out of the vehicle and scurried (with John limping) into the studio back door.

Upon entering, they heard the thumping sound of bass and drums reverberating from Studio 4 (which luckily was the only studio they needed to pass on their way to Studio 2). They felt relieved that it appeared no one had seen them enter the studio. Studio 2 was reminiscent of the layout of the Abbey Road studios. It seemed that Geoff knew it had a similar feel and had most likely requested this particular studio. In they walked, and they were immediately greeted with a big smile from a big man.

"Hello mates!" exclaimed Mal Evans. He then hugged both as if they had mystical powers he could somehow transfer to himself.

"Hey Mal!" said Paul.

"It's been way too long," said Mal.

"Malcolm, I know we would all like to sit and chat, but we want to get right at it. Will you get our gear out of Paul's car and set it up for us, please?" Mal was stunned. He didn't think he had ever heard the word "please" out of John Lennon's mouth.

Mal whisked away to grab John's Gretsch 6120 guitar and Paul's famous Hofner 500/1 violin-shaped bass. After a few minutes, the gear was set, and Geoff took control of the soundboard. John went directly to the baby grand piano that had adorned the studio floor. Paul picked up his bass and played some warmup bass lines. But then he put the bass down.

"Maybe I should put down a basic drum beat while you play it through," said Paul.

"Yeah, that'll work," exclaimed John. Finally, after almost thirteen years of hiatus, Lennon and McCartney were again recording! This was the moment every Beatles fan had been waiting for since they'd split in 1970.

Nine takes in and they were satisfied with the basic track. Geoff added some reverb to Lennon's vocals and then made some suggestions to Paul as to how he wanted to record the bass. Typically, at this point, guitars would be added, but John needed a break. He was emotionally drained. On one hand, it felt good to record again. On the other, it brought back memories of that dreadful December night in New York. So he stepped out of the studio with Mal to grab some food. He had put on somewhat of a disguise with a ball cap, a long overcoat, and sunglasses. He was certain some of the musicians standing in the hall recognized him as he limped passed.

Geoff told Paul he wanted the bass amp placed in the coat closet. He then closed the closet door and put a microphone right on it. Paul had been thinking of a bass line for the song from the minute he heard the first notes. He placed the cans (headphones in studio jargon) over his ears and went at it. Knowing how Paul was the ultimate perfectionist, Geoff sat back and expected this to be a long afternoon. On the first take, Paul played one of the most incredible bass lines the engineer had ever heard come out of the former Beatle. But Paul was not satisfied. He was also not pleased with takes two through seven (even though Emerick was amazed at each attempt). Finally, take eight was the one.

One hour into what the engineer had thought would take all day, it was complete. Paul entered the control room to give it a good listen on the massive studio speakers. Slowly, a smile grew upon McCartney's face. He knew he had nailed it. Emerick was bursting at the seams and said, "Paul, do you realize what we just accomplished?" Paul nodded with reserved approval. The bassist's mind was racing around what should happen next. Obviously, they needed to add a guitar and harmony vocals. But he had other questions:

Could this lead to a Beatles reunion?

Would we record an entire album?

What about touring?

Should we do a television show?

What will George say if we ask him to play? He hated this band at the end.

But wait. What does John really want to do with this? That was the first order of business, after recording the guitars and harmony vocals.

Mal and John returned with some leftover fish and chips from the restaurant down the street and offered it to Paul. "No, thanks. Do you want to hear what we've got so far?" Paul asked.

"Yeah, roll it," John said.

The song definitely sounded like a Beatles song.

"We should call the general," said John.

"Do you really want that?" Paul asked.

"Yeah, but I don't want this overproduced. No *Abbey Road* shit. And no Montovani rubbish, either!" stated John.

With that, John made the call to George Martin. Judy Martin answered the phone with her warm, welcoming tone. "Hello Judy, it's John Lennon. How are you?"

"Oh, hello, John! How are you feeling? We were so worried for you," she said.

"Well, I'm doin' much better now, love. Is George available to talk?"

"He's not here at the moment but should return within the hour. Shall I have him phone you?"

"Yes, please. We're at the CBS Records studios. But please don't let out word of this call, okay?"

"I will absolutely not say a word. I'll have George call when he arrives. It's so nice to hear your voice, John!"

By the time George called back an hour and a half later, John had laid the guitar tracks and they had started working on harmony vocals. "Hello, this is Pizza Express. How may I help you?" chuckled John.

"Is this John?" asked Martin.

"Of course, mate. How's it going with ya?" he asked.

"John! It's great to hear your voice! Thank God you were not more seriously injured in that tragic incident. What is on your mind, John?" George asked.

"Well, I'm down here in the studio with Paul" (as Paul yelled out over the back of John's head, "Hey, George!").

"Is that so? What prompted this reunion with your former mate? And what can I do for you?"

"Well, let's not get into what bit my arse to get down here, but we just recorded a new song."

Martin was stunned—and speechless. He had witnessed the ultimate highs and the absolute misery with these lads.

"I'd like your input, if yer don't mind."

"But John," George interrupted, "I'm still on contract with EMI. I'm not certain they would be pleased to hear I'm working with their competition."

"George, you have pull and you know how to use it. Please do what you can. We're in Studio 2 and will be here all night," pleaded John.

It was 11 p.m. when George Martin arrived in the studio. He was happily surprised to see John and Paul again, but he was absolutely over the moon that they had recruited Geoff Emerick. Geoff was so easy to work with, thought George. They had worked together so well in the past that he was not only pleased, he was excited at the prospect of working with him again. George settled in and listened to the track they had recorded. John and Paul could tell he approved and could see that his mind was going in a hundred different directions. "That is just brilliant!" exclaimed Martin.

"What can you do to make it more Beatle-ee?" John asked.

"The only thing I might suggest, John, are some strings. I can hear an arrangement in my head, if you'll allow."

John hesitated a bit. "Well, George...have at it, my friend. I only ask that it doesn't end up sounding like we're *trying* to be the Beatles. I guess the trick will be to make it Beatle-ish without seeming as if we're forcing it."

"Will do," replied George as he started notating his arrangement down on paper. "We'll have to get a few players from the London Symphony Orchestra."

"Okay. Get 'em in here fast, Georgie," teased John.

Paul sat like a schoolboy on the last day of school before summer break. His excitement was enhanced by the swirling thoughts he could not suppress about what was to come.

May 15, 1982—The night creeped into the next morning as George Martin had secured three of the best violinists in town. Two of them showed up together just after 2 a.m. with the third following just before 2:30 a.m. George explained to them his arrangement and the feel he was hoping to accomplish for this soon-to-be masterpiece. There were more takes than George expected, but the hired hands were not used to performing so early in the morning. Finally, after eighteen takes and almost three hours, George was satisfied with the result.

John and Paul had left with Mal just after midnight. They were heading to get a celebratory beer at a small pub down the street. The Pig Sty was the perfect little pub for them to discreetly have some harmless fun. John had always been known as a bad drunk—he was the definition of the phrase "Instant asshole. Just add alcohol." But this was different. John didn't want to get drunk. He just wanted to unwind with some old mates.

Mal bought the beers and brought them back to the table. The pub was small, and it didn't take many to fill it to the legal maximum. Tonight, there were only a handful of patrons and none seemed to notice the two most famous musicians in the world. "Cheers, mates!" shouted Mal with a grin that could light up London. They all clanked their mugs, then chugged a taste of the malt and hops.

"This has been an incredible day," Paul finally let out. "I can honestly say when I woke this morning, recording a song with my former partner was the last thing in the world I expected!"

John jumped in, "So, are you regretting it now?"

"No, no, no. This is something I've thought about for some time, but just never imagined would happen," said Paul.

It was now approaching 2 a.m., and three beers later, John asked, "Hey, Mal, got any change?" Mal searched his pockets and then produced a few shillings that he threw on the table.

"Here ya go," said Mal. John grabbed one and waltzed over to a payphone in the corner of the pub. He smiled at Paul and Mal as he began dialing.

"Hello?" said the awoken voice on the other end.

"Hey, Ring! It's me."

"John?" said Ringo Starr.

"Yeah, yeah. What's new with you?"

Ringo sat up in his bed, shaking off the sleep in his head and wondering what was wrong. At this hour, he felt something bad may have again happened. *John wouldn't call at this time of night unless it was an emergency,* thought Ringo.

"Hey, I'm here with Paul and Mal. We're having a little fun after laying down this new tune," John said.

"John, are you serious?"

"No, I just wanted to wake your fucking arse! Of course I'm serious. It's nice, and Paul laid down a drum track, but I really think it needs your backbeat."

Now, Ringo stood and started walking in small circles. Barbara woke to see her visibly shocked husband. "You know I'm there for you anytime, John," he said.

"Great, I'll see you in the morning. CBS Records, Studio 2 around 10 a.m. or so. Can I count on you, bloke?"

"Of course, of course, I'll see you there."

With that one phone call, the Beatles were almost officially reunited. John returned to the table, laughing. Mal and Paul, curious as to the inside joke John had volleyed upon his return to the table, asked, "What's up, bloke?"

"We got Ring back!"

They looked at each other and burst out laughing. This was all too surreal. But it was real. The night that would eventually go down in music history, ended with a hushed goodbye and some warm handshakes. Paul and John returned to Paul's vehicle and sped off back to John's flat. Mal, on the other hand, sat in his car for more than ten minutes trying to get a grasp on the events that had just transpired. Flashbacks went through his mind of the heights of being with the Beatles, to his own brush with death in 1976. Six years earlier, drugs and depression had taken its toll on him when he pointed an air rifle at a Los Angeles policeman, who in turn shot him in the stomach.

His life was about to change for the better. His head was spinning, but he couldn't take that huge smile off his childishly round face. They were back!!

Chapter 3

May 18, 1982—Approaching George Harrison with the idea of making some music with his old bandmates was going to be a colossal undertaking. They all knew how miserable he was at the end and it didn't go unnoticed that George's first solo album, *All Things Must Pass*, went straight to No. 1 and then went platinum six times over. A writer had once dubbed George "a major talent unleashed, one who'd been hidden in plain sight all those years" behind Lennon and McCartney.

So, John was hesitant—but determined. The phone rang at the Harrison residence.

"Hello?" answered George.

"George! How are you doing, my friend? It's John!"

"Well hello, Beatle John. How are you doing?"

George's tone toward his former mate had softened after the Dakota incident. Out of all the Beatles, he was the first and most adamant to address the dangers they faced touring. He had dreamed of incidents like the one that happened to his former band leader. John knew this and also knew that George would not just jump into the water with both feet without some good old-fashioned nudging.

"George, we've made a little record—Paul and me. It's a good one and we've asked Ring to play some drums on it. It wouldn't be right if you didn't at least come and give it a listen before we release it."

John felt George immediately withdraw, but he persisted. "Look, I'm not saying there should be a Beatles reunion. I just felt it wrong to have Paul and Ring involved without giving you a call."

George pondered for a moment and came back saying, "John, you know I love you like a brother. But you also know how difficult it was for me to be in that band toward the end."

John calmly acknowledged that sentiment and assured George that things were different now. George also internally recognized that he hadn't had many hits as of late.

"Okay, I'll come down. *But*...I don't want this to be a Beatles reunion. I don't think I'm quite ready for all that."

George was in—at least partially.

May 20, 1982—George Harrison showed up at CBS Records on this Thursday morning with tea in hand. He was the master of disguises, so no one had recognized him at first. The long scarf over his head and his spectacled sunglasses denied the view of those deep, mysterious eyes.

"Hey, Paul," George said to the former bandmate who was mostly the reason for his misery during the end stretch of that band.

Paul was happy to see George in good health and in good spirits. "How are you, George? It's been so long. How is the family?"

"We're all great. Wasn't sure I wanted to do this after all the chaos of those last recording sessions."

Paul felt uneasy at the idea of broaching this subject...especially so soon into their greeting. "Yeah, well I think we've all grown a bit since then." Paul had been no slouch over the years. His solo albums had done relatively well, and Wings had numerous hits. Paul's first album *McCartney* went to Number 1 on the charts, as did *Red Rose Speedway*. Wings' albums *Band on the Run* and *Venus and Mars* also topped the music charts. Paul could still write great songs and George knew it.

The control room was now getting a little crowded as Ringo waltzed in. Geoff Emerick was busy setting up microphones and didn't notice George. "Hey Geoff!" George yelled through the control room microphone. Geoff turned to see the lead guitarist waving through the glass of the room.

George and Ringo exchanged pleasantries, and soon George Martin walked in. "What?" exclaimed a surprised George Harrison.

"Hello George," said the famous producer.

"How ya doing, George? Still don't like that tie, you know!" Harrison was always the joker and never hesitated to be cheeky at any given chance. But he was now more concerned than ever as this was definitely shaping up to be a Beatles reunion.

Paul could sense the tension displayed by the lead guitarist. He knew George wanted nothing to do with a reunion. "George, we all got together at John's request and we'd at least like for you to give this one a listen, to see if you can add your tasteful guitar," Paul calmly stated.

George looked around and didn't see John. "Where is he?" he asked.

"Oh, he's up talking to one of his old record exec friends in the offices here."

Just then, John sauntered in. "George!!" he shouted to his friend. They hugged and George seemed sincerely happy to see John.

"Geoff, get your arse in here so George can get a listen to what we've got!" said John. Emerick came back around the equipment and into the control room. A warm but sturdy handshake greeted him from the remaining Beatle he had yet to see.

As the song began, George showed no expression. It appeared as though he was elsewhere and his mind was wandering to other more important things in his life. In reality, Harrison knew this was destined to be a hit and was battling his inner demons about how to respond. "That is a very good tune, John. Is this new, or something you've had around?"

"Just wrote it, my boy," John cheerfully announced. Not another word was spoken as George meandered into the studio and picked up his rosewood 1967 Fender Telecaster. Mal was not at this session, so Harrison was not aware of his involvement at this point. He fiddled with the small amp, turning some of the knobs until he got what he thought would be the perfect tone for this song. He used his signature Maestro Fuzz-Tone pedal to create that familiar Harrison tone.

In the early years of the Beatles, George would typically require fifteen to twenty takes or even more to get a guitar solo they would all agree upon. But years had gone by and George had gotten better by leaps and bounds. The first take was as near perfect as they could have imagined. George stepped back, practiced another lick he thought would complement the song...and then went at it again. Take two of George's solo was the one. It was reminiscent of his style on the *White Album*, which had transformed what most had thought of his musicianship from above average to outstanding. Since Ringo had previously re-recorded the drums onto the track, Harrison's solo was the last, and most fitting, piece to the musical puzzle.

At precisely 11:47 a.m. London time, the song was complete. A new Beatles song was almost out of the oven and into the hungry hands of every music aficionado. This was a major accomplishment and was a bit hard for even the Beatles themselves to wrap their minds around. They all four sat in the control room with Geoff and George Martin. It was George Martin who broke the silence. "Should we mix it now, boys?"

John looked at the others and asked them what they thought. Again, this was not something anyone who had dealt with Lennon in the past would have expected out of his mouth. Usually, John's word was it...especially when it came to his own songs. Paul was the first to respond. "I love it and yes, let's get to mixing!"

John rarely wanted anything to do with the mixing process. He felt it was the studio's job and he couldn't be bothered with such trivial details. Today, though, John wanted to be there to offer any assistance he possibly could. The boys gave each other a surprised look and shook their collective heads in disbelief. Paul's immediate feeling was to stay and help, as he had become quite the producer over the years. But he realized that this might be a good thing for John to have input on one of his songs throughout the entire process. So, Paul, George, Ringo, and then Mal Evans (who had just appeared in the studio) went out for tea and biscuits.

Almost two hours had passed, and the entourage returned to the studio to see John and Geoff yucking it up, having the time of their lives. The song had been mixed down in record time, as Geoff Emerick now found it amazingly easy to work with John. He had listened to some of John's subtle requests of how he wanted it to sound and again carved a timeless Beatles creation. The song now started on the control room speakers as they all listened intently. After three minutes and fifteen seconds, the song ended to an outburst of approval in the control room. The most excited was Paul, as this was everything he had secretly hoped would happen for years. George Harrison was a little subdued, as he still struggled with anything Beatle related. Meanwhile, George Martin couldn't remove the smile from his face as he was certain this would not only be a huge hit but could be the beginning of another era for the former moptops from Liverpool.

They took home copies of their new song, "Given to Fly," and knew they were to keep it close to the vest. Any word of this getting out could be detrimental to its release and subsequent reception. The problem was that there was no way for this to stay secret, and sure enough, CBS Records employees had caught wind of what was going on in Studio 2.

May 25, 1982—Five days later, news broke of a new Beatles song. The TV stations were all trying to be the first at breaking this incredible music news. By 6 p.m. that night, word had spread around the globe.

Riiinng.... "Hello," said John.

"Hey," said Paul. "Since the world now knows what is going on, should we announce it on our own to dispel any other rumors?"

John thought it was a good idea and said he would schedule a news conference...the most anticipated news conference in the history of pop music. Before John scheduled it, though, he contacted Ringo and then George. Knowing George would always be the hardest nut to crack, John cautiously approached him last. As John figured, George was against it and made his displeasure known to John.

"The cat's out of the bag, George," stated John as a matter of fact.

George suggested they all meet at one of their houses to discuss what the next steps should be. "We can meet here at Friar Park (George's residence)." John agreed to tell the others of the upcoming meeting at George's home.

May 27, 1982—At 10:30 a.m. on that Thursday morning, Paul and Ringo showed up simultaneously while John limped in a few minutes later. George offered up tea to all. They grabbed a quick biscuit and headed to the living room area of George's beautiful mansion. George started the conversation.

"I'm happy to have recorded this with you all and feel a certain sense of pride we were able to accomplish it without almost coming to blows. Having said that, I've said from the start that I want to avoid anything Fab Four related. Now it seems as if you want to get the band back together again. It doesn't interest me."

They knew this was coming from George, but Paul had expected it and knew just how to coerce the quiet ex-Beatle.

"George," started Paul. "We know how we all acted back in those days, and while I don't like to spend much time on regrets, I do regret that we didn't give you a fair shake. It is obvious that we made a mistake."

George didn't have to say a word. He knew they were aware of how many of his songs the Beatles rejected that eventually made their way onto his No. 1 album after the breakup.

"This is what I'd like to propose," Paul continued, "and I've yet to say this to the others so I'm just throwing it out there. From now on, if we do decide to make a go of this, any song you bring to the table will hold the same weight as everyone else's songs. No exceptions. Also, it's time to ditch the Lennon/McCartney concept of our songs. Songs should be credited to the writers, period. If John, you and I write a song together, the credits will reflect that. If Ring adds a part to a song that I wrote, the credits will reflect that as well. No more Lennon/McCartney monopoly!"

George was shocked to hear the person he considered to have the largest ego of anyone he knew capitulate to the fact they were all equals. This was definitely a turning point as George now loosened up and even joked, "So it's possible to have an entire Harrison/Starkey record if we choose?"

The others smiled, and Paul responded, "Exactly."

John had been sitting and listening the whole time but seemed pleased with the conversation. His only addition to this exchange was, "That is a fantastic idea!" Ringo was also eager and willing to give it a go.

George was silent and still unsure about this venture. Calmly he stated, "I will commit to recording a few more songs with the Beatles and that's it!"

Before they parted ways, they agreed to hold a news conference to let the world know they would once again become the Beatles! But, not before George threw a little wrench into the mix. "I'd like to not be at the news conference, though." John didn't mind, but Paul was a little concerned as he felt this could be a sign of things to come. They agreed that George didn't have to be present, and it was official—the Beatles had reunited!

May 31, 1982—This last day of May was bright and sunny. The spring flowers were starting to bloom and the sound of birds whistling their unique songs floated through the breeze. The news conference had been so anticipated that the boys were now forced to hold it in London Square. This time, hundreds of press and photographers came. More than eight thousand fans clamored around the square to hear what they could hear; see what they could see. CBS Records had executed an ad hoc contract stating that at this point, the boys were represented by them. In doing so, CBS then committed to assisting in this conference. So, they had a massive PA system installed prior to the news conference. The goal was for everyone to hear it right from the horses' mouths.

The excitement built up by the media coverage was unmatched in music history. Even their historic landing at JFK Airport in 1964 paled in comparison to this announcement. It was a beautiful spring day with the temperature reaching a comfortable 74 degrees Fahrenheit. Fans crushed against the police barricades. The screams of excitement made the crowd electric and created an uneasy pulse of its own. Homemade signs were abundantly displayed by the thousands of attendees... all showing support for their beloved Beatles. One young woman in front held a sign saying, "Ringo, will you marry me?"

Standing out front was CBS Records President Allen Davis. He began the news conference with a few short words. "Hello, everyone! How are you all doing? Today may be one of the most important days in music history. I'd like to introduce to you... again, the Beatles!!!"

With that, the entire area exploded with cheers and screams of joy. Then, out of nowhere, appeared the lads. First John, then Yoko who was holding onto young Sean's hand, followed by Paul and Linda and then Ringo.

"Good everything!" announced John in another wordplay moment that caused his bandmates to giggle. "We've come here before you all to say we're not through yet!" Again, the crowd erupted. Photographers could not take pictures fast enough as they struggled to capture every millisecond of this event. "We wanted to let you all know that we have indeed recorded a new song and are thinking about making a go of this thing...again!" Every sentence ended with an uproar from the thousands of onlookers. "Paul wants to say a few words now. Hey, Jim, your turn!" John said as he backed up a little to make room on the tiny platform for his new and past songwriting partner.

Paul was visibly ecstatic, and his smile was contagious. "Hello!" he screamed into the microphone. "This is something we hadn't really planned, but somehow, here we are, right?" Another round of applause. "Now, we want all of you to know this is different from the sixties when we were constantly able to break ground, and much of that had to do with equipment. We were able to form our own sounds as we tweaked with the limited technology available to us at that moment in time. I think that was what made some of those recordings so special. We're not going to claim to be breaking any new grounds here now. We just want to write music again together and see what can become of it."

This time, the applause didn't stop for almost three minutes as Paul paced the small platform, throwing his hands up in the air to match the excitement the crowd felt. What an event to behold. Most people could not believe what they were seeing and hearing. This was every Beatles fan's dream—they were getting back together to make music! The only thing that could possibly be better was to see them play live again. But there was no mention of a tour, as recording an album was already bound to be a monumental task for the boys to navigate through. Ringo wouldn't say a word today, leaving that to the two main songwriters.

This news conference, which lasted less than ten minutes, had the music world abuzz. Much of the media reaction was one of excitement, but there were many skeptics. Some of the reservations voiced in the media outlets were...

"Why wouldn't they just leave well enough alone?"

"Why take a chance at ruining that reputation?"

"How could they possibly recapture their old magic?"

"Where was George Harrison? Is he even back with them?"

"Could they go forward as the Beatles without George?"

The band was again nightly news for some time to come. They had certainly piqued the interest of the media, their peers, and of course, the fans. It had been more than twelve years since the band was in the studio and eighteen years since a fifteen-year-old from Silver Spring, Maryland, named Marsha Albert pestered a disc jockey on WWDC-Radio to play the Beatles for the very first time in America. There was no way to tell if the band could again achieve the success they once had or if they would flop, but every fan welcomed the chance to embrace the Beatles once again. It was now official, and the world would hold on for the ride!

Chapter 4

June 10, 1982—On this fabulous spring day, it was Beatle George who made the first move. His call to John that morning started off, "I've got a couple of songs I have been working on that I think would be perfect for this thing."

John now felt the newly found warmth in Harrison's voice to be a reassuring thing. He had always used Paul as his bounce board for not only music, but for the rare moments he would allow his emotions to surface. Now, he started to feel that George was the one who could provide the stability that had been missing in his childhood. John felt a deepened sense of gratitude to Harrison that he could not express. "That would be fantastic!" said a jubilant Lennon. "I'll phone the others and get us into a studio."

The band had recently been offered a new record contract with CBS Records Music for a four-album deal at $6.5 million per record. This was by far the most lucrative musical contract in history. They were already millionaires, and this would coat their pocketbooks for years to come. As expected, George initially refused to sign the deal. He claimed that he could only guarantee his involvement for one album. The CBS Records' attorneys then carved out a new clause for George and the two sides hammered out the details throughout the first week in June. The clause stated that George guaranteed his services for one album, but after that he would be able to walk away with no retribution from the label. The executives wanted Harrison to be part of this, but they knew who their Golden Tickets were. It was certain George could still write a good song, but they needed John and Paul. It would never be close to the Beatles without those two.

June 17, 1982—As the summer of 1982 was on full display, the boys again found themselves in the homey confines of CBS' Studio 2. Everyone was in good spirits and there was a sense of enjoyment one gets at a family reunion. They now, for whatever reason, felt closer to each other than they had been when they first arrived in America, and those around them knew it. "Good morning, gents," said the always jovial Mal Evans, after he had completed the equipment setup. He was even more excited to see his friends making a go of this again. He had witnessed the in-band fighting and could never understand why none of them would give an inch. Mal would just shake his head and think, *These fools don't even know how good they have it with each other.* It seemed he was aware of something that had not crossed the minds of these music icons—they needed each other.

Geoff Emerick began placing microphones here and there in the studio, hoping to get a sound they had yet to discover. All four Beatles and George Martin exited the control room and entered the studio to give Harrison's new song a good listen. He sat on a stool with the others standing as close as possible without crowding the guitarist.

G-G-G-G-D-D-C-C-G began the opening chords on his vintage Gibson J-160E acoustic guitar. *"It's hard to find the words to your heart...,"* sang George. The soft ballad had a beautiful melody, and the lyrics seemed to ebb and flow right alongside the music of this moody creation. It was a wonderful song, with a memorable chorus and even a nice, recognizable break...recognizable in the way that most Beatles fans would find appealing to the ear. George announced that this new song was called "Solitude."

The song ended to a brief silence while they all began to ponder what they could add to George's new hit. John was grinning. "You know, George," he said, "seems like you've picked up some of my tricks over the years!"

They agreed to get right to the recording process. John grabbed his Epiphone Casino electric, Paul picked up his Hofner bass, and Ringo sat up straight behind his Ludwig kit. George walked through the chord changes with John. Paul already knew them just from watching George's run-through, and within minutes the song had blossomed into another incredible Beatles creation. It had initially started as a soft ballad, but Lennon could not help inserting his rocking upbringing into the mix. Before they knew it, the song was turning into the kind of rock song John had been groomed on, and George was wise enough to allow that to happen. They had been able to keep the original acoustic guitar sound in place even after adding John's rocking guitar part.

After six takes, the basic track was complete. George then added a brilliant guitar solo to the middle break. He made a few attempts at the main vocal and John suggested some lyrical changes. John felt some of the words were a little jumbled, but he knew the sentiment of the song was good. So, after a verse change, Paul and John added harmony vocals. Five and a half hours later, the song was complete. It had grown to become more of a Beatles rocker than most of their "Phase 1" recordings. John had coined the terms "Phase 1" and "Phase 2" to reference their first successful journey together, and now their current path. The song gained momentum within the studio walls as some executives were allowed a sneak preview.

In the control room, Geoff Emerick was so pleased with the sound he had captured from the boys' new record, he almost immediately started the mixing process without confirming it with the songwriters. They all came into the control room to hear what they just crafted. George Harrison was the most pleased and was smiling from ear to ear. John and Ringo were also happy with their performances. Paul was a little more reserved. He felt he had not given this song his most dedicated effort. He asked if he could give it a few more attempts as his perfectionist ways were once again surfacing. This was the kind of suggestion that might have caused a row during Phase I, but now things were different...and Harrison welcomed Paul's eagerness for perfection.

Paul picked up his bass, put on the cans, and began another take on George's first Phase 2 offering to the group. Paul's mind immediately went back to George's song "Something," where he was alone with Geoff Emerick in the studio and created one of the most melodic bass lines in Beatles history. He was alone because the others had no intention of supporting each other at that point in the band. With that recording session in mind, Paul closed his eyes and put down some fabulous bass lines on the next four attempts, but it was Take 5 that made the hairs on the backs of their necks stand straight up. It may have been even better than the bass on "Something."

The three Beatles and George Martin celebrated in the control room. Paul could see the happy faces and returned to give the new take a listen. This take pleased Paul, as well. He had given his friend George the best present he could give—his best effort from the heart. "Solitude," by Harrison/Lennon, was scribbled in marker on the 3/4" tape reel container. This was certainly a different time for the Liverpudlians who had changed the world in the '60s. Phase 2 seemed destined to repeat history.

August 31, 1982—With the new Beatles album complete, it was Ringo who offered up a title: *Back Drop*. They liked the references of that title. It created images of their current situation as they were back again; of the incident that had occurred at The Dakota where John was shot in the back; and was also a tongue-in-cheek nod to their previous run at the top (using Drop instead of Top for a twist) of the music industry. Paul and George had initially balked at this title as they both felt the reference to John's shooting was not in good taste. But John asserted that he loved it and was not bothered at all by the reference. He appeared to have turned the corner from that incident and felt at ease confronting it head-on.

Eleven songs filled this new Beatles record—three from Lennon, three from McCartney, two that Paul and John collaborated on, one Harrison composition, one by George and John, and one by all four ("Rite of Passage"). When Paul had come up with the song "Mr. Sampson," he had thought about changing the name as to not be so literal. In 1966 while recording "Eleanor Rigby," Paul had decided to scrap the use of what he initially penned as "Father McCartney" to "Father McKenzie." At that point in their careers, the use of abstract lyrics always prevailed in their writings. But now with age had come a more direct approach. They felt it did need to remain "Mr. Sampson" and not "Mr. Simpson" as Paul had half-heartedly suggested. John loved this McCartney track that praised and almost even paid homage to the gentleman who may have saved his life.

Back Drop *(produced by George Martin)—CBS Records Music (1982)*

Rite of Passage (Lennon/McCartney/Harrison/Starkey)
Given to Fly (Lennon)
Devil's Cauldron (Harrison)
My Foils (Lennon/McCartney)
Deeper (McCartney)
Free as a Bird (Lennon/McCartney)
Solitude (Harrison/Lennon)
Real Love (Lennon)

Seeds of Love (McCartney)
New York (Lennon)
Mr. Sampson (McCartney)

Mike Sampson had since become a global hero for his quick actions on that December night in New York. He had refrained from interviews, and the only clip any network could muster was one of him saying, "Anyone in my position would have done the same thing. Please direct your attention to John's recovery." This was the sort of chivalrous attitude that endeared all four Beatles. Being in the background had made Mike even more of a folklore legend.

The mystery that clouded this private hero grew and grew until the public view of Sampson had become something he could never really live up to. CBS Records executives had contacted him shortly after signing the Beatles and had agreed to pay him a hefty sum of money as a reward for saving the life of John Lennon. When they offered him $125,000, he almost dropped the phone. He wanted so badly to accept, but in his heart, he couldn't do that. He meant what he had said—that anyone in his position would have done the same thing. He politely refused the offer (to his wife's dismay—who had been listening intently and was desperately begging him to accept). But she knew the character of the man she had married and admired that, even though the money would have changed their lives forever. He begrudgingly accepted the offer of a new car (a brand new red 1982 Lincoln Continental Mark VI Signature Series), as his beat up 1971 Dodge pickup had seen better days, for sure.

September 6, 1982—John, at first, felt indifferent toward Sampson. He knew the man probably had saved his life, but he still never called to properly thank him. George Harrison tracked him down that afternoon as the boys were back in New York to promote the new album.

"Hello?" Mike said as he picked up his phone.

"Hey, Mike, this is George Harrison."

Sampson wasn't certain if this was a prank, as he was forced to change his phone number after the hundreds of calls for an interview and also calls from random Beatles fans. "Is this really George?" asked Mike.

"Yes, mate. We'd like you to come down to the CBS Records offices in Manhattan. Can ya make yer way round here today sometime?"

"Sure, Mr. Harrison...I mean, G-George," Sampson stammered.

At a little after 2 p.m., the office receptionist phoned into the conference room where the boys had been having some laughs with a few label execs. "Mr. Sampson is here to see Mr. Harrison," the voice over the intercom declared.

"Good. Send him in," replied Tony Vozza, the youngest and closest exec to their new stars.

The door to the conference room opened and there appeared Mike Sampson. The boys had not yet met him but were in awe of the fact that his stature was smaller than what they had pictured. Maybe all the news coverage of him had created a larger-than-life image. Lennon couldn't help but wonder how a man of this size could have taken down a guy the size of that crazed shooter. Mike was thirty-two-years-old, stood just over five-foot-six, with a head of thick, curly red hair and a mustache.

"Welcome, welcome," said the boys, with John leading the greetings.

"Mike," started John, "I owe a debt of gratitude to you for what you did that night."

"Oh, Mr. Lennon, there's no need for a 'thank you,' and if that is why I was called down here, I am truly humbled. But again, a 'thank you' is not necessary."

"No, Mike," said Paul. "There are two reasons we wanted you here today. First, we want you to be the first one to own a copy of our new album...signed by the four of us (with a special thanks from John). The other reason is that we are hoping you'll work with us going forward."

"Work with the Beatles?!"

"Yes," George continued. "You see, we're giving Derek Taylor a position to more or less manage us, and with that, we've created a new position that will make his life a little easier."

"I apologize, Mr. Harrison..."

"Please. Call me George," he replied.

"Um, okay. Well, uh, George...I'm not familiar with who Derek Tyler is."

They all had a good laugh and tried to calm him down as Mike's nervousness was obvious.

"It's Taylor," said John, "and it's absolutely perfect that you don't know of him. What we'd like is for you to be his assistant. He'll need someone to do some of the legwork here in the States while he handles day-to-day operations back in England."

Sampson was confused and as nervous as could be, but also excited about the opportunity and quite a bit shocked. He had no idea what a band manager did, let alone an assistant manager... and he had no experience whatsoever in the music industry. The band explained that it was better if he didn't know anything about the job. They could help him along any way he needed, and they would also be able to mold him into the type of assistant manager that would be beneficial to Derek as well as the band.

All four Beatles assured him that he would be in good hands throughout the training process, and that each one would make themselves available to assist if he ran into anything he couldn't handle. Mike sat for a minute, not knowing what to say but aware that this was an opportunity he could not refuse. He stood and not so calmly replied, "Yes. Yes, of course I'll do it. Thank you all very much for this!"

They went on to discuss some of the details—how much they would pay him, where his office would be in New York, and Derek's personal contact information. He was told to call Derek any time of day or night if he had questions. The one thing Mike kept thinking was, *I'll have to quit my job at the shop. I can't wait to do that! No one at the shop will ever believe this.*

Mike had worked at a machine shop for the past six years. It was a tough life, but he never complained. He was an old-school type who believed in a good, hard day of work. He had no issues with getting his hands dirty and sometimes coming home to his family smelling to high heavens. Mike knew his wife would be ecstatic of this news as she had always been pushing him to get better work. They had a small child at home and were expecting another addition to the family by the end of the year.

Mike then shook all of their hands and started on his way back to his home on Long Island. Before he exited the conference room, though, John pulled Mike's arm back gently and handed him the signed copy of *Back Drop*. The chills he received at the sight of this new Beatles record was only surpassed when he flipped it over to see song No. 11: "Mr. Sampson." He could no longer hold in the emotions that he had so desperately hidden from everyone, including his wife, regarding all that had happened to him over the past year and a half since the shooting. The media attention, the Beatles fans trying to track him down, the onslaught of any passersby who recognized him...it was all too much for this quiet hero. An uncontrollable stream of tears now flowed steadily down his cheeks. Paul was the first to walk over and put his arm around Sampson. The others followed and wrapped their collective arms around him. There they stood—a Beatles sandwich with Mike Sampson (their new assistant manager) as the main course.

Chapter 5

September 9, 1982—*Back Drop* was released on this day and went immediately to No. 1 on the U.S. Billboard charts. It sold 350,000 copies on the first day alone! Radio stations now inundated the airwaves with old and new Beatles material.

The two tracks that the boys decided upon as the ones to promote were "Given to Fly" and "Mr. Sampson" (with the Harrison/Lennon composition "Solitude" getting even more airplay as it was deemed "the ultimate Beatles rocker" by one disc jockey). The boys had regained control of the airwaves and the music charts. They had four songs in the Top 10: "Given to Fly," "Mr. Sampson," "Solitude," and "Free as a Bird".

Billboard Charts – Week of September 12, 1982

THIS WEEK	LAST WEEK	2 WKS AGO	WEEKS ON CHART	ARTIST LABEL	TITLE	PEAK POSITION
1	NEW ▶		1	THE BEATLES CBS RECORDS ★ ★ No. 1 ★ ★	GIVEN TO FLY	1
2	1	7	18	EURYTHMICS RCA	SWEET DREAMS (ARE MADE OF THESE)	1
3	6	2	12	MEN WITHOUT HATS BACKSTREET	THE SAFETY DANCE	3
4	4	3	12	TACO RCA	PUTTING ON THE RITZ	4
5	NEW ▶		1	THE BEATLES CBS RECORDS	SOLITUDE	5
6	7	5	7	BILLY JOEL COLUMBIA	TELL HER ABOUT IT	3
7	3	1	15	THE POLICE A&M	EVERY BREATH YOU TAKE	6
8	NEW ▶		1	THE BEATLES CBS RECORDS	FREE AS A BIRD	8
9	NEW ▶		1	THE BEATLES CBS RECORDS	MR. SAMPSON	9
10	5	4	16	DONNA SUMMER MERCURY	SHE WORKS HARD FOR THE MONEY	3
11	15	8	9	BONNIE TYLER COLUMBIA	TOTAL ECLIPSE OF THE HEART	8
12	10	10	8	MICHAEL JACKSON EPIC	HUMAN NATURE	9
13	9	9	11	CULTURE CLUB VIRGIN	I'LL TUMBLE 4 YA	9
14	13	11	7	ASIA GEFFEN	DON'T CRY	11
15	12	12	15	THE HUMAN LEAGUE A&M	(KEEP FEELING) FASCINATION	15
16	NEW ▶		1	THE BEATLES CBS RECORDS	SEEDS OF LOVE	16
17	14	13	10	JACKSON BROWNE ASYLUM	LAWYERS IN LOVE	7
18	17	14	6	STRAY CATS EMI AMERICA	(SHE'S) SEXY + 17	14
19	18	15	7	AIR SUPPLY ARISTA	MAKING LOVE OUT OF NOTHING AT ALL	15
20	12	16	11	MEN AT WORK COLUMBIA	IT'S A MISTAKE	6

They were hotter than ever, and calls from around the globe came in for offers to play at the Royal Palace in London, the Coliseum in Rome, and even the Red Square in the USSR. These were all intriguing offers to the boys, and while they were pleased at the attention and demand for their music, they weren't quite ready to play live...at least not yet. Paul was always the one who loved to perform live. After Phase I, he played more live gigs in one year than the other three did combined in ten years.

Harrison had only gone on one tour and that was in 1974. On that tour, his voice gave way to strep throat and he was forced to cancel some dates. His nerves had also gotten the better of him, and he spent an evening in Phoenix in cold sweats due to anxiety. He hated performing in front of a live audience, and it wasn't because he was shy or lacked confidence...he was terrified of the dangers he would be exposed to.

Now, as they sat in the offices at CBS Records in London, Paul approached the others with an idea. "I have been thinking about something that might be fun for us all. And we could also pull a quick one on some of our fans," he said. "We could show up at a small pub unannounced and play a quick set. Then rush the hell out of there before anyone catches word of it."

The thought of playing anywhere live brought a knot to the stomach of Harrison. Again, they all felt his not-so-subtle retreat. George stood up, stared directly into McCartney's eyes, and said, "I've agreed to this whole circus again, but this is where I draw the line. This isn't going to happen...not with me, anyway."

The others weren't surprised by George's response, and John let it be known that he wasn't keen on the idea either. Paul continued, "Come on, mates. It'll be a blast. And I've already made contact with some British agents who would comb out the area and make sure...actually guarantee our safety. We all want that. George, you don't think I want to put any of us in danger, do you?"

With that, George sat and relaxed a bit. He thought about it for a minute and said to Paul, "If I can meet with these agents to hear their plan and then feel it would be safe enough, I might consider."

"That's all I'm asking of you!" said Paul.

November 13, 1982—Four agents from the British Royal Armed Guards showed up at the CBS Records offices that morning to discuss their proposed security measures. Ringo was the only

Beatle absent from this meeting as he was with Barbara, who was having a medical procedure that day. The agents started their presentation to the band. They had prepared a storyboard that contained sketch after sketch of the street layout and how they would assign agents to patrol those areas. The pub they chose was called The Loose Goose and was on Mathew Street in Liverpool... just down the road from the now closed but world-famous Cavern Club (where the boys had carved their chops to become one of the tightest pop bands in the country).

Agent Samuel Willard was heading the presentation. "You see, men, this is the area of most concern," he said as he pointed to a sketch of the side alley to the pub. "Now, we'll have agents on each end of the alley, two or three on the rooftops of these adjoining buildings. Five or six will cover the perimeter within about seventy-five meters, and then two agents will guard each entranceway."

Derek Taylor had sat intently, listening to the strategy, and knew this would be an expensive undertaking. "Pardon me, Agent Willard, but do you have a rough estimate of the cost of this endeavor?" he asked.

"Yes, we have worked out what we believe to be a fair price. It will be £500 per agent for the night. We anticipate approximately 15 agents, so that would come to £7,500." That made some eyes in the room a little wide as it was a substantial amount to be paid for them to perform a gig. They did find it somewhat comical that a band of their stature would not get paid for a gig but must pay out a good sum of money to play.

Derek realized that this was necessary to get past the hurdle of touring and possibly have the band generate more income with a small tour. "That's fine," replied Derek. "Well, boys, what do you think?"

John was feeling the sudden thrush of anxiety at the thought of being in front of a crowd again in that environment. He asked the others if he could sleep on it and let them know the next day. George, who had been completely against this, seemed to soften to the idea.

"John," began George, "if you are against this in any way, I completely understand and support your decision. But this does sound safe. You know my feelings on it and even I think we'll be okay." John nodded and they parted ways.

November 14, 1982—John woke that morning, fed Sean breakfast, and then sat with Yoko over a cup of tea. "Well, Mother, what are you thinking about this adventure?"

"John, I'm concerned. How can these agents guarantee your safety?"

That was the one question Lennon himself was struggling with. He didn't reply—just sat staring out the window of their spacious flat. "I have to face this demon eventually, you know," he told her.

"Do you?" was Yoko's response.

John knew she was right, but he also knew that was not the way he approached things in his life. He was always one to face something head-on as if he was the one to fear. "Listen, I think I should do this. I think it's safe enough and on a small enough scale to be good for the lot of us."

Yoko knew she couldn't change the mind of her headstrong husband. She smiled and said, "I will do anything to help, John."

Paul McCartney's phone rang just before 11 a.m. "Hello?"

"Hey mate, I'm in!"

Paul almost jumped out of his seat. "That's fabulous, John. Can I call the others?"

"No, let me do it. I want to make sure everyone understands my reservations and concerns."

"Absolutely!" replied Paul. John then made calls to the others and spent the most time talking with George. George had almost gone completely the other way overnight. He was even more anxious about this than Lennon appeared to be yesterday at the meeting.

"Well, I'm not so sure now, John. I understand Paul's desire to play live, and I think we all enjoy certain aspects of that. But I'm having trouble feeling at ease with this thing. I just don't see how anyone can guarantee we'll be safe."

"I'll tell you what, Georgie my boy. We'll hold hands the entire time," chortled John. He then got serious. "Let's meet one more time with the agents and voice these concerns before making any decision." With that, George had agreed to another meeting.

November 17, 1982—The meeting at the CBS Records offices that morning went quickly, and the boys felt more comfortable after the agents' second presentation. After a few minutes, they all agreed to the plan and signed an agreement with the Royal Guards. The date they agreed upon was November 21, 1982, as they didn't want to push it too far forward in fear of word getting out. Paul and Ringo felt an excitement they had missed for well over ten years. They both loved to play live. John and George, while both reserved about this escapade, were settling into the idea. John especially tried his absolute best to embrace it with open arms. It was not an easy hill to climb as they were both more anxious about this than they had been over anything in years.

November 21, 1982—The morning of the night of the surprise gig brought some tension for the four lads from Liverpool. Each one knew what the day would bring and weren't sure if they were ready for such chaos. Mal had one of the band's close friends, Peter Asher, go down to the pub to tell them he was going to start setting up some equipment for a show that would happen that night. When the manager of The Loose Goose, Jimmy Scott, heard this, he immediately stepped in. Jimmy was thirty-six-years-old, had long, dark hair, a thick mustache, and had an edge to him obtained through his many years as a bar manager.

"Look, bloke, I don't know who you are, but you can't just start setting up equipment in my bar."

The band's attorneys had been prepared for this and had sent along a nondisclosure agreement with Mr. Asher. He reached into his briefcase and produced the document. "The intent of this agreement...," it started. By the second paragraph, Scott's jaw dropped wide open. "The fucking BEATLES?!" he exclaimed. Peter was thankful they were the only two within earshot as the manager had almost screamed this at the tops of his lungs.

"Yes, the fucking Beatles, mate," replied Peter. He went over the details of the brief agreement, which simply stated that if he were to mention this in any way to anyone, or even hint at this event, the pub would get sued and they would most likely lose the establishment. Jimmy's mind was about to explode at the thought of the most famous musicians in the world playing a short set at their small pub. *How could he not tell anyone? What if there was no one there to hear it? After they started playing, was he allowed to contact anyone?* The answer to that last question was a resounding "No" from Asher. This would only be for the lucky few in attendance. Anyone who then caught wind of this would be the extent of outreach that would happen.

It was 9:15 p.m. at The Loose Goose and maybe 25 to 30 people were in the pub, which had a legal maximum of 175 people. The stage area was dimly lit, and no one had even noticed the musical equipment hidden underneath the red sheets that Peter Asher put in place. The microphones were hidden offstage as Mal Evans and Peter Asher entered the area. The pub patrons barely noticed the two setting up the final pieces of the equipment—placing the mics out front, turning on the amplifiers, and then removing the red sheets from the equipment.

The band had recruited Nicky Hopkins to sit in and add keyboards to the complex songs they would not be able to perform without. Since not many people would recognize Hopkins, they had him appear first to give a small introduction. He positioned himself behind the keys, pulled the microphone closer, and began, "Ladies and gentlemen, tonight is a very special night, indeed. I know my words can't correctly emphasize what you're about to witness..." With that, he had definitely got the attention of the pub patrons, who were now staring toward the stage. "I'd like to introduce for your listening pleasure...once again...THE BEATLES!!!" There were a few laughs but mostly people just sat and thought, *What is this buffoon talking about?*

Paul McCartney walked onto the stage first, followed by Ringo and George. Finally, John limped his way to the stage. Two regulars sitting at the bar turned towards the stage and almost fell off of their bar stools at the sight of The Beatles. Scott had been bursting at the seams and could now finally let the cat out of the bag to the patrons. Yes, this was The Beatles and he explained to some regular customers that he was informed of this earlier in the day. The crowd was stunned, and as the excitement grew from the reality of what was happening, they frantically rushed to the stage to get a better look at these music legends. It was the type of moment that scared the shit out of Lennon and Harrison. But besides having agents inside the pub, big Mal Evans was a buffer to be feared as he stood guard out in front of the stage.

Bam, ba-ba, bam, ba-ba, bammmm.... "Roll up, roll up for the *Magical Mystery Tour, step right this way...,*" sang John. A collective scream came out of every mouth that was witness to this incredible spectacle. Nicky Hopkins spun his whirling keyboard sound around to give it the same texture heard on the original Lennon/McCartney classic. *"That's an invitation...to make a reservation..."*

The patrons could not believe what they were seeing and hearing. This was historic and the band sounded incredible. The

Beatles' vocal harmonies, which they had become so famous for, were still spot-on, and this first song proved they could still sing together. Within minutes, people were swarming into the pub in droves. The smile on Scott's face went from sea to sea. He still could not believe this was happening at his pub. *What a stroke of luck that they chose our establishment to play a surprise show!* he thought.

By the end of the first song, "Magical Mystery Tour," more than two hundred people had crowded into the small, smoked-filled pub. John and George were becoming anxious about this, but Paul and Ringo were delighted. The agents knew this was crunch time for the band and were on high alert. While they were all confident of their abilities to protect the boys, the agents were uneasy as the crowd gained momentum outside of the pub. By the end of their second song ("Given to Fly"), the crowd outside had swelled to nearly one thousand people. Word spread like wildfire, and surprisingly, Eric Clapton was informed by a friend who lived close by the pub. The Beatles ran through a short set of older and new material including "Come Together," "Solitude," "Sgt. Pepper's Lonely Heart's Club Band," and "With a Little Help from My Friends" (for Ringo to have a turn at lead vocal).

The boys were just about to finish up the song "Mr. Sampson" when John spotted Clapton in the crowd, which had swelled to well over capacity for the small pub. "Eric! Eric!" yelled John over the hysteria. The former Cream guitarist approached the stage, greeted his friends, and was given a Gibson SG to play. Paul suggested they do "While My Guitar Gently Weeps," and off they went. *"I look at you all, see the love there that's sleeping...,"* sang George. And then Paul and George: *"While my guitar gently weeps."*

This was just surreal. The Beatles? Playing live at this small pub? And now with Eric Clapton? Every person who was able to get in the door of the pub that night felt they'd hit the jackpot. How could one not feel that way? This was guaranteed to be worldwide news, and even those who weren't a fan of the Fab Four knew the significance of the events of the night. George only forgot one line of the song they had not planned to play, but no one noticed.

Nine songs and just over thirty-five minutes later, the Beatles disappeared into the night. The crowd that had grown to over two thousand people lined the streets outside of The Loose Goose hoping to somehow get inside. Most were unaware that the boys had already scooted out the back with the assistance of their agent friends.

BAM!! exploded a sound from out back. All four Beatles dropped to the ground. Luckily it was only the sound of a garbage dumpster lid being slammed down at a restaurant a few doors down. They got up, dusted themselves off, laughed about it, and whisked away to have some drinks.

John had suggested again going to the Pig Sty, as he assumed it would provide adequate protection for them. George didn't like the thought of going out with his bandmates and felt they had pushed their luck enough that evening. But with a little prodding, he was coerced into at least one pint. There sat Paul McCartney, John Lennon, George Harrison, Ringo Starr, Eric Clapton, Nicky Hopkins, and Mal Evans at possibly one of the most famous pub tables ever assembled. John was incorrect about this being a quiet little establishment that night. Since word of their appearance at the Goose, the London streets were overflowing with fans and people trying to latch onto the excitement that had been generated a few kilometers up the road. George had the insight to invite one of the British agents along to have a pint with them. This turned out to be a wise choice as the agent had to intervene immediately upon their arrival when two drunken fans barreled their way to the table.

The boys laughed about the night's events and the reaction of the crowd that had witnessed the show. John, never one to care much of what others thought, was the first to bring up that he saw men and women coming to tears at the sight of their playing together. This made him genuinely happy. The usually stoic Lennon seemed to be softening up. During the entire run with the Beatles, he had never paid much attention to the impact the band had on people—musically or otherwise. To him, it was a burden to be labeled by what others might think or expect. But this was different. Age had changed them all, and while John had just turned forty-two years old, he wanted to appreciate the most of what life had to offer. His tolerance for others, especially his fans, was constantly growing. He had found himself enjoying the interactions he had with the crowd that night as he inserted his comic sense of being into the mic every chance he could. Each quip had been met with laughter and cheers.

George stuck to his guns and decided to part after one pint. He invited the others back to his place and they all gladly accepted. Eric went along with George as he needed a ride, seeing he had been dropped off at the door of The Loose Goose. The others stayed for a few more pints until the crowd became overwhelming and the one agent could no longer keep them safe.

They all headed back to Friar Park for more cocktails. When they arrived, George had produced a large joint for them to smoke. Paul's eyes lit up as he had always been a proponent of marijuana. The boys had gone from taking all sorts of drugs (cocaine, LSD, heroin, etc.) to now just the occasional joint. So, they all participated and sat back to enjoy the drug's creeping effect. Finally, at 3:25 a.m., they all clinked glasses for one final toast and then parted ways. On the way home, Paul was grinning, thinking about the events that had transpired that night. He couldn't have been more pleased at the result, and while they were a bit rusty with their live show, he knew they were now better than they had ever been during Phase I.

Set list—*The Loose Goose Pub (November 21, 1982) with the singer listed next to each song:*

Magical Mystery Tour—Paul with John

Come Together—John

Solitude—George with John

With a Little Help from My Friends—Ringo

Given to Fly—John

I Want to Tell You—George

Sgt. Pepper's Lonely Heart's Club Band—Paul with John

Mr. Sampson—Paul with John

While My Guitar Gently Weeps—George with Paul
   (and Eric Clapton on guitar)

Chapter 6

November 28, 1982—David Geffen had been unusually bothered that morning. Not only had he dropped John Lennon and therefore missed an opportunity to sign the reunited Fab Four, he was feeling the impact they had made with their unannounced performance. He felt sick as the thought of the Beatles possibly touring drove home the miserable reality that he'd fucked up... bad. "Get Davis on the line," he yelled out to his assistant.

"Do you mean Mac Davis?" was the response.

"No, no...Allen from CBS Records."

After a few minutes, each of the respective assistants connected the two label CEOs.

"Hello, Allen. I'm certain you know the pretense of this call". Davis most assuredly knew. "All I really want to ask is that you allow Geffen Records to help promote a tour, if the band chooses to pursue one."

These two music moguls had a history that was what most would consider strenuous at best. "Look, Dave, I do feel bad that you dropped John from your label, and I would like to help you in some way. But I really don't see that happening."

"What do you mean by not happening? Do you mean them touring? Or not letting us be involved?" Davis tried to be as cordial as he could, knowing the impact his next sentence would have on Geffen. "I'm sorry, Dave, but if they do tour, CBS Records will have exclusive rights."

With that, Geffen slammed down the phone. "FUCK!!" he screamed to no one in particular.

December 5, 1982—Paul received a call from Derek Taylor, who had been in contact with CBS Records President Allen Davis. "Paul, we've received an offer for a small tour that I think might be too lucrative to refuse," said Taylor. He went on to explain the details of the 15-show tour, starting in the U.K. with some shows scattered around the globe. It was to be spread out over a period of five months as to not put too much intense traveling on the boys. The selling point was the money they would make. Taylor called it the "50-50" deal. Each band member was guaranteed £50,000 a show, and the band would then split 50% of the door proceeds. The ticket prices for their shows would start at £50 apiece for the larger venues and £100 for the smaller ones. As Paul let those numbers dance around in his head, it dawned on him that this would most likely be a once in a lifetime offer.

"Well, Derek, I think it sounds wonderful. I'm not so certain the others will see it like that. What cities are they proposin'?" asked Paul.

There were the usual U.K. stops (London, Wales, Belfast, Glasgow) and then Tokyo, Paris, Berlin, Moscow, Sydney (2 shows), with five shows in the U.S. (Detroit, Chicago, Los Angeles and two shows in New York). Paul immediately suggested a meeting with the others, but Taylor thought it best to phone them himself. He knew this was going to be a difficult task and thought presenting it in a meeting setting seemed a bit like sabotage.

The phone calls were made to the other three and each one was given time to air out concerns, ask questions, and briefly contemplate this offer. As expected, Ringo was in and didn't need any persuasion. John was surprised and laughed out loud at the outrageous money they were offered. He told Derek he would consider this and talk with Yoko before committing to anything.

George, on the other hand, told Derek, "Fuck off. Not a chance." And hung up.

Derek felt he had let the others down by possibly not presenting it to George in a manner that would have been easier to digest. Derek was not one to mince words and had trouble at times being tactful when approaching a touchy subject like this. He put his head in his hands and then again called Paul. "Paul, Ringo is in. John is thinking about it, but George...."

'He wouldn't do it, right?" asked Paul.

"You got it. He hung up on me."

Paul mildly chuckled as he imagined the conversation. "Okay, let's give it a day or two, then I'll phone him," said McCartney.

"Sounds good," Taylor replied before disconnecting.

December 9, 1982—John was in a jovial mood that morning, as he had been playing with Sean and that always made him happy. So, he let Paul know he would contact George about the possible tour.

"Not doing it, John" were George's first words.

"I know, I know. Believe me, I spent the past two days trying to come up with as many reasons as I could to not do this. But the bottom line is that it will be worth it...for us all," replied John.

"Listen, I'm not budgin' on this. I played for you all at that pub, but this is out of the question," said the now not-so-quiet Beatle.

After Paul was informed of George's response, he phoned George. At this point, Paul was a little frustrated with his bandmate's constant refusal to do anything Beatles related. He could not understand why Harrison wouldn't give back a little to the band that had opened so many doors for him.

"George, I've got a suggestion to make this a little easier. You can do any show you'd like to choose from on this tour and the other dates, we'll ask Eric to play."

George's silence proved that Paul still knew how to pull the strings of their lead guitarist. He knew that while George and Eric were good friends, there was still intense competition between the two. When George's wife, Patty, was in the midst of falling for Eric, a half-drunken Harrison invited Clapton over for an impromptu jam that turned into an unspoken guitar battle (which Clapton handily won).

George thought this was hitting below the belt. Paul knew having Eric replace him would not sit well with the guitarist. "Paul, I've tried to come to terms with all of this and it keeps coming down to safety...you know that."

"I've already put some numbers together for the amount it would cost us all for the extra security we feel is necessary to consider something of this magnitude," stated Paul. He explained that each Beatle would surrender £5,000 from every gig. They would then pursue another £15,000 from the promoters of the venues, and £15,000 from their label (CBS). This would free up £50,000 a night to pay for the best security money could buy. George agreed that this was needed, but still wasn't about to give in.

"How do you know Eric would even do it?" George asked.

"We don't" was Paul's response, although they both knew he would jump at that opportunity. George relaxed a bit at that as he had expected McCartney would have already secured Clapton.

"Okay, well let me think about it," George said as they hung up.

Four hours later, George called back. "Paul, I'm not signin' anything that will lock me in for an entire tour. If I do a show or two and don't feel comfortable, I'm done."

"Great, George. It'll be a blast, I'm certain of that!"

Paul first called the other Beatles to inform them they were going forward with the tour and then called Derek Taylor. "We're gonna do it, Derek," said Paul.

"Fantastic!" stated Taylor. The manager then got busy with the details. He immediately contacted the CBS offices to inform Allen Davis of their decision to pursue the tour and of the security plans they had demanded. Davis agreed to pay the extra amount and then had his people get to work on starting to set up the security while also squeezing another £15,000 from each promoter. Not surprisingly, every promoter paid out that sum without hesitation. They were slated to make an incredible profit even after surrendering the extra cash.

After recruiting Eric Clapton as a backup, an agreement was written for each venue, and in it was a clause that allowed for George Harrison to be replaced by Cream's former lead guitarist. That seemed to be an issue for every destination. Each was concerned that Harrison would not appear, but having Clapton as a backup was certainly an amazing alternative.

December 15, 1982—All four Beatles were present for this last-minute press conference they had hurriedly put together. Since it was such late notice, only a few dozen photographers were present for this announcement.

"Hello," said John to the small crowd gathered inside CBS Records Studios in London. "We've decided to play some live shows." Cameras clicked, and people pushed their way to get better position for this event. "We're going to do fifteen shows over a five-month period starting in January at the Royal Albert Hall."

The cameras clicked away, and the crowd grew with people swarming into CBS Records. The murmurs and whispers soon blossomed into a full-on assault of questions. Every reporter wanted to know the details, but they weren't going to get any from the band. This was their manager's duty or possibly the label's job. Either way, their focus was to finish getting ready for this tour. They still weren't ready to play live…even though they had already been rehearsing for the last month and a half.

The new year was fast approaching, and there wasn't much time to prepare if they again wanted to become the incredible live show they once were. The song list for each show was being hashed out, and there were some mild disagreements about what to include. They decided on a good variety of old and new songs, with an eye on not playing too much new material. Paul was always the one to please crowds by knowing which favorites the fans wanted to hear and inserting those songs into the set lists. George and Ringo were similar in that sense, but John was always seeking something out of the ordinary...something that could grow his street credentials with their peers. But he also knew this was a new era and the tour was brief enough that playing some of their "Phase I drags" (as he referred to them) wouldn't be that horrible.

With an unmatched catalog to choose from, the set lists started to resemble a greatest hits package. When some CBS executives stated that they wanted a say in the songs the band would perform, all four Beatles nixed that notion without pause. The set lists were theirs and theirs alone to create and modify as needed. Each one would vary only slightly for the different venues, and some of the latter shows would have the same list as they had previously used.

Since each Beatle could do one solo song a night, Mal urged Ringo to play "You and Me (Babe)" off of his *Ringo* LP. The song had been written by Harrison and Mal Evans, and he held great personal pride in assisting in that creation. "We'll see," said Ringo, smiling and putting his hand on the big man's shoulder.

Finally, they had agreed on the set lists for every show. This was an important task and it was vital for all of them to rehearse these songs. Some of the songs (especially the solo ones) were unfamiliar to the others, who had not played them previously. These were the biggest hurdles to get past. When they sat back to review the lists, they were more than pleased, almost excited at playing some of these tunes that a live audience had never witnessed.

January 10, 1983—The night of their first live gig since Candlestick Park in 1966 (excluding their rooftop foray for the *Let It Be* album and movie in 1969) was encased in excitement. News channels around the world had been talking about this tour at every turn and were firmly planted outside of Royal Albert Hall in London. The audience included a who's who of music and entertainment. The star power showed up in full force—Mick and Keith (and the other Rolling Stones), Clapton, Bob Dylan, Jeff Beck, Jack Nicholson, Dustin Hoffman, Harry Belafonte, Phil Spector, Clive Davis, Michael Jackson, Diana Ross, Paul Simon, Stephen Stills, Graham Nash, David Crosby, Pete Townsend, Harry Nilsson, Billy Preston, and Stevie Winwood to name just a few. It was *the* place to be in the entertainment world that night.

No one knew what to expect. *Will they suck? Will they play old hits? How long will they play? Can they still perform at a high level live like before?*

Shortly after 9 p.m., the boys wandered onto the stage to a standing ovation that lasted almost five minutes. They positioned themselves and prepared for what they had hoped would be a success. They weren't certain, either, how they would sound as their last rehearsal in the studio did not go well. John and George got into a little row about their guitar sounds. Lennon thought George's guitar was not distorted enough while going over "Come Together" and because of this, they didn't even rehearse it. That last rehearsal had become a nightmare for all involved. It wasn't just that George and John were in disagreement; no one had put any effort into sounding good at all that evening. The two people most concerned about this were Paul and Derek. Their manager worried that the venue would not bear witness to the boys performing at their best, while Paul was forever in a state of worry when it came to their live shows. He took an immense amount of pride in their live sound.

But now it was time to play. The audience settled into their seats and the band began the thumping opening to "Come Together." The crowd exploded in unison as they sang every lyric. The song had a small misstep in the first chorus as George fumbled a chord change. After that mistake, the night was flawless. They mixed a good portion of old and new with each one taking their turns singing. As promised to George, he had more of a spotlight than they had previously allowed him. He sang two of his Phase 1 Beatles records, one Phase 2 song, and one solo song. Ringo belted out "Boys" and then later sang "It Don't Come Easy" (a Starkey composition that was mostly written by Harrison, but uncredited to him). The rest of the songs were sung by Paul and John. Their harmonies were so tight that some of the other greatest harmonizers in music history (i.e., Paul Simon and CSN) watched in awe. These were stars who weren't easily impressed yet they were on their feet cheering and screaming alongside every other fan that night.

The boys played a ninety-minute set (more than an hour longer than their Phase 1 sets). They slowed only once to do John's reflective "In My Life." After the final notes of "Hey Jude" rang out, the boys gathered at the front of the stage, did a Beatles bow, and waved to the crowd before scurrying off. They had again proved that when they were on their game, no one was better in a live performance.

Backstage was a madhouse, and everyone wanted to be part of it. Michael Jackson talking with Paul; Bob Dylan hanging with John; Crosby and Nash snuggling up to Harrison; while Ringo danced around pouring champagne for all. Dustin Hoffman made his way backstage to greet Paul, who he had befriended some years back. They had met in New York when Hoffman was witness to Paul's writing of "Picasso's Last Words (Drink to Me)."

Derek Taylor had come backstage with a smile on his face and two letters in his hand. He stood on a stool and yelled over the crowd to try to gain their attention. "Please, please," he begged. "Please let me have one minute of your time. We just received two faxes and I'd like to quickly read them." The star-studded backstage grew quiet as they could see the Fab Four perk up to listen to their manager. "Congratulations, men, on an outstanding performance tonight. All of us here at Buckingham Palace are thrilled you have begun performing together again. Bravo! Sincerely yours, Queen Elizabeth." There was a loud laugh among the room with some scattered boos.

Derek continued, "I think you might like this one a little better... 'Hello, boys, I heard you put on a dynamite show tonight. Congratulations and please look me up if you're ever in Vegas!' Signed, Frank Sinatra." With that, the whole room erupted in cheers. Sinatra still carried incredible weight in the music industry, and the boys were overjoyed that he took the time to write. Things couldn't get any better for the band...or could they?

Set List: *Royal Albert Hall (January 10, 1983) with the singer listed next to each song:*

Come Together—John
Get Back—Paul
Given to Fly—John
Boys—Ringo
Think for Yourself—George
Gimme Some Truth—John
Seeds of Love—Paul
The Word—John
Real Love—John with Paul
I Want to Tell You—George
It Don't Come Easy—Ringo
The Night Before—Paul
In My Life—John
Getting Better—Paul
Solitude—George with John
Maybe I'm Amazed—Paul
Yer Blues—John
Can't Buy Me Love—Paul

Encore

Wah Wah—George
Mr. Sampson—Paul with John
Hey Jude—Paul

Chapter 7

January 21, 1983—The Theatr Felinfach in Wales would be the smallest venue the boys would perform in during their thirteen-city/fifteen-show tour. It was a beautiful theater with the most amazing acoustics a musician could want. The show that night had been sold out in less than twenty minutes after tickets went on sale. They were in great spirits that Friday evening and were getting along famously.

Since re-forming, they had been careful not to be too intoxicated before performing. But they had all felt at ease with their playing and decided it wouldn't hurt to indulge in a few cocktails prior to the show. It was John, the most unexpectedly responsible Beatle, who suggested they slow down to make sure they could all be at their best. Again, the others saw a change in not only John's demeanor but also in his newly found responsibility to their product. He wanted them to be the best Beatles they could possibly be for their audiences. George seemed to think that was attributed to the large amounts of money they were being given. Paul thought differently. He felt that John's brush with death had rattled him to the core, and even though Lennon would never admit this, his whole perspective on life had done a complete 180-degree turn.

As the boys readied themselves to walk onstage in Wales, John called the others together for a quick huddle. "Where are we going, boys?" They all laughed at the memory of John's famous picker-upper line when things would get tough during Phase 1.

"To the toppermost, Johnny!" was their response.

"The toppermost of what?" asked John.

"The toppermost of the poppermost!" replied the others as they laughed at the almost forgotten saying.

Derek had ordered a video slide show to be put together of the boys back in the '60s, through their solo years, and up to the present day. As this three-minute video ended, the boys started onto the stage to another standing ovation that would this time last nearly seven minutes. The Wales crowd was warm and accommodating. The boys felt at home in this theater, which reminded them of the Royal Albert Hall, only more comfortable. The balconies were small and close to the stage. The scent of ladies' perfume and cigar smoke filled the theater as they started into the first notes of "Sgt. Pepper's Lonely Heart's Club Band." For this night on stage with them, they had recruited the services of Nicky Hopkins again. He would remain with them for the rest of the tour...albeit slightly in the background. Paul was more than capable of playing the keyboard parts, but his bass playing was essential to their sound. So, having Hopkins would give them more options of songs to perform.

The audience was incredibly moved by this unbelievable performance. Even some of the toughest Brits found themselves shedding a tear at the sight and sound of this unreal spectacle.

The night went without error or incident as their ninety-minute set seemed to end in only minutes to everyone who had witnessed the historic concert. This show would go down as possibly their favorite of the whole tour. Spirits were high in their camp. It wasn't only the boys who felt the joy; it was their manager, the road crew, and all who had worked the theater that night. Paul tried to keep his giddiness under wraps, but deep inside he was bursting with pride.

All who really knew the band were aware that while John was considered the leader of the group, it was really Paul who was their musical leader. John had always made way for Paul to direct the music because he knew how talented the bassist was and how keen of an ear he had. Paul truly felt like the Beatles was "his baby."

Set List: *Theatr Felinfach (January 21, 1983) with the singer listed next to each song:*

Sgt. Pepper's Lonely Heart's Club Band—Paul
Something—George
Given to Fly—John
Boys—Ringo
Hey Bulldog—John
Blackbird—Paul
Here Comes the Sun—George
Seeds of Love—Paul
Imagine—John
Real Love—John with Paul
It Don't Come Easy—Ringo
Dark Horse—George
In My Life—John
Fixing a Hole—Paul
Solitude—George with John
Live and Let Die—Paul
Revolution #1—John
Can't Buy Me Love—Paul

Encore

You Can't Do That—John
Mr. Sampson—Paul with John
Hey Jude—Paul

January 22, 1983—The London *Times* review of the Felinfach show raved about the band's energy and the warm atmosphere they created with the audience. It praised their constant interaction with the adoring fans and called them the "...living legends of live performance." The reviewer wrote about each song from the night and described in microscopic detail the sounds, sights, and smells. It was as glorious a review as they'd ever had written about one of their performances.

Every reporter who had witnessed the event described the warmth of that night and the unbridled joy felt by the ticket-paying customers. The attention now garnered from these reviews preceded them to every destination of the tour. It was having a snowball effect and the mania kept growing with every stop. The boys read the review in the newspapers that John brought into the CBS studios the next day, where they would resume rehearsing different material. The others read it and then did a faux celebratory cheer using the copies of the newspapers as the cups of their achievement.

There wasn't much time to celebrate that day, though, as they had a full schedule of songs to rehearse. George had brought two new songs to the others and Paul was excited to try them out. They went through a few oldies ("One After 909," "Don't Let Me Down," and a slower, much dirtier version of "Twist and Shout") when Paul asked if they could give one of George's new tunes a shot. They were all eager to learn and play new material. So, they jumped right into it. The song was entitled "Wallows of Sound," a tongue-in-cheek nod to the sound Phil Spector had become so famous for creating.

This song sounded more like John and Paul than did any of their new material. It had "Beatles" written all over it. George had asked a friend whom he had met through Ravi Shankar (Bishan Dyal) to accompany him on this track. The two had gone over the sound George was seeking a few times prior to that day. The song began with the swirling sound of the Shehnai (an Indian wind instrument that creates a canopy of sound mostly used as a droning background for a song). That alone set the others' minds off with ideas for a song they knew was something special.

After the opening sounds of the Shehnai, George asked Ringo to put a heavy backbeat to the song. He explained that while the intent was to create an image of peace in the listener's head, he still wanted it to rock. It took Ringo a couple of tries to get the beat George had heard in his head. It was Paul who helped translate that sound to Ringo as he understood what George wanted. George then turned to John and quickly ran over the chord progression. It was in the key of D and George wanted the sound to be what guitarists refer to as "ballsey." That put a smile on John's face as it was right in his wheelhouse. The guitar chords went from D to F back to D and then G. It wasn't difficult but John struggled to get the rhythmic Indian tempo just right. After a few minutes playing it with George, John was ready to give it a shot.

"Wallows of Sound" was rehearsed, recorded, and mixed within ten hours of learning the song. It was by far their most bare (in terms of production) yet complex song they had ever tracked. The intricate harmonies over interesting chord changes throughout the song gave it that complexity, although it included little in terms of overall instruments, having only the two guitars, bass, drums, and the droning Shehnai. This would incite an inside joke with the boys: The idea of recording this song exactly the opposite of the way Phil Spector would have done it, while naming the song after his technique, was a hoot to them all.

It may have been the Indian instrument that really hit the nerve of listeners as they sat back in the control room like proud papas. Geoff Emerick turned to George and said, "This is absolutely terrific, George. I think you've touched upon something that possibly no one has yet to do." George smiled and thanked Geoff for engineering a sound that was different yet undeniably the Beatles.

As the four Beatles discussed their musical direction with George Martin, it became clear that another album could be in the mix. The producer was all for it, but warned of too much, too soon. He was concerned that the quality of songs being brought in would diminish if they felt forced to come up with new material. This had once not been a problem as the ideas while in their twenties seemed to flow out nonstop. Now as they had gotten older, songs and song topics were not appearing as fluently as in the past. There was no rush to write new songs. The label had signed them for four albums, and the one that was already in the books firmly sat at No. 1 on the music charts. The band made sure when they signed their record deal to not have timelines associated with the release of any of their upcoming projects. That allowed more time and space for creativity without the weight of a deadline looming over their collective shoulders.

They were all about to go home for the night when Paul asked George Martin to stick around for a minute. Paul had been leery of bringing in new material at this time because he knew he had a tendency to be overbearing when it came to how he wanted his songs to sound. He didn't want to rock the boat as things had been going extremely well for them all. So, he thought running through the new songs and addressing his reservations with the producer would help guide him as to how to proceed.

"George, can you give these two new songs a listen and tell me what you think?"

"Of course, Paul," said the always professional Martin.

Paul ran quickly through the first one—a soft and melodic ballad in the same vein as "Mamunia" from Wings' *Band on the Run* album. *It was good!*, thought Martin. Paul started into the next new tune, but then stopped. "It'll most likely be played on the piano, but I'll run it through on this acoustic," he stated.

This song was reminiscent of "Golden Slumbers" on the *Abbey Road* album. It had the most beautiful melody and built up to a crescendo that sounded anthemic to Martin. George's mind raced to how he would arrange the song.

"Paul, I think both of those songs are fabulous. Shall we present them to the others?"

"I'm not so certain yet...I really have in my mind how I want these to sound, especially that last one. And I don't want to force the others to play what I want them to play."

Martin knew this was the reason Harrison had so badly wanted out of the group in the 1960s. He realized the delicate waters they would have to tread. Both agreed on how the song should end up sounding and it was now up to the producer to make the suggestions Paul had requested of him. They talked in length about these two songs, and about whether they should now think about beginning their second album since their historic return to the public eye. It was the kind of nice conversation that had always seemed to take place when the two were in the studio alone.

There had been a time when Martin had felt resentment toward McCartney for pushing his way into the control room and Martin out. The boys had relied on Martin to help form their sound up until a point where Paul could no longer sit back and allow anyone to produce his numerous hit songs. Even though Martin had felt uneasy about this situation, there wasn't much he could do as he knew McCartney had now become proficient at producing his own material. Almost simultaneously, when Martin finally came to terms with this, McCartney began again giving free rein back to Martin to produce as he had always done.

They agreed to step lightly about presenting these two songs to the others. They still had 13 shows left on their 1983 tour and there were many songs that needed to be worked on to be comfortably prepared. For now, they were both satisfied with keeping a conversation about the new album on the back burners.

The producer and the star parted ways that night both feeling a renewed sense of camaraderie. There were no hard feelings between the two even though there had been some contentious moments in the past. They both realized that not only were things going great at this point, but they still needed each other. The roll that the band was on would not slow anytime soon.

Chapter 8

January 29, 1983—The boys were in Belfast, Ireland, to play that night at the historic Ulster Hall. This concert hall on Bedford Street had opened in the late nineteenth century and was the host to some of the world's top acts. The four Liverpudlians were looking forward to playing that night as they were all quite aware of the history surrounding the venue. It had hosted acts such as the Rolling Stones, the Kinks, the Who, Pink Floyd, and Cream. Recently, it was the host to mostly local acts and bands on the cusp of making names for themselves. As the hall opened and began filling, Paul took a peek through the stage curtains to see the grand hall in its current glory. He was surprised at the nervousness he felt about playing this wonderful venue.

The show started like all of the rest on this tour—with the three-minute video that Derek Taylor had created for them. The Irish crowd stood from the moment the house lights went down and the video began until the very last song of the night. This tour had already become the stuff of legends. The crowds that would now gather outside the venues were swelling at each show, even though no tickets were to be had. This night was to become another memorable show for the band.

They started with "Magical Mystery Tour," which would end up becoming the opening song for most of the tour. It sounded just as it did on the 1967 album and possibly even better as Ringo's drumming had become more proficient with each show. The boys knew that Ringo was always the key to their performances. If he played well, they sounded fabulous. If not, they tumbled alongside their lovable drummer.

The others knew Ringo had taken a turn for the best while playing "Lucy in the Sky with Diamonds." It was during the part in the song when the drums led into the chorus with a *thump, thump, thump, thump...* *"Lucy in the Sky with Diamonds..."* On this night, however, there were only three thumps when Ringo rolled into a triplet that spun his bandmates' heads immediately around as if to say, "Holy shit!! That was brilliant!" Ringo sat straight up, smiling and playing as if he had always known how to do a triplet on the drums. He had been watching some videos of Buddy Rich, and while Ringo knew that Rich was a better drummer by far, Starr studied his triplet technique.

Ringo, being a left-handed drummer playing a right-handed kit, started many drum fills on what other drummers would call the "wrong drum." This created many of his unique drum fills, but also caused the drummer much difficulty playing some of the normal drum fills others could easily do. So being able to now play a triplet (even though as unorthodox as it would end up being) gave Ringo a new sense of confidence in his playing. This new drum fill would not go unnoticed by the reporters who wrote their stories the next day.

The show had only one hiccup and that was when John broke a string on his sunburst Epiphone Casino guitar during "I Want to Tell You." Mal Evans was quick to grab the Epiphone from John and replaced it with his legendary Beatles Rickenbacker 325. He then set out to restring the Casino for his onstage boss. Most in the audience barely noticed the quick switch and Nicky Hopkins was there to rescue John. He changed the sound of his keyboards to imitate a guitar to cover for the absent instrument.

The final notes of "Hey Jude" rung out in the hall and the boys again gathered at the front of the stage to bow for their adoring fans. It was another success in a string of successes that had now become commonplace again for the band.

Set List: *Ulster Hall (January 29, 1983) with the singer listed next to each song:*

Magical Mystery Tour—Paul
Come Together—John
Given to Fly—John
With a Little Help from My Friends—Ringo
Taxman—George
Watching the Wheels—John
Seeds of Love—Paul
Lucy in the Sky with Diamonds—John
Real Love—John with Paul
I Want to Tell You—George
You and Me (Babe)—Ringo
Good Day Sunshine—Paul
Nowhere Man—John
Can't Buy Me Love—Paul
Solitude—George with John
Let Me Roll It—Paul
I'm Only Sleeping—John
Please, Please Me—John and Paul

Encore

All Things Must Pass—George
Mr. Sampson—Paul with John
Hey Jude—Paul

February 3, 1983—The Beatles were scheduled to rehearse on this morning when they received a phone call from Olivia Harrison. George had been in a car accident. While his injuries were not severe, he would need a few days to heal. She assured them he was fine and that he was just rattled a little to go along with some bumps and bruises. At first, the others thought about canceling the rehearsal but then decided to go ahead anyway at the urging of the future Sir Paul. He thought this might be the perfect opportunity to introduce the two new songs he had played for George Martin when they were in the studio alone a few weeks back.

Paul sat down in the studio with an acoustic guitar and began playing the chords to his new song, "Jewel of the Heart." John and Ringo sat listening intently. This was also unusual for Lennon as his previous disconnect to Paul's songs had been replaced with a sincere ear. He now wanted to help form this new song in the same manner that Paul had always done for him.

Ringo was the first to speak. "What kind of beat would you like on this, Paul?" he asked.

"Well, Ring, I was thinking it would be best to have a drum sound that is kind of in the background. Almost the same as what you did on 'Till There Was You.'"

With that, Ringo decided upon the sound he would create—he tossed the drumsticks aside and played the drum toms with his bare hands. That turned out to be the perfect backbeat to this melancholy song. John then took over the acoustic guitar part as Paul picked up his bass. The song flowered and bloomed over the next nine takes until it had grown into another McCartney masterpiece. It did have the same type of feel as "Mamunia," like George Martin had thought when he first heard the song. There was little production needed for this one and the only piece left was an added guitar solo from George. Paul had envisioned a slide guitar part that George had become so good at playing.

The three Beatles were pleased with the new song but again Paul wanted a few more takes at the bass line. This took little time as McCartney had it down by the fourth retake of the bass part. Paul then told the others he'd like to show them another song. Paul held this one a little closer to the vest as he thought it was the best tune he had written in years.

It also just then dawned on him that George may not be the unhappy one with this new song—it was most likely to be John as the song cried out to be produced in the way that George Martin made them famous for, but was also the type of "rubbish" Lennon loathed. John had stated his displeasure more times than he could remember about songs being over-produced. He despised all the tricks, gadgets, and studio sounds that would end up on the songs he created to be much more bare and raw sounding. His roots were rock and blues music, so the classically trained George Martin at times stood in his way like a human Mt. Everest. Martin would not soon forget a fiery Lennon telling him, "I don't want any of that over-produced shit from the *Pepper* record" as they were about to record *Let It Be*. That one sentence had made Martin withdraw as he found it almost impossible to balance Paul's desire to have a massive sound and John's hatred of that style of music.

So, when Paul sat at the piano and started the introduction to what would soon to become the immortal "Follow You," he did not let on to the ideas he had previously discussed with Martin. This song really did sound like "Golden Slumbers" and the other two Beatles realized that.

To Paul's surprised pleasure, John complimented him by saying, "I love it! Are the words done?"

"Not yet," was Paul's reply.

He knew if he let John be part of the writing process that Lennon would be much more invested and interested in recording it. John told them that he had some good lyrics sitting around that he'd like to add to this new tune. So, after a few run-throughs, the three were ready to record. Geoff Emerick moved microphones here and there, setting one inside a small shoebox just in front of Lennon's amp. He was always looking for different sounds that had not yet been touched upon. This idea caused Lennon to laugh. He thought, *How on earth is that going to sound coming from a shoebox?* It did create a sound as if Lennon was playing far away in an empty auditorium. This pleased them all. After thirteen takes and almost six hours, the basic track was done.

George Martin stood in the control room of Studio 2 and called the band in from over the microphone to come and give it a listen. Martin thoughtfully began, "You know, Paul, I think this one could use some strings and maybe even the old Mellotron (which was so recognizably distinct as the beginning of "Strawberry Fields Forever")." This suggestion even caught Paul off guard as the producer had been silently pondering this direction. John was all for it. That made the rest of the recording go as smoothly as any song they had previously done.

The thing that made it a bit difficult for John and Ringo (and then George when he showed up two days later) was the amount of time it would take to complete the entire track. Every new song that had been recorded for their Phase 2 sessions was done in less than a day. They had chosen this new path because the Fabs all had family now and weren't so inclined to spend unlimited hours in the studio. But they all knew this song could become one of their greatest efforts if no one got in the way. They spent the next two days in the studio working on "Follow Me" and were getting close to completion, but the song would have to wait until after their next performance. The band left Emerick to fix some recording issues on the song as they prepared for the next gig.

February 6, 1983—Their next show was scheduled for this night in Glasgow at another historic venue—the Barrowland Ballroom. This ballroom and dance hall was built in 1934 and subsequently burned to the ground in 1958, leading to a complete rebuild in 1960. This room did in fact look more like a dance hall than a concert venue. The selling point, though, was the acoustics. The ceiling of the ballroom was lined with echo-reducing panels and formed a uniquely warm sound that would allow any instrument played underneath to resonate wonderfully. This room had a marvelous environment for concerts and could hold 1,900 attendees, making it the largest venue to date on this tour. The boys were all in fine form that evening and were pleased that George's accident didn't hinder his playing ability. They were also eager to get back to recording, as the new song that was still in the oven, so to speak, was beckoning them back into the studio. Even Harrison was aware of the buzz generated around Paul's new song and welcomed the opportunity to add his guitar to it.

The night was another success and the Scottish fans in attendance sang until they were hoarse. The Beatles completed their tour of the United Kingdom and were again on their way to proving they were the best live band on the planet. It was now time to travel a little more extensively—something that Harrison dreaded but the others accepted. The Barrowland show went without a flaw, but there had been a bit of an issue backstage after the show. George was not happy with McCartney and claimed the bassist was playing too loud for the others to even hear their own instrument. John was indifferent about this and Ringo was just plain used to not being heard. But to George, this was a battle that had to be fought. He felt he could not properly focus on the notes he was playing if his main concern was being heard at all. Paul didn't hesitate to defend his stage volume and demanded that George just turn up his own volume. The argument became so heated that Ringo, Mal, and Derek all had to step in to separate the two. John mildly chuckled at the sequence of events. He had always thought that confrontation was okay and at times even important to the dynamics of the band.

Set List: *The Barrowland Ballroom (February 6, 1983) with the singer* *listed next to each song:*

Magical Mystery Tour—Paul
Come Together—John
Given to Fly—John
Boys—Ringo
Taxman—George
Imagine—John
Seeds of Love—Paul
The Word—John
Real Love—John with Paul
I Want to Tell You—George
It Don't Come Easy—Ringo
Let It Be—Paul
Nowhere Man—John
Fixing a Hole—Paul
Solitude—George with John
Maybe I'm Amazed—Paul
Rain—John
Lady Madonna—Paul

Encore

Give Me Love (Give Me Peace on Earth)—George
Mr. Sampson—Paul with John
Hey Jude—Paul

February 9, 1983—The boys were back in the studio on this day to add George's guitar and vocals to "Jewel of the Heart," and then they were to finish work on "Follow You." It didn't take George long to create a perfectly fitting slide guitar solo to "Jewel." He had heard Paul's request for a slide solo and had created a tone on his guitar that was crunchy, warm, and full. It was reminiscent of many songs from George's *Living in the Material World* record that had once and for all quieted the critics who claimed his guitar prowess was marginal at best. George's guitar playing, and especially the way he played slide, had now become something of a goal to attain for any aspiring guitarist.

With that song complete, it was now time for him to turn his attention to this amazing new song that had generated so much attention from the others and George Martin. Harrison listened to "Follow You" for the first time in the control room and was moved to the point of sadness. It took him a few minutes to figure out why he was sad, but it dawned on him that while he knew that he could write a great tune himself, he wasn't so sure he could write something this incredible. Still, he was eager to add what would end up being one of his best guitar solos ever, let alone on a Beatles record. George sat in the studio alone with the headphones on and was immersed in the overall sound that had been groomed by the others and George Martin. They had added strings and the Mellotron to the basic track. It only lacked the final vocals and George's solo. Four takes in, George decided to use the wah-wah pedal and that altered the entire dynamic of the solo.

The celebration from the others in the control room showed George he had played the perfect part for the new McCartney composition. This was destined to be the best and most elaborate song of their careers. Even John didn't mind the over-production of this instant hit. The song needed it and they all agreed (after the vocals were recorded) that it was done and ready to be mixed.

It was getting into the evening at this point and the boys were tired from working most of the day in Studio 2. All four Beatles, along with Mal and Derek, made their way to the slowly becoming famous Pig Sty for a round of drinks to celebrate their achievement. At the table, they laughed about recent events, and all raised their mugs to a loud "Cheers" from the lot. Derek and Mal sat quiet but smiling the whole time as they watched the boys launch volley after volley of jokes, digs, wordplays, and just plain ridiculousness. It was the kind of thing that had endeared them to the public during the film *A Hard Day's Night*.

George spoke seriously for a minute. "Maybe it's time to do another album." There was an enormous sense of relief that hit Paul at that moment as this heavy burden had been lifted off his shoulders. This had been on his mind almost constantly and he had avoided approaching the subject too soon. Now that George had suggested it, they were sure to go forward with the project.

Before any of the boys had a chance to respond, the swell of pub patrons that begun to swarm around their table had escalated to a dangerous level. A full pint of beer was knocked out of the hand of an onlooker and landed directly on John and Ringo. Ringo became quite upset, but John just laughed. He then turned to the beer spillers and proceeded to dump the rest of his beer over his own head. Lennon had suddenly become a happy drunk, and the patrons burst into laughter at his antics. The others, however, felt that they were now in danger and retreated to their vehicles with the assistance of Mal, Derek, and the pub manager (whom they had now become friendly with).

It was George again who suggested they carry on at his mansion. They all agreed and spent the next four hours listening to music, drinking, and smoking weed at Friar Park. It was as joyous a night with each other as they could remember. Even Clapton showed up to join in on the fun.

Chapter 9

February 13, 1983—The Beatles were on a plane headed to Tokyo that morning. John was excited as Yoko had been waiting for this show since they announced the tour. This was the country where she was born, and while spending many years in London and New York, she still considered Japan to be her home.

When they arrived at Tokyo International Airport, another huge crowd had gathered. The Japanese media had been headlining each evening news for the past two weeks talking about the Beatles' arrival. Paul suggested that Yoko exit the plane and head down the airstair first to allow the group of reporters quick access to their hometown hero. She had always been in the background of any Beatles event, but this time her status was nearly that of the boys in the band. The reporters yelled out their questions and formed an immediate circle around her, almost pushing the Fab Four aside.

This made John proud, as his wife had been persecuted by the press for years after their breakup in 1970. Most thought that she was the catalyst for the breakup and were unrelenting in their blame of her. John felt it was unfair and he had for a time soured toward the media because of this. He now felt she was getting the recognition she deserved. Paul was on the other side of the aisle, thinking she did in fact play a big part of their split. He held his resentment toward her inside and would never let on to John about that. Back in the late '60s, it was George and Ringo who would confront John about bringing Yoko to all the recording sessions that were once forbidden to any outsider. John didn't get over that for many years. It was after the shooting that he seemed to let that anger dissipate.

February 15, 1983—The gig at Nippon Budokan in Tokyo that Tuesday night went exceptionally well, and the lads had again worked their magic on the 14,102 fans in attendance. This was by far the largest venue at this point of the tour. The screams of the audience brought back memories of many Phase 1 shows where numerous teeny boppers would pass out from the excitement.

Yoko had invited her family members to join her for the show and then to come backstage afterward. The backstage room where the boys would have their usual after-show gathering was large and appeared to be a separate auditorium (in fact, it was a gymnasium used for sports exhibits and the like). Food and drinks were abundant with waiters in tuxedoes offering up delightful dishes. The aura of the backstage party was electric, and the boys noticed many people leaning over to indulge in what they later realized was cocaine. The drug had become popular at that time for the younger generation, and the Japanese youth seemed to eagerly embrace it. All four Beatles had experimented with coke in the late '60s but had long since stayed away from it and other hard drugs. They had all taken their fair share of LSD and other mind-altering substances but now only occasionally smoked pot.

That night, though, George decided to put some up his nose. This did not sit well with Paul, who was against the drug. He approached George and said, "What the hell are you doing, bloke?" He was incensed and let Harrison know this.

George immediately barked back, "Fuck off, Paul. I'm not a child anymore and I'm definitely not your responsibility." This enraged Paul to the point of wanting to replace their lead guitarist and began a new tension between the two that would lead to troubles down the road.

March 16, 1983—The boys had played Paris on this night to a somewhat subdued crowd. The French enjoyed the Beatles but were the most reserved bunch they would perform for on the tour. John had always felt uncomfortable in Paris because of their lack of enthusiasm and what he thought was a superiority complex. The show went well, and they then made their way to Berlin, Germany, to an equally enormous success.

The Berlin show was another highlight for the boys because of their musical beginnings in that area. The famous Star Club in Hamburg was where they became such an incredible live act. Most bands would play anywhere from an hour to three hours a night in a live environment. The Beatles would play eight- to ten-hour shows. It was madness but these long hours honed their live skills and molded the young men into a single, tight unit that would eventually earn them the nickname "The Four-Headed Monster." After the Berlin show, they moved on to Moscow, Russia. The USSR had been off-limits for any popular music as the Cold War was still being waged. Moscow was beginning to show signs of Western influences, and the Russian audiences were as thirsty for popular music as any country the boys had toured.

April 6, 1983—The Moscow performance stood as the largest crowd they would play on this tour. The band performed their ninety-minute set at Luzhniki Stadium (a football stadium that held approximately 81,000 people). Realizing the significance of this event, the boys had invited Eric Clapton and Mick Jagger to join them for two extra songs ("While My Guitar Gently Weeps" with Clapton and Harrison trading off guitar solos at the end, and then a rocking version of "Back in the U.S.S.R.," which brought the house down). The crowd sang along to every song, and like with most other shows, tears of happiness were scattered throughout the stadium at the amazing event. The audience knew they were witnessing something special that they would most likely never again see.

This was a grand moment for the lads from Liverpool. They had broken ground in a place where few acts were allowed to perform. This was pleasing to the band, and for now the tension between George and Paul had been replaced with the joy of the moment. The Russian press praised the group with an intense fervor that escalated their status to one of dignitaries. They were called "honorary citizens" by one of the writers who had made a plea to the readers to petition the government for this to come to fruition. The four were elated at the warm welcome they had received but had not expected from the Russian media.

April 17 & 18, 1983—The Beatles had been to Australia in 1964 and had an amazing experience, so they scheduled two shows at Sydney's Hyde Park for this tour. Each show drew over 55,000 people and was broadcast on closed-circuit television throughout the continent. Derek Taylor had made a deal with the Australian network that distributed the event on pay per view to obtain 25 percent of the proceeds. This was another lucrative offering along with the already record-breaking amount they were receiving from the venue. Taylor had caught wind of the closed-circuit showing only after seeing it advertised on the local TV stations. It appeared the network was trying to keep this information from the band in hopes of cashing in on them. At first, Taylor threatened with a lawsuit but then settled for a quarter of the money made through the closed-circuit screenings.

The money they would make from this far surpassed that which they made from the venue, which was the most they were ever paid for a live performance. Each show at Hyde Park resulted in the band making well over £475,000 per man with the venue paying £100,000 and the network paying the rest. It was a massive amount of money, even for them, and while they were pleased with this, Taylor and Beatles lawyers would later in fact file a suit against the Australian Broadcasting Company. The suit would be settled out of court after a three-year battle. The settlement amount put the grand total for each Beatle after the two-show extravaganza upwards of £1,000,000! Most touring bands would not make that amount per person in a year's time.

Both shows were fantastic and met with a wild Australian enthusiasm the boys had so fondly remembered. Two shows in two nights did have an adverse effect on them, though. They were tired and now were losing some of the initial excitement of playing in front of live audiences. This was not a byproduct of the Hyde Park shows; it was now starting to become more tedious instead of just fun. Paul was not as tired of the routine as the others. He enjoyed the strenuous challenges of being on the road and was the only Beatle to attend both after-show parties. All four had attended the party after the first show, but only Paul appeared on the next night to the delight of the eight hundred people in attendance. Even he left after only a brief time, deciding it was probably a good idea to get some rest.

April 20, 1983—After staying an extra day in the Land Down Under to enjoy some of the sights, they were now on their way to the states. The first stop was Detroit, where they would play Cobo Arena. This concert hall was known among touring bands for having great acoustics for its size and for the enthusiastic crowds it would house. The boys landed at Detroit's Metro Airport to another mob of fans and reporters. This seemed to be a common theme now at every airport they made their way through. Mike Sampson met them at the airport. He had been excited, but nervous, because he had not seen the band since their meeting last August in New York. The boys were elated to see their new assistant manager and friend. They always seemed to become extra cheery when an outsider joined the mix (and especially since they admired the quiet hero from Long Island).

It was cold and rainy on that Wednesday morning as the boys checked in at the Pontchartrain Hotel. Detroit was a blue collar town that loved its sports and music. The rock crowds there were rowdy and wild. The band spent most of the day with Sampson and paid a visit to Hitsville USA on Grand Boulevard. This was the home of Motown—the recording studio that created its own genre of music. The Beatles had been so influenced by this sound out of Detroit that they covered three Motown songs on their second album (*With the Beatles*): "Please Mister Postman," "You've Really Got a Hold on Me," and "Money."

After their video had completed, the boys came up onstage to an uproar from the 12,483 in attendance. The standing ovation and screaming that greeted the band lasted over ten minutes. It was even more hysteria than what they had already been experiencing on this tour. The Detroit crowd was truly living up to its name as one of the best. People were holding signs showing their appreciation to the band. The one that made Lennon laugh and point out to the others was held by a young man that read, "My grandma is here!!" It was a multi-generational experience, and the decibels reached by this crowd were almost "Shea Stadium-type" ear piercing.

They played their usual set along with the regular three-song encore, but the fans would not leave...even after the house lights came on! No one was budging—they wanted more and weren't going anywhere. After ten minutes, the house lights again went down. The eruption of the crowd nearly blew the roof off the arena. The band had not expected such a riotous reaction and were eager to get back onstage for a second encore.

Paul approached the microphone and said, "Wow! Wow! This is purely incredible. What an audience! Thank you, Detroit!" They played two more songs ("I've Got a Feeling" and "I Want You (She's So Heavy)")—both of which they had previously rehearsed but not played on this tour. The songs ended in a frenzied mania that kept increasing in volume as the fans again showered them with screams of praise. All four came to the front of the stage, bowed simultaneously, and made their exit. This time the house lights came on immediately, as it was already past II p.m., the city-imposed cutoff time for concerts.

The boys were backstage having a drink and celebrating with local celebrities and others lucky enough to know someone connected with the band. Suddenly, they heard rhythmic chanting and screaming coming from the hall. The audience had not gone home...after fifteen minutes of screaming at the tops of their lungs. *This is absurd*, thought McCartney as he turned to the others to ask if they wanted to play more. Finally, the house lights once again went down, and the astonished group of English lads came back out onto the stage. This time, they were greeted with a volume that was now approaching one of a Lear jet. It was truly deafening. They had not remembered a show where they played even one encore after the house lights came on, let alone two, which they were about to embark upon.

They stood in front of the adoring audience and were blindsided by a sense of gratitude they had not yet felt on this tour. Every other show had its share of excitement from start to end, but this was different. Their appreciation of the fans this night made it an easy decision to come back out for a third encore. John grabbed the microphone this time and gave out his most sincere thanks to the people of the Motor City. Paul had suggested the final two songs that had not been played live on this tour: "Penny Lane" and "Day Tripper." Prior to coming back out, they quickly went over the two songs.

The final notes of "Day Tripper" rang out, and even though the volume of the crowd was still on the rise, the boys were done. They were beat from this show, which had lasted over two hours and ended at 11:40 p.m. It had been monumental in many ways, and the most spectacular moment may have been getting Smokey Robinson to come onstage for fabulous versions of "You've Really Got a Hold on Me" and "Please Mr. Postman." The Beatles were also influenced by Elvis, Buddy Holly, and Chuck Berry, but Motown was indeed a special place for them all. Detroit had a reputation for having some of the best rock audiences in the land, and this night was no exception. This was a show that the band would not soon forget.

Set List: *Cobo Arena (April 20, 1983) with the singer listed next to each song:*

Magical Mystery Tour—Paul
Come Together—John
Given to Fly—John
Boys—Ringo
Taxman—George
Imagine—John
Seeds of Love—Paul
The Word—John
Real Love—John with Paul
I Want to Tell You—George
I'm the Greatest—Ringo with John
Can't Buy Me Love—Paul
You've Really Got a Hold on Me—John with Smokey Robinson
Please Mister Postman—John with Paul and Smokey
Solitude—George with John
Lady Madonna—Paul
Rain—John
All My Loving—Paul

Encore #1

What Is Life—George

Mr. Sampson—Paul with John

Hey Jude—Paul

Encore #2

I've Got A Feeling—Paul with John

I Want You (She's So Heavy)—John

Encore #3

Penny Lane—Paul

Day Tripper—John with Paul

Chapter 10

April 25, 1983—The boys were back in New York for an interview with Geraldo Rivera, where they again captured the viewing audience with their charm and wit. The boys were funny, engaging, and candid. The interaction with each other had been one of respect and maybe their most appealing quality. Viewers could sense the closeness of the group, and their inside jokes dominated the interview. The band enjoyed Geraldo and he seemed to bring out the best in them.

"So, John, how are you doing now? Are you completely healed?" asked Rivera.

"Well, as you know, Geraldo, they removed part of my brain along with the leg. So, what was the question again?" The crowd laughed and politely cheered.

"It seems they didn't remove the part of your brain that controls humor!" replied Geraldo.

"Oh yes, they did remove that, Geraldo!" George intervened to another round of laughter. Rivera was extremely thorough with his research of the boys as each Beatle had his share of turns answering his questions.

Getting back around to Lennon, Geraldo asked, "John, how are things with you and Julian?"—touching on a subject that was bound to be quite delicate. John did not have a good relationship with his first son until recently when he slowly started reappearing in the twenty-year-old's life.

"Well, we went on holiday last year—Yoko, Sean, and Julian. I'm happy to say we're now closer than ever. I wasn't around much when he was small, ya know?" he said, slyly grinning at the studio audience, which again caused some laughter.

The media had reported on numerous occasions how the two were not close. Julian never had the father he had always hoped for, and John now seemed determined to make up for lost time. John's father was a merchant seaman and therefore was also not around much during his only son's childhood. Making amends in that sense was rewarding to John, even though it took him seventeen years to getting around to it.

Julian had become a musician and was working on his own material at the time. "I asked the others about this before the interview and they all agreed to it, but now I'll ask you...would you perform a song for us? With Julian?" Just as Geraldo finished the question, out came a wide-smiled Julian to a standing ovation. John stood and almost tumbled over as his left leg had been hurting from sitting for so long. He hugged Julian and the young man made his way around to greet the others.

"Well, I'll be damned. You mean just me and him? What would we do?" was Lennon's response. Paul jumped in to say, "We've already worked it out with Jules, John. We want to do 'Hey Jude' with him on piano."

"Fantastic!" Lennon marveled.

"Hey Jude" had in fact been written about Julian when his parents were going through a divorce. Paul had always been like an uncle to John's son and sometimes more of a father than his own. As the boy grew and became aware of this, he had felt a special closeness to McCartney, knowing that one of the most famous songs ever was written to comfort him.

The Beatles plus one made their way to a small stage where their equipment had been set up. They went through a wonderful version of the song, which always made an audience sing the ending anthem part in unison. It was a proud moment for the elder Lennon to have his son perform live with the Beatles. The others were just as delighted to have the son of their friend playing alongside in front of an audience.

John's mind raced and he asked Geraldo, "I know he's been working on some music and he played me something the other day that I'm wonderin' if you'll allow him to do a bit of right here...."

"Dad, no" was Julian's response. But Geraldo, always quick to recognize a great TV moment, urged the younger Lennon to play his new song. The studio audience stood and cheered until Julian finally gave in.

"Okay, okay. I'll give it a go. But I've only just recently completed it. So, I'm not certain how it'll turn out!"

All four Beatles and Geraldo gathered around the piano to hear Julian play his soon-to-be hit "Valotte." The song left the other Beatles, Rivera, and the studio audience in amazement as it sounded like it could have possibly been a Beatles release. Julian even sang like his old man. If one closed their eyes, they could have easily mistaken the younger Lennon for the world-famous one. After a healthy round of applause, the boys noticed a tear coming to the elder Lennon's eye. They had never witnessed the stoic musical genius come to a tear, but this was certainly a proud moment for Julian's father.

May 2, 1983—The band was now in Illinois to perform at the newly opened Allstate Arena in Rosemont, just on the northwest side of Chicago. There was a little tension in the air that evening as the band had been spending a bit too much time together and it was showing. The jovial atmosphere that often surrounded the boys was not present, and in its place arose scowls of displeasure at every comment.

George had been indulging in a little too much cocaine again for Paul's liking and the two were not speaking. John chose to stay quiet and somber instead of bashing away at the others as was his inclination. He now felt the need to drink...and that he did on that Monday night in Rosemont. The band wandered onto the stage fifteen minutes later than usual at approximately 9:30, making the crowd restless and uneasy from the start. They ran through the first half of their set in spectacular fashion, making no mistakes and giving their all even though their hearts didn't feel like it. But, coming from such a riotous crowd in Detroit, this audience seemed to lack energy, enthusiasm, and appeared plain bored. That was enough to set Lennon afire. "If yers don't like it, you can all sod off!" he yelled at the crowd off the microphone but loud enough for many to hear.

From that point, what started as a mild disconnect turned into an all-out battle between the band and the Rosemont crowd. The heckling wasn't so bad, but when objects started being hurled at the stage, all four Beatles walked off. At that point in the show, they had played fifteen of the twenty-one songs on the list for that night. The promotor, in an attempt to quiet the crowd, got on the microphone and pleaded with the boys to come back out to play more. His pleas would fall on deaf ears as the band had already left the building.

On the way back to their hotel in their limo, George defiantly pulled out some cocaine and started to snort it right in front of the rest. Paul immediately knocked the open package out of George's hand to spill the expensive drug all over the plush carpet of the limo. George lunged at Paul and the two wrestled to the floor with Ringo and John pulling them apart, but not before blood trickled from McCartney's nose.

"Pull over!" yelled an angry McCartney to the limo driver. The driver pulled over and Paul jumped out. "I'm not riding with that fuckhead anywhere. Matter of fact, I'm done playing with you!" he screamed at Harrison. Ringo also got out and decided to walk with

Paul back to the hotel. The two talked the whole way back and were not noticed by the few people they passed. They made sure not to speak when strangers did walk by as their British accents would have easily given away their cover. That night would eventually be a turning point, as a seed of the tensions to come had been planted for a band that had conquered the world—twice.

Set List: *Allstate Arena (May 2, 1983) with the singer listed next to each song:*

Magical Mystery Tour—Paul
Come Together—John
Given to Fly—John
With a Little Help from My Friends—Ringo
Taxman—George
Imagine—John
Seeds of Love—Paul
Lucy in the Sky with Diamonds—John
Real Love—John with Paul
I Want to Tell You—George
It Don't Come Easy—Ringo
Good Day Sunshine—Paul
In My Life—John
Get Back—Paul
Solitude—George with John
~~Let Me Roll It—Paul~~
~~I'm Only Sleeping—John~~
~~Please, Please Me—John and Paul~~

~~*Encore*~~

~~All Things Must Pass—George~~
~~Mr. Sampson—Paul with John~~
~~Hey Jude—Paul~~

May 3, 1983—The band was scheduled to fly into Los Angeles that day, but high-tailed back to England. It was time for a short break from each other. All four did whatever they could over the next week and a half to avoid anything Beatle related as it had again become a difficult environment. Paul was still livid over George's use of the drug and even more upset that Harrison put it in his face so defiantly. Paul had always looked at George as inferior in more ways than one—musically and culturally. Being a few years older had made McCartney feel like he was the big brother that could order Harrison around as he pleased. Besides, it was Paul who got George into the Beatles, and he felt he was never properly appreciated for opening that door.

At the same time in New York, the Beatles new assistant manager, Mike Sampson, received a call from Allstate Arena manager Jim Cook. The arena manager was furious about the band walking off the stage before their set was completed and threatened Sampson with a lawsuit. Sampson had always been quick on his feet, so he told the manager that one of the band members had been hit in the head with a set of keys that opened a cut. "Bullshit!" was Jim's response. He went on that if someone in the band got injured, there was a complete medical staff on hand to help get them back out to play.

They argued back and forth until Mike offered to give back the $23,400 the manager had paid the band for the extra security. Cook almost took the deal but instead again threatened a lawsuit and hung up. It would soon be up to the lawyers to hash out. This issue would stay in the court system for the next three and a half years, ending with the band settling out of court and giving $46,800 back to the venue. Sampson was getting some valuable on-the-job training that would later help him navigate the often-turbulent waters of band management.

May 12, 1983—McCartney knew he had to make amends before their next show in Los Angeles. So, the day before they were to fly to California, he phoned George in an attempt to straighten things out.

"George," he began, "I was wrong for telling you what to do on your own time. But you must understand this is having an adverse effect on your playing and is making it impossible to have rational conversations with you."

Harrison paused to ponder Paul's sentiment and then explained how the pressures of the tour were getting the better of him. He knew Paul was right and really didn't like the drug much anyway. It was getting to be just a habit...and a bad one, at that. The conversation lasted less than ten minutes and George agreed to abstain from the drug for the final three shows of the tour. They also agreed to revisit the next steps of the band after a two-month hiatus when the tour ended. There was trouble brewing and all four knew it.

It was Mike Sampson who again came to the boys' rescue. He could sense the in-band friction and invited them to a home-cooked family meal at his residence between their final two shows in New York. They had decided to play two nights in New York at John's request. He wanted to give back to the city he called home for many years and to its people who had nurtured him like he was their own.

But first they had to get through the Los Angeles show at The Forum. This was to be a monumental task as the tension in the band was at an all-time Phase 2 high. Ringo wasn't getting along with Paul, and quietly John had become disillusioned with George, thinking maybe Paul was right that the cocaine was detrimental to the lot. It remained to be seen if they could pretend as if nothing were wrong and continue to be the fun-loving blokes from Liverpool while performing for a live audience.

May 14, 1983—The day of the gig at The Forum was a glorious Californian day. The sun shone brightly, and the temperature was in the low 70s. It was a perfect day and the boys took advantage of it as each one went out to enjoy the warm sunshine. Harrison met up with David Crosby and Graham Nash to smoke weed and play songs out on Nash's back patio. McCartney looked up a friend and visited a local art museum while John took Yoko for a walk by Grauman's Chinese Theatre in Hollywood. Ringo was going to be more of a concern as he tracked down Harry Nilsson, who happened to already be on a three-day drinking binge with Mickey Dolenz. The other three Beatles showed up at The Forum by 7 p.m. for their 9:15 show, but Ringo didn't waltz in until 9 p.m. and that angered the others. Besides being fashionably late, he was also very much inebriated. The 17,119 screaming fans were ready to witness history, and the boys could only hope to give them some... at least good history and not bad.

They started the night with "Magical Mystery Tour," which fed right into the Lennon hit "Come Together." The crowd went crazy as the band sounded great and was everything they had hoped to see. Ringo's playing started off fine, but by mid-set, the drummer had become sloppy—so sloppy that it prompted Lennon to half-jokingly ask the crowd if there were "any drummers in the audience." That comment was met with some laughter and dozens of raised hands from the many capable drummers in attendance.

Paul was quiet and uncomfortable as he fiddled around on the bass, pretending not to notice the elephant in the room. Ringo went from happy, even giddy, to somber and miserable. He had always been acutely aware that his playing on the best of days wasn't as elaborate or precise as many of his peers. He had been known for his great backbeat, solid playing, and could always hold a tempo well. But he had been unfairly compared to drummers like John Bonham of Led Zeppelin, Keith Moon of the Who, and recently Neil Peart of Rush. These other drummers were usually found at the top of most lists of the greatest drummers ever and that bothered Starkey. He felt he held a spot as one of the best if only because he helped make the Beatles the greatest band in the world after their years of struggling with Pete Best behind the kit.

This night had become the sort of disaster for Starr that would later leave him to only get gigs with friends and people who wanted the chance to play with a Beatle. Ringo straightened up as much as he could and made it through the second half of the show without too many mistakes.

Backstage would turn out to be the most star-studded of the tour. The Hollywood elite came out en masse to see the only West Coast stop for the band. It didn't take much looking to find a celebrity—in one conversation would be Jack Nicholson, Paul Newman, Al Pacino, and Doris Day...in another there was Clint Eastwood, Tom Hanks, Meryl Streep, Bob De Niro, and Charlton Heston. The atmosphere backstage was electric for all, except John, Paul, and George. Ringo dove right back into the bottle as the final notes of "Hey Jude" rung out and became the happy drunk most would recognize him for being. Paul put on a happy face for the crowd, but John and George weren't about to do that. The two were visibly not pleased with the goings-on in the band and felt no real need to be socializing just so everyone there could say they partied with the Beatles.

George and John left for the hotel after only a short time. Paul stayed for over an hour and had gotten tired of smiling while he was miserable inside. Ringo stayed the whole evening until the Forum workers politely asked them all to move the party elsewhere. When Doris Day offered up her home in Bel Air, many of the now drunken attendees jumped at the chance to continue this festive night.

It would be a pivotal night for Ringo as he wound up being

arrested by the Bel Air police at 4:45 a.m. for public drunkenness, disturbing the peace, and resisting arrest. The incident stemmed from a comment made by a way too drunk Jack Nicholson about Ringo's sloppy playing that evening. Ringo confronted Nicholson only to be pushed back in the face by the actor. This caused quite the stir at the Day residence, and those closest to Ringo escorted him outside, where the trouble further ensued.

It was Mal Evans' duty to corral the drummer from the police station that night but not before Ringo had gotten into a scrap with another drunk prisoner. When Evans arrived at the holding cell, he saw bruises and cuts on Starkey's face. It looked like he had taken the brunt of the beating. Things were unraveling before their eyes and the Beatles were hanging on by a thread.

Set List: *The Forum (May 12, 1983) with the singer listed next to each song:*

Magical Mystery Tour—Paul
Come Together—John
Given to Fly—John
With a Little Help from My Friends—Ringo
Taxman—George
Imagine—John
Seeds of Love—Paul
Fool on the Hill—Paul
Real Love—John with Paul
I Want to Tell You—George
It Don't Come Easy—Ringo
Oo You—Paul
In My Life—John
Get Back—Paul
Solitude—George with John
Sgt. Pepper's Lonely Heart's Club Band—Paul
I'm Only Sleeping—John
I Saw Her Standing There—Paul

Encore

Dark Horse—George
Mr. Sampson—Paul with John
Hey Jude—Paul

Chapter 11

May 19, 1983—The band was in New York for the final two shows of the tour that had many successes to go along with the in-band tension that was acutely visible to all who were close to them. Ringo had been embarrassed by the events in Los Angeles and was out to prove his worth to the band. In his eyes, these last two shows were his chance to do just that.

They agreed to do a brief radio interview with Murray the K, as he was an integral part of their music saturating the American airwaves in the '60s. The boys liked Murray as he was delightful to be around—funny, engaging, and, as with many residents of the Big Apple, brutally honest. The band had avoided most television, newspaper, and radio interviews, but Murray was different—they appreciated what he had done to promote them when they were unheard of in the states.

They even fielded a few calls from the listeners. The call that got the most attention was from a thirty-four-year-old Marsha Albert (now Marsha Boucha). The boys vaguely remembered that it was a fifteen-year-old Marsha who prodded disc jockey Carroll James Jr. at radio station WWDC-AM to play "I Want to Hold Your Hand" for the first time in the United States. They had some laughs with her and asked if she was calling to "claim royalties" as John poked fun at her. She simply wanted to talk to them as they had briefly met long ago before the band's first show in America. This conversation led to them tracking her down the next day. She had so happened to be in New York with her husband and two small daughters doing some sightseeing.

May 20, 1983—Mike Sampson had been in contact with Marsha and asked if she could come to The Plaza Hotel where the band was staying. He asked her to bring the family and any luggage, etc., they had brought on their mini vacation as the boys wanted to put them up in a suite at the "Plaza." Marsha was excited to meet them again but had wished her daughters were a little older, as the six- and four-year-olds would not have vivid memories of meeting these music legends. Sampson had invited some photographers to capture the event. It was the kind of feel-good encounter with celebrities that many hoped for, but few would realize. They chatted for almost thirty minutes with cameras clicking and the boys being as charming as ever.

Ironically, it was now Mike Sampson who was in the position of offering a job to Marsha to work with the Beatles. He offered her the job of press secretary to the band. The stunned look on her face was then followed by a series of questions: "What does a press secretary do?" "Will I have to relocate?" "Would this be full-time or part-time?" (She was still raising two children.) Mike and the boys laid out for her what they had recently discussed about this role. It would mostly entail keeping the Beatles in a positive light to the press. The media could be ruthless to them, even though they were still considered to be the greatest pop band of all-time.

After a few more minutes of discussion regarding her new position with the band, she gladly accepted. She had been a stay-at-home mother since the birth of their second daughter in 1979 and was beyond excited that she only needed to work part-time, mostly from home. There would be the occasional trip to New York or London or the West Coast, but for the most part it appeared the boys only wanted her on their payroll. Anything she could then add would be above and beyond their intentions.

This had been another idea Lennon pushed for as he continued to follow through on his overwhelming desire to give back. Paul had spent much of the time playing with the two little girls, who knew him only as the "nice man with a funny voice." He played hide and seek with the girls, tried (and failed) at some magic with a coin, and then put them both on his lap as he made up a story about castles and dragons. The little girls were mesmerized by his story—one of the things McCartney was adept at...creating visual imagery. The gang gathered for a group photo from a meeting that would forever change the lives of Marsha Boucha and her family.

May 21, 1983—The first show at Madison Square Garden was another phenomenal show that would go down as one of their best on the tour. The boys were glad it was coming to an end and in hindsight believed the five-month stretch was a little too spread out. The extra time between shows created some issues that had placed more pressure on them all. They were now of the mindset that it should have been done in about three months' time. This would have given them time to relax and not rush to each show, but not too much where any of them could find trouble. It was easy to find trouble for these most popular fellows. Any hanger-on was eager to get a name for themselves at the expense of the boys from Liverpool.

On this night, the band had invited some musical friends to join them onstage. The artists were endless, and it almost seemed like an "open jam" for popular musicians. The names included Billy Joel and Michael Jackson (both of whom McCartney had befriended in the '70s), Elton John and David Bowie (with whom Lennon had scored the No. 1 hits "Whatever Gets You Through the Night" with Elton, and "Fame" with Bowie), Mick Jagger, Tina Turner, Joe Cocker, Phil Collins, Glenn Frey, Don Henley, Stevie Nicks, Ray Davies, and Eric Clapton. Almost half of the set list for the night was ignored as they found themselves playing whatever the other musicians would suggest. This made for an ambivalent night for the sold-out MSG audience. The bad was that they would not hear some of the vintage Beatles songs that had been so praised by the media in previous shows. But the crowd would also be witness to some of the greatest jam sessions ever assembled.

The Beatles were joined by Clapton, Joel, Bowie, Davies, and Stevie Nicks to do a raucous version of "Blue Suede Shoes" and Ringo's "It Don't Come Easy." Then Elton, Mick, Turner, Michael Jackson, Frey, and Henley joined the band for an extended version of the Motown song "Money," right into "I Saw Her Standing There." The kicker that night may have been Chuck Berry showing up unannounced and leading the way through "Roll Over Beethoven" with every inch of the stage taken up by the world-famous musicians that gathered to show their affection for the Beatles. That song lasted nearly fifteen minutes as each performer took turns at a solo on their respective instruments or sang a verse to the immortal song. The highlight of the song might have been when George, Eric, and Chuck Berry circled each other to trade off solos. George and Eric each made an unsuccessful attempt to imitate Berry's memorable "Duck Walk." Chuck stepped in to show the other two how it was done. It was all in good fun as the three legendary guitarists had a laugh about it onstage.

Set List: *Madison Square Garden (May 21, 1983) with the singer listed next to each song:*

Magical Mystery Tour—Paul
Come Together—John
Given to Fly—John
With a Little Help from My Friends—Ringo
Taxman—George
Real Love—John with Paul
In My Life—John
Another Girl—Paul
Solitude—George with John

Sgt. Pepper's Lonely Heart's Club Band—Paul

I'm Only Sleeping—John

Blue Suede Shoes—the Beatles with Eric Clapton, Billy Joel, David Bowie, Ray Davies, and Stevie Nicks

It Don't Come Easy—the Beatles with Eric Clapton, Billy Joel, David Bowie, Ray Davies and Stevie Nicks

Money—the Beatles with Elton John, Mick Jagger, Tina Turner, Michael Jackson, Glenn Frey, and Don Henley

I Saw Her Standing There—the Beatles with Elton John, Mick Jagger, Tina Turner, Michael Jackson, Glenn Frey, Don Henley, Phil Collins, and Joe Cocker

Encore

Roll Over Beethoven—the Beatles with Chuck Berry, Eric Clapton, Elton John, Mick Jagger, Tina Turner, Billy Joel, Michael Jackson, David Bowie, Joe Cocker, Phil Collins, Glenn Frey, Don Henley, Stevie Nicks, and Ray Davies

May 22, 1983—The first show at the Garden was superb, and the *New York Times* had a sparkling review the next day on the front page. The reporter had written how the excitement of the evening kept growing and growing as more and more celebrity musicians were announced to come join the band. He went on to say that while the audience knew they would see the Beatles (which alone was unbelievable to anyone lucky enough to own a ticket), they would also witness "...more musical interactions than the London Symphony Orchestra." The boys were in great spirits this night and were on their way over to Mike Sampson's home for the evening. Mike's wife, Trish, had cooked a nice homemade meal for the band and their wives.

The four Beatles arrived with their wives at around 6 p.m. and were greeted at the door by Mike and Trish. They had taken the kids (three-year-old son Joshua and newborn daughter Alexa) to

Trish's mother's house for the night. Mike had a large family with an older brother, two younger brothers, and a younger sister but it was his older brother, Dennis, who was the only one that knew of this dinner. The older Sampson loved the Beatles' music and was ecstatic when he and his wife, Sharon, were asked to join them. The house was small, but comfortable. They had two separate eating tables and had removed a large couch from the living room to have more space to eat. Later, after dinner, they would change it back for all to socialize and have cocktails.

At one table sat Paul and Linda, John and Yoko, and Mike and Trish Sampson. At the other was George and Olivia, Ringo and Barbara, then Dennis and Sharon Sampson. Lennon immediately noticed the turntable in the corner and snooped around for an album to play. Bingo! Fats Domino's *This Is Fats Domino* album made its way under the turntable needle. As the opening notes to "Blueberry Hill" echoed into the small living room, John grabbed Yoko to perform a limp-ridden waltz around the dining table.

With dinner complete, the gang gathered in the living room to listen to music, have drinks, and tell stories and jokes until the wee hours of the morning. It was simply the nicest evening they could have imagined. This kind of night was exactly what the doctor had ordered. There had been quite a bit of pressure to perform well and there was also an immense amount of self-induced pressure due to being in such tight quarters together for long periods of time. It turned out that the Sampson brothers and their wives were the perfect distraction to what had become quite the chore again. This gathering had made the band a little closer as they had let their guards down a bit toward each other.

The wives of the band most likely played a part in that happening. The boys were usually on their best behavior when their wives were involved, and this night was especially important in their eyes to behave properly. The Sampsons were gracious

hosts who had expected nothing from their celebrity guests—
they only wanted to offer their home for a short reprieve from the
madness of a tour. And that is exactly what happened this night
before the last show of their 1983 tour.

May 23, 1983—This was the day they had been secretly wish-
ing would come since the tour started and especially since the
Rosemont show. Tonight would be the final show of the tour and
they were pulling out all the stops. They had spent a few days
after the show in Los Angeles rehearsing what they would play
on this night. They chose to make it the most memorable of the
tour in the musical sense that they were going to omit solo songs
and anything from the new album (which had now gone Platinum
three times over). They would play their personal favorites from
the Beatles Phase I years. The only other musician allowed on the
stage that night was Nicky Hopkins, who had played every night
on the tour except the first show at the Royal Albert Hall.

In the dressing room before the show, the boys were poking
fun with some jovial banter when in walked Bob Dylan. Bob was
always in a precarious situation with his fans because of his folk
roots. That had caused many audiences to boo his performances
when he decided to play an electric guitar instead of an acoustic. It
also was not "cool" for the folk-hippy-eclectic-poet scene to like the
Fab Four, but he had secretly liked their music...and furthermore,
he was their friend. Dylan would never admit this, but he was
certainly proud that the most acclaimed pop songwriter of their
time was influenced by him and even went through what Lennon
would call his "Dylan period" during *Rubber Soul*. Bob produced
a nice-sized joint, which he shared with the four lads before their
final show.

The Beatles walked onstage at 8:25 p.m., which was earlier than
the other shows because of their added songs to the already hefty
set list. There was electricity in the air—the kind of excitement

felt at a professional sporting event where a championship is at stake. They would play about four or five songs from the "normal" set lists on this tour, but most everything was a new venture for the boys to play live. "Magical Mystery Tour" started the night in grand fashion and was met with a thunderous round of applause. The band went directly into "I Call Your Name." This was one of Lennon's personal favorites as he had considered it to be one of his best.

The night continued with Ringo and George taking turns at the microphone to sing a song. After "Wait," the boys gathered in the front of the stage with Ringo taking a short break to sing an a cappella version of "Because" (with Nicky Hopkins playing quietly in the background). This song was a thrill for all who witnessed, and it boldly showed off their vocal prowess. "I Want You (She's So Heavy)" was next, and the long, mesmerizing end part was beyond powerful. It was the kind of performance that defined the Beatles—raw, edgy, melodic, and rocking. This song was said by many who attended to be their favorite of the night.

Each song seemed to get better and better. Then, the band completed the two-hour set with "Penny Lane" and "Strawberry Fields Forever." These last two songs had garnered so much attention when they were released in 1967 that they had been given credit for changing the entire recording industry. It was "Fields" that would eventually become the song that inspired the *Sgt. Pepper* album. At first Lennon didn't want the production added to his masterpiece. He had written it on an acoustic guitar and had not intended all of the extra production by George Martin, but he allowed it anyway. The others loved it and at that time, John was open to their suggestions.

The band left the stage to another huge standing ovation and came back on five minutes later. The audience had thought they had seen the best, but the best was yet to come. They began their encore with a song no one would have expected—"Tomorrow

Never Knows." This was a difficult song to perform, and even though the song only contained one chord, the studio effects had made it almost impossible to mimic in a live environment. It was also one of the only songs Lennon would admit was heroin induced. They played the song in a much stripped-down version because that was how John had initially envisioned it would sound. Nicky Hopkins added some of the psychedelic swirling sounds you hear on the recording, but it was much closer to the writer's original intent. *"... all play the game existence to the end, of the beginning, of the beginning, of the beginning, of the beginning..."* The audience screamed in delight as the song ended in spectacular fashion.

The last two songs were medleys from *Abbey Road*, and while Lennon despised medleys, he knew this would "knock their socks off" as he was heard saying before the show. Hopkins produced the sound of crickets chirping to begin the song. The lights were low, and a slow but steady stream of fog covered the stage. A dimly lit deep blue light hit Lennon as he started his haunting guitar (which almost sounded like a bass) at the beginning of "Sun King." The others were hit with dim lights as Paul and George now harmonized with John. The boys' vocals were at the heart of this song and they sounded amazing together.

The moody "Sun King" gave way to the heavy drum intro of "Mean Mr. Mustard." The stage lights became brighter as the song grew and the band dove right into another Lennon rocker, "Polythene Pam." By the time the song came to its crescendo ending, prior to McCartney's "You Never Give Me Your Money," the stage was as bright as the sun. But instead of going into the next song, they held the A chord right after Paul yelled "Oh look out!" It was a dramatic ending and one that helped escape the obvious transition into "You Never Give Me Your Money"—a song they chose to omit.

The band was to continue the *Abbey Road* medley section of the night and went right into "Golden Slumbers." At this point of the show, the audience was in a trance-like state. There were people crying, people arm in arm, all singing this beautiful McCartney tune. Everyone who knew this medley hoped they would play the whole thing. It would be a pity if the band only played "Golden Slumbers," but the crowd somehow had a feeling they would not be disappointed.

As had been the hope, the boys went right into "Carry That Weight" and played it fabulously. They then began the opening to "The End," but not before Klaus Voorman appeared onstage to grab Paul's bass. McCartney grabbed a guitar from a stagehand and Ringo went into his only drum solo ever recorded on a Beatles album. This live solo would last more than twice as long as the original recording. The band joined back in to play the A7 to D7 chords on guitar with Paul and John singing "love you" over and over. There stood John, George, and Paul in a circle all wielding a guitar to trade solos that would last nearly three minutes. It truly seemed like a guitar battle. Lennon had a crunchy sound on his guitar, McCartney's tone was bright and full of treble, and then Harrison had a full, warm tone. If this was indeed a battle, Harrison would have been crowned the champion as his guitar playing had definitely improved over the years. This was the defining moment of the tour with the three Beatles battling it out on guitar for all to see. It was pure magic and everyone in attendance knew it. The Beatles' 1983 tour was now officially over.

Set List—*Madison Square Garden (May 23, 1983) with the singer listed next to each song:*

Magical Mystery Tour—Paul
I Call Your Name—John
With a Little Help from My Friends—Ringo
Savoy Truffle—George
Wait—John with Paul
Because—John, Paul, and George (a cappella)
I Want You (She's So Heavy)—John
Eleanor Rigby—Paul
Across the Universe—John
All My Lovin'—Paul
Something—George
Rain—John
Helter Skelter—Paul
Happiness is a Warm Gun—John
Fixing a Hole—Paul
Get Back—Paul
Yer Blues—John
I Me Mine—George
Hey Bulldog—John
Sgt. Pepper's Lonely Heart's Club Band—Paul
Dig A Pony—John
Penny Lane—Paul
Strawberry Fields Forever—John

Encore

Tomorrow Never Knows—John
Sun King/Mean Mr. Mustard/Polythene Pam—John
Golden Slumbers/Carry That Weight/ The End—Paul

Chapter 12

May 24, 1983—Word had spread rapidly about their final show at Madison Square Garden, and every newspaper in the country had an article about it. This show was not even 24 hours into the books and was already deemed "legendary" by many reporters who had witnessed the spectacle. The lads read as many articles as they could find about their final show of the tour while on the plane back to England.

It was now time for some well-earned rest and relaxation. All four had made their own plans for a holiday and couldn't wait to be somewhere other than "Beatle-land." There was little chatter amongst the lads on that private chartered jet provided by Pan Am Airlines. The one issue that was discussed regarded possibly going back into the studio to record more music. At this point, it was the only thing any of them had even a remote interest in doing. They wanted nothing to do with live shows, interviews, press conferences, television appearances, and the like.

Even though George had once again become the most miserable of the bunch, he recently had written numerous new songs he wanted to present to the band. So, they all agreed to meet back at CBS Records on July 18 to discuss the next steps for the band.

As eager as George had been to get back to recording, Paul was not. He was going through what could be described as a sort of post-tour depression. McCartney never hid the fact that he enjoyed playing live, and Ringo was the only other Beatle who shared that sentiment. Paul felt that their time together onstage created a buffer between them all, which prevented more internal skirmishes. But now that the tour was over, McCartney struggled to think about walking into the studio with the others. He was certain tensions would again rise and make it almost impossible for him to stay focused on any one thing. He would withdraw like a child avoiding something that they might be afraid of or not like.

July 18, 1983—The morning started off with a phone call from George to Paul.

"Paul, I'm getting ready to head to the studio and wanted you to know I've got more songs I'd like everyone to hear." Paul pondered why Harrison would call to tell him that instead of showing up with the songs and presenting them then. The answer came in George's next sentence. "I'm telling you this now because I'm hoping to avoid the same issues I had dealt with in the past."

Harrison would bring a song into the band just as the others would but his songs would never really be taken seriously until he forced his hand. He was hoping to avoid what he considered to be disrespectful treatment by informing Paul upfront instead of catching him off guard when they entered the studio. This was a wise tactic because it certainly may have been the element of surprise that made Lennon and McCartney clam up when it came to Harrison's songs.

The boys arrived at the studio to see George Martin talking with Geoff Emerick. Something about these two made them feel more comfortable in the studio with each other. Paul thought that it would be an impossible environment to be in without the producer and the engineer. They exchanged cordial greetings and Lennon was in good spirits as he joked with the others. After the lads grabbed some tea and Mal Evans finished setting up equipment, they began to discuss a plan.

Harrison started, "Not to be the bearer of bad news here, but no more tours for me." The others nodded in agreement. Even if there might be a tour in their future, now was certainly not the time to broach that topic. "As I told Paul earlier on the phone," continued George, "I have some songs I'd like for all of you to hear."

Everyone was eager to start writing and recording more, and now that Harrison had a slew of new songs, the boys were excited to get at it. John mentioned he had a few new songs and even Ringo had one he had been working on. Paul mentioned he might have a song or two in the works, but nothing completed yet. It was quite a surprise to the others that Paul didn't have anything ready to record. He was usually the one with a plethora of songs in his portfolio. He hadn't felt up to writing anything for quite some time after the tour ended. He almost completely withdrew from music except to listen to some of the old standards that he enjoyed so much.

George's first offering was a song he titled "Most Days" and had a sound like many of the songs from his *All Things Must Pass* gem. He picked up his Fender Telecaster and started into this rock song that strayed from the softer side he had put on display over the past few years. *"Most days, I am here for you...most days you appear for me..."* The others immediately liked it and Paul was the first one to start playing along on this new tune. It was a little melancholy as there were minor chords strewn about the somewhat complex song. It started in the key of F minor to B flat minor and stayed there while George explained what he ultimately wanted it to sound like. He was still interested in the Eastern/Indian sounds he had immersed himself in for so many years, and this was the sound he was seeking during that part. He suggested a sitar background and the others agreed that it would enhance the mood of the song.

John quickly came up with a guitar lick that sounded as if he'd stolen it directly from Jimmy Page. The raunchy-sounding guitar part that he played over the minor chords was pure genius and added layers to the already growing song. The middle part of the song was even more complex as it went from a B chord to a G and then to a C sharp to a D. That whole progression, with the melody he had written over it, had McCartney amazed at what he had just heard. Paul was now starting to feel more open to writing and recording. It was as if this one song pulled him back out of his musical shell.

The boys went over "Most Days" numerous times until Ringo had found the perfect beat. It was similar to his drums on "Tomorrow Never Knows." This was destined to be another massive hit, and everyone was at their very best to try to make the tune what it would eventually become...a masterpiece. After four hours on this song, which had grown by leaps and bounds since their first attempt at it, they took a short break.

George played another one on his acoustic guitar that was called "Drawn Apart." The others immediately knew the lyrics were directed at the band and mostly toward Paul. *"It was once such an easy thing...now it's so hard to sing...giving you my all...waiting for your call..."* John especially read into the lyrics to see that this was George venting about them and he didn't mind. As a matter of fact, it was the kind of intimate feelings that Lennon had admired from any writer. He loved the genuine vulnerability of digging down deep into one's soul for creative fodder. Paul could have easily crawled back into his shell, but he did not let the new song bother him. His excitement from the first song that George had presented to the band was still in the forefront of his mind and he again felt the musical juices flow.

They spent about twenty minutes listening to the new song and writing down suggestions. George Martin had ideas for this one and wanted to add cellos or a baritone sax. All four Beatles were happy with what was going on in Studio 2 that day. They took a break for lunch and surprisingly all ate together. It was getting harder to go out in public so Mal brought back some delightful Mediterranean vegan food for them to enjoy.

The boys sat around the studio break room eating hummus and tabbouleh while talking about the new songs. They were family, and times like this cemented that fact. Families fight. Families split. Families get back together. Families love each other. This was all true for these famous musicians. Mal was correct in thinking about how much they needed each other and didn't realize it. The boys spent an hour and a half eating and enjoying each other's company. It felt good again to be a Beatle, if only for a short time.

They reconvened in Studio 2 to hear more suggestions for the new Harrison songs from both Martin and Geoff Emerick. Geoff always had ideas and was very courteous about how he would approach them with the band. He had thought of new ways to record the drums and guitars. He wanted the drums alone in another studio down the hall that was never used for anything but large orchestras. He would clear out the room entirely, place Ringo's kit in the middle, and set microphones on the outskirts of the room. This would make it sound like an echo chamber. The band loved it. His idea for the guitars was to put the amplifier in a large moving case with it open slightly and the microphone placed directly outside of it. The boys weren't sure about that idea but as always were willing to hear what it sounded like. It turned out to be an overwhelming success. The sound the amp produced by being enclosed in a large moving case was like nothing they had ever heard. It created a reverb sound and gave the guitar a natural distortion that felt warm to the ear. It was another magical studio creation by Geoff Emerick, and everyone involved was excited at the new sound.

It was now John's turn to share one of his new tunes with the others. He started on the piano. It sounded like a honkytonk song in the same genre as New Orleans jazz. He played some interesting chords over the beautiful melody he had written. The lyrics were complete, but Lennon had forgotten most of them while doing this first run. He had not completed the music and Paul was ready to add what he heard in his head for the missing middle part. After the quick run-through, Lennon explained that while the piano sound would be reminiscent of the swamp music out of the Bayou, he wanted the guitars and drums to give it a rock edge. The boys had fun with this one and spent the rest of the afternoon into evening working on it.

Even though the tapes were always rolling when they were in the studio, nothing was recorded yet that would end up on the new album. George added some distorted guitar to the background and then overdubbed some climbing arpeggios that sounded like the ones he'd played at the end of John's "Dear Prudence" from the *White Album*. This new song that had no name yet (and would end up being called "Intuition") was slowly becoming another marvelous Lennon composition. It had a memorable melody over chords that contained notes that would crawl down a musical scale like so many other hits he had written. The crawl-down notes were reminiscent of the ones that dominated his Top 10 hit "Watching the Wheels" from his *Double Fantasy* record.

That night after the band had left the studio for their homes, Paul was so inspired by the day's events that he immediately sat at the piano at his Blossom Wood Farm mansion in Peasmarsh East Sussex. Linda had been preparing something for her husband to eat as the two didn't believe in maids or butlers or chefs. They enjoyed making their own food and experimenting with different vegan dishes. Paul loved the spices and food from the Indian cuisine, so Linda had made some garlic naan and vegan Biryani for her husband. He was hungry but only accepted the tea she had offered as he sat intently at the piano.

Just as with the song "Yesterday," this song seemed to be channeled through him from some unexplainable source. He felt that sometimes he was only the medium in which these songs were generated. This one was no exception, and while the sound was not at all like the soft-sounding "Yesterday," it was pure McCartney.

After about forty-five minutes at the baby grand piano that sat in his large living room, the music and melody were complete. Realizing the inspiration came through him in the same fashion as "Yesterday," he gave it a working title of "Today's Road." The title led him into the beginning lyric, *"I once travelled alone, but that was yesterday...today's road is not so grey..."* As Paul wrote down lyrics and sipped his tea, Linda asked if he would like to eat some of the food before it became too cold to eat. He politely declined as he felt he needed to get these new lyrics down on paper. An hour later, the entire song was finished to Paul's satisfaction.

Linda, who was usually quite reserved about her husband's songs, told Paul that she thought the song was fantastic and asked if she could be in the studio when he recorded it. This took Paul by surprise as she had never requested to be in the studio before. This time around, the band spent their days in the studio without any outsiders, not even Yoko. But McCartney knew the others wouldn't object if he asked them prior to her coming.

July 20, 1983—The band had taken a day off to do some personal things and mostly because John had a doctor's appointment to monitor the progress of his leg and hip. He had been in quite a lot of pain, but never complained. He was happy to be alive and would never forget how close he had come to dying at The Dakota in New York. Paul phoned John early that morning.

"Hey John, what did the doc say?" he asked.

"Well, I think I'll live. He said I'm doing great and to keep stretching and walking as much as possible. What's on yer mind?" asked Lennon.

"I've got a new one I'd like to go over today if that's okay."

Lennon knew there was more to the story than that, so again he asked, "Okay, now what's really on yer mind, son?"

"I want to bring Linder down today to the studio and I was hoping you would be okay with that."

John smiled as he was well aware of the grief caused by Yoko being at all the recording sessions in the past. The old John would have barked back some sort of refusal at that idea. But the new John said, "Of course, Paul. You know we all adore yer lovely Linder!" as Lennon quoted the title of Paul's opening song on his first solo album, *McCartney*. Paul laughed and sighed in relief. He thought this might turn into a battle over who was allowed in the studio but was pleasantly surprised that John didn't fuss over it in the slightest bit.

When they arrived at the studio, George had been excited to play more of his songs. But Paul kindly asked if he could show them a new song he had written only two days prior. Since Paul had brought Linda into the studio and appeared to be excited about the song, George smiled and said, "Yeah, let's hear it."

The other Beatles plus George Martin gathered in Studio 2 around the piano to listen to Paul playing his new tune while Geoff Emerick and Linda stayed in the control room. The song started in the key of C and went to A minor, then F to G. He played through the entire tune and sang the lyrics he could remember. It was an amazing song and the others knew it. They knew this song would end up being one of the best on the new album.

Harrison was the first to say something. "Paul, where did you come up with this beauty?"

The song sounded like a combination of everything McCartney had written in his later Beatles years and some of the Wings' best. Paul just grinned and said, "I dunno. I think the gods had something to do with it!"

George Martin asked Paul how he wanted the recording to sound. Paul didn't want too much production but suggested maybe a French horn or something similar. He definitely did not want strings or an entire orchestral ensemble. The band went right to work on "Today's Road" with the same enthusiasm that was present during the "She Loves You" session (which Geoff Emerick would later write in his book about his time with the Beatles "Here, There and Everywhere"). Emerick would go on to write how the "She Loves You" session was "...one of the most exciting recordings of the Beatles' entire career." This new McCartney endeavor was certainly in that same spirit as the boys threw themselves into the tune with every ounce of energy they could muster.

The song was slowly being sculpted and before they all knew it, four hours had passed. Paul was extremely pleased at all the suggestions and the enthusiasm displayed by his musical partners. After a break for lunch, John suggested they start recording the new song. Paul was ecstatic and backed off from his habit of producing to let the others add what they felt would enhance the tune in any way. This musical freedom added to the enthusiasm of the session and brought down some of the walls that usually were up when recording a McCartney track. George realized this as he had previously been on the wrong end of Paul's demands to the lads on how he wanted every single note played to his songs. This was a new Paul to go along with the new John. It was refreshing, and they all truly enjoyed being around each other on that day.

George pulled Paul aside after most of the recording was complete. "Paul," he began, "I wanted to say that I know I've been a royal pain in the arse and I sincerely feel bad about that. I know how the coke affected my ability to be reasonable and I take full responsibility for that." Paul was stunned and simply smiled at his friend. "I also want you to know that I no longer do the stuff. It's not because of your hatred of it. I just tired of the whole scene."

Paul was shocked, surprised, and happy to hear this news. He thanked George for opening up to him and for the sincere apology, but George wasn't done.

"You know, I never did properly thank you for getting me into this band in the first place. It changed my life for the better, and while there was a lot of misery along the way, I'll be forever grateful for the opportunity you gave to me."

The street-tough Paul almost came to a tear as he grabbed Harrison to hug the guitarist. The others couldn't hear the conversation but saw their warm embrace and wondered what had gone on in their private meeting. This day was another turning point in the relationship between Paul and George. He knew what it took for Harrison to apologize so sincerely and would from that point on treat George as the equal he always was.

Chapter 13

September 7, 1983—This day in the studio would mark the commencing of the recording process. The band had spent almost every day over the past month and a half rehearsing the new material and was ready to go. John had brought in three songs, George had four (with Paul's help on one and John's on another), Ringo had one (with all four contributing), and Paul had written two for the new album. They also had two new Lennon/McCartney songs, with one of those ("Sweet Liz") written like in the old days—face to face. It was bound to be another chart-topping release. They had already recorded Harrison's "Wallows of Sound," McCartney's "Jewel of the Heart," and the McCartney/Lennon composition "Follow You."

Now they turned their attention to another one of George's songs, "Most Days." This song would take the better part of two days to complete but went so smoothly that the boys barely noticed. George added a sitar to most of the song, but some of it would eventually be mixed into the background, barely to be heard. Even still, it added layers and depth to this track. Lennon's Jimmy Page-style guitar lick turned out to be the most integral part of the song. It fit perfectly over the minor chords and George couldn't stop smiling at John while this part was being recorded.

Paul loved the chord changes in the middle break of the song, and he asked George if he could add some harmony vocals. Harrison was thrilled about that. Some of his best Beatles songs had that amazing McCartney voice in the background. The song "While My Guitar Gently Weeps" was ignored by the others until Harrison brought in Eric Clapton to the sessions. When they did finally record the song, it was Paul's harmony vocal that helped make it the classic it became. George realized how important it was back then and felt the same was needed on this new one.

September 11, 1983—The next track they worked on was Mc-Cartney's "Today's Road," and the momentum from the previous recording session continued throughout this song. George had been working on this one for some time and had created a guitar solo for it that reminded the others of his solo on "Something." That solo was perfectly carved for the song and is always considered one of the main highlights from the No. 1 hit.

The first few run-throughs weren't bad, but there was definitely something missing, they all thought. Paul had been right about adding the French horn, so they tracked down Alan Civil who had played the memorable horn solo in Paul's song "For No One" on the *Revolver* album. The fifty-four-year-old eventually made his way into the studio to the delight of the boys. They had remembered Civil well from that 1966 recording session even though their drug intake at that point was at an all-time high. This time, however, the horn player wasn't brought in for only the solo part. He was asked to play along with the entire track and to create a high end that would come across as a "heavenly sound to the listener" (McCartney explained).

It took him three takes and less than a half hour to play it exactly the way Paul had instructed the elderly gentleman. "Today's Road" was written partly about Linda as had been so many other McCartney hit songs. This tune had flowered into what everyone involved knew it would become—legendary Beatles that could challenge even their best from the Phase 1 years. Two more songs were recorded and mixed in three days' time. They were on another roll musically that would keep going for some time to come.

September 14, 1983—John had approached Paul with a song he had written a few days earlier that had no lyrics, just a few chords. Paul liked it and the two sat down to finish it off. Just then they saw some activity in the control room. It turned out that Brian Wilson had accepted their offer to join them in the studio. When Wilson entered the studio, the band was in shock to see the talented musician/producer in such bad shape. He was almost unrecognizable and stumbled a bit as he approached them. Brian had fallen on hard times emotionally. He had been struggling with mental health and drug problems.

They shook hands, sat, and talked for a while. John couldn't help but feel sad for this musical legend. It appeared to him that Wilson's best days were behind the former Beach Boys leader. They discussed the song they were working on and asked if Brian would help finish it. Immediately after showing Wilson the chords, the producer/musician came to life. He was considered a musical genius by his peers and had been one of the main inspirations for what many believe is the greatest album of all time, *Sgt. Pepper*. Paul added words and Brian showed him a melody to follow. He then had John sing a lower harmony while he took the upper harmony using his high falsetto vocals. Before the two Beatles knew it, Brian had taken over. He wrote an intro, a middle bridge, and an ending. He also added more background harmonies to fill out the new song, "Existential."

George and Ringo had been watching the creation of the song in amazement. They had heard how Wilson would work in the studio and were witnessing it firsthand. They were now ready to record. They spent the next three hours recording the music for the basic track and then another four hours on the vocals. It progressed into an incredible combination of the Beatles and Beach Boys sound. John and Paul's voices blended perfectly with Brian's. The vocal performance with the three of them was spine-tingling. The boys were thrilled at the sound of this song, and even though Brian was not quite himself, his true genius shone through. It would be another chart-topper and would stay at Number 1 for six weeks.

November 2, 1983—This would turn out to be the final day of recording as the band had been at it for almost two months straight. They would be adding the last bits to the Harrison/Mc-Cartney song "Final Words" and then recording "See You There" (the song Ringo had written with the help from the others). "Final Words" had been brought in by George, who then approached Paul to help him finish.

This song was focused on Harrison's twelve-string guitar and had a similar feel to that of "Apple Scruffs" from the *All Things Must Pass* album. Paul came up with a nice electric guitar accompaniment and created a most beautiful bass line for the song. John was absent from this early session but later added some piano and harmony vocals to go along with George and Paul's already recorded vocal tracks. They spent nearly five hours finishing and then mixing the song. It had both a new and old sound to it. One could hear the evolution of the new music and the reminders of the old in this single track. It was an astonishing achievement for them, and they were more than proud to have recorded such a brilliant song.

After lunch, John appeared in the studio to start work on the new Ringo tune. This had started off with Starr playing a few chords on the piano and then morphed into another fantastic composition the band had crafted. They ran through the song for the basic track with each member on their usual instruments (Ringo on drums, Paul on bass, and both John and George on guitars). Then Ringo added his original piano part to the tune followed by his lead vocal. John, Paul, and George then added backing vocals. They all felt it needed more, so they grabbed different percussive instruments such as the morocco, wood blocks, tambourine, and even jingle bells. This added a new layer that George Martin knew should be placed in the background of the song. They all had a hoot playing the different instruments and experimenting with them at the same time. It was another happy moment for the boys and after almost six hours, the song was recorded and then mixed. The album was complete! Now for the name...

No one had put much thought into naming this new record, although it would be another Ringo malapropism that surfaced to become the title *Nocturnal Rocks*. Starr had recently read an article about the indigenous rocks on the Hawaiian Islands and had a bit of trouble relating the story to the rest. The record was mastered and then pressed in no time at all.

The CBS Records executives had only heard bits and pieces of the record but were now given the full album to hear. They were amazed that this new record seemed to be even better than the last album that topped the music charts for almost two months. They couldn't believe that the band kept producing such quality music at this juncture of their careers. Every time they questioned whether or not their most important and popular act still had what it took to make a good record, the answer was a resounding "Yes!"

The Beatles had delivered their most groundbreaking record since *Sgt. Pepper*, and everyone who heard it knew that was the case. The execs had wrongly assumed it was John and Paul who were their Golden Eggs. In reality, Lennon and McCartney would not have been who they were in Phase 2 without George especially, and Ringo to a certain extent. Everyone who worked at CBS Records was all smiles for the following weeks and months. This was surely the hit record they were hoping to receive from the band, and in turn, the record execs decided to give the boys a surprise bonus in the amount of £250,000 per member. This was the largest bonus by far that CBS Records would ever give to any artist on their label.

December 19, 1983—This day in December 1983 would feature the release of the Beatles new album *Nocturnal Rocks*. There had been many discussions about releasing this recording on the new format, compact disc. CDs were slowly gaining momentum and some people thought they would replace record albums. John and Paul especially were against this. They wanted to maintain the integrity of the recordings by keeping them analog and not digital. They would be right, and wrong. They were right that the analog sound is much fuller than the digital sound, but the CD would eventually replace record albums by the early 1990s. So they refused to record it digitally and missed the opportunity of being the first artist to release a compact disc.

The album would arrive in stores before the Christmas shopping rush as would be the case for many of the band's projects. The release was met with worldwide acclaim, and critics from all over the globe raved about this remarkable achievement. It was certainly groundbreaking in every sense for the music industry. There were studio techniques created that would become industry standards for years to come, to go along with the escalated complexity of each song. One writer noted, "There was a time when we all thought the heights of the Beatles' songs had already been reached with no return in sight. This one record dispelled all of our doubts. It may even challenge 'Pepper' as the greatest record of all time."

Nocturnal Rocks *(produced by George Martin)—CBS Records Music*
(1983)

Most Days (Harrison/Lennon)
Today's Road (McCartney)
Final Words (Harrison/McCartney)
See You There (Starkey/Lennon/Harrison/McCartney)
Less Is More (Lennon)
Drawn Apart (Harrison)
Follow You (McCartney/Lennon)
Existential (Lennon/McCartney/Wilson)
Wallows of Sound (Harrison)
Jewel of the Heart (McCartney)
Intuition (Lennon)
Sweet Liz (Lennon/McCartney)

Billboard Charts – Week of December 25, 1983

THIS WEEK	LAST WEEK	2 WKS AGO	WEEKS ON CHART	ARTIST LABEL	TITLE	PEAK POSITION
1	NEW ▶		1	THE BEATLES CBS RECORDS ★ ★ No. 1 ★ ★	FOLLOW YOU	1
2	1	9	11	HALL & OATES RCA	SAY IT ISN'T SO	1
3	5	8	3	DURAN DURAN CAPITOL	UNION OF THE SNAKE	3
4	7	10	8	YES ATCO	OWNER OF A LONELY HEART	4
5	3	7	15	LIONEL RITCHIE MOTOWN	ALL NIGHT LONG (ALL NIGHT)	1
6	4	5	14	BILLY JOEL COLUMBIA	UPTOWN GIRL	3
7	NEW ▶		1	THE BEATLES CBS RECORDS	TODAY'S ROAD	7
8	6	6	14	PAT BENATAR CHRYSALIS	LOVE IS A BATTLEFIELD	5
9	NEW ▶		1	THE BEATLES CBS RECORDS	MOST DAYS	9
10	11	13	8	OLIVIA NEWTON-JOHN MCA	TWIST OF FATE	8
11	13	8	7	ROLLING STONES ROLLING STONES	UNDERCOVER OF THE NIGHT	10
12	NEW ▶		1	THE BEATLES CBS RECORDS	WALLOWS OF SOUND	11
13	10	12	15	MATTHEW WILDER PRIVATE I	BREAK MY STRIDE	9
14	12	19	9	ELTON JOHN GEFFEN	I GUESS THAT'S WHY THEY CALL IT THE BLUES	11
15	15	20	12	THE ROMANTICS NEMPEROR	TALKING IN YOUR SLEEP	12
16	14	10	10	CULTURE CLUB VIRGIN	CHURCH OF THE POISON MIND	10
17	16	15	14	PETER SCHILLING ELEKTRA	MAJOR TOM (COMING HOME)	14
18	NEW ▶		1	THE BEATLES CBS RECORDS	INTUITION	18
19	9	12	15	QUIET RIOT PASHA	CUM ON FEEL THE NOIZE	5
20	17	16	8	THE POLICE A&M	SYNCHRONICITY II	16

December 21, 1983—The Beatles' new album sat firmly atop the Billboard charts. The band was elated, and their label was beside themselves with joy as record sales on the first day alone reached 500,000 units. Today they were to meet at CBS Studios to discuss the plan going forward. Derek started the meeting by congratulating the band on their new album and the reception it had gotten. He then suggested another tour to promote the new album. John, George, and Ringo were adamantly against that idea.

Paul didn't say a word. So Derek told them of interview requests from radio and TV stations as well as newspapers. Even *Rolling Stone* magazine wanted to do another story on the band's return to the top. That was the one thing they were interested in doing... another *Rolling Stone* interview.

"Oh, one more thing," said Taylor. "*Late Night with David Letterman* has been calling and is offering up an enormous sum of money for you boys to appear on the show." George was against this, but the others said they would think about it. After spending the past four months in the studio, it was again time for a break from Beatledom. Each member of the band went their separate ways. John and Paul went on holiday, while George and Ringo decided upon going home. Time for that much-needed reprieve.

March 14, 1984—It had been nearly three months since *Nocturnal Rocks* was released, and the album was still at the top of the music charts. It would remain at the Number 1 spot for a whopping twenty-three weeks. The song "Follow You" was still atop the singles chart when John and Paul were to appear on *Late Night*. They enjoyed the humor of David Letterman and had finally given in to his persistent requests. George wanted no part of it and Ringo was having cataract surgery, so the two planned to play some acoustic songs for the taping.

Letterman decided to have no other guests that night, and after his usual Top 10 list (this night would be "The Top 10 Rejected James Bond Gadgets"), John and Paul came out to a thunderous round of applause.

"So how are you guys doing?" the host started.

"Just peachy, Dave. Thanks for havin' us" was Paul's response.

"So I'm just curious, John...do you now carry a submachine gun when you come back to New York?"

The audience laughed along with both Beatles.

"Well, Dave, Paul is now my personal bodyguard. It states it right on the album notes!"

Letterman cracked up with that infectious laugh of his. After a slew of jokes and stories, he asked them if they would play a song. The audience responded wildly at being able to witness this intimate performance.

They both were handed acoustic guitars with John sitting on the right, Paul on the left. They would always be in that position because Paul was left-handed and John was right, so their guitar necks would point away from the other. They sat, adjusted their microphones, and said a few words to the crowd.

"Hello there," Paul began. "We're going to play some acoustic songs for you and here's a new one."

The two began an amazing acoustic rendition of "Follow You." The song highlighted both of their vocals while also showcasing some guitar proficiency as they played off of each other. It was a phenomenal performance. They then decided to play "Given to Fly." This song would be a meaningful song to them both as it was the catalyst that brought the band back together. During some of the dynamic musical pauses, the audience was so quiet, it was deafening. The crowd appeared to be mesmerized by the sounds coming from these two musical geniuses.

After another long-standing ovation, they decided to play a Beatles Phase 1 song. They got rid of one of the microphones, put the remaining one in between them both, and went into "Two of Us." The audience screamed so loudly when they started singing, they had to stop singing and repeat the beginning guitar parts as no one would have heard their vocals. They smiled and then shared the mic to sing this song for the first time to a live audience. It was another unbelievable performance and Letterman stood to cheer along with the studio audience.

Dave then invited the boys up for more one-on-one questions. He joked about them going forward without George or Ringo. "Who needs those guys anyway?" he said. Before they were to close the show, John and Paul went over to play a song with Paul Shaffer and the house band. They decided to do "Hey Bulldog." It was a superb song to play with the band and also to end the show. Paul's incredible bass line drove this song as John and Paul harmonized to one of their best rockers.

The cameras were about to fade out when they all of a sudden faded back in. It appeared the cameraman was told not to fade out by a producer of the show. They didn't want to cut off this extraordinary performance and were willing to get fined for doing so...which they did by the FCC. The headlines the next day about the fines they received gave both the network and the show an increased audience. Most people thought it was a great thing that they kept the cameras rolling for the viewers and didn't mind taking the heat for it.

July 11, 1984—All four Beatles decided to participate in the *Rolling Stone* interview with Robert Fricke. The interview took place at the CBS Records offices in London. Fricke was just making a name for himself and wanted the band to be as candid as they could. He asked tough questions like "What happened at that concert in Illinois?" and "What happened in Los Angeles with Ringo?" and "Where was George for the Letterman performance?"

These were the kinds of questions that made them avoid interviews. They mostly danced around the ones they didn't feel comfortable addressing, and at one point George spouted off at Fricke about a question he didn't like. "What kind of question is that and what do your readers care? This is a music publication, not a tabloid, right?" With that, Fricke backed down and then stayed on track with music-related questions. This was not the interview they had expected, so they ended it prematurely. It would be the last magazine or newspaper interview they would grant as a band.

Chapter 14

November 9, 1984—Almost a year had passed since the release of their last album. The songs "Follow You," "Final Words," "Today's Road," and "Wallows of Sound" each reached the No. 1 spot on the charts. "Follow You" topped the charts for an amazing eighteen weeks.

Julian Lennon had released his solo album *Valotte* in October 1984 and it reached No. 17 on the music charts. John was proud of his son and called him this morning.

"Hey Jules, how are ya doing?"

"Hey, Dad. Things are great. I was just offered a deal for a second record!"

John was ecstatic for his son. He offered to help him any way he could, but Julian wanted no help from his famous father. Jules had been trying to distance himself from his dad's work. Some in the media had thought it was actually the famous Lennon who wrote Julian's hit song. So Julian wanted to make sure that his father was not involved in any way on the new album.

"Okay, well I'd like to see ya sometime. Let's get together soon," said the now responsible father.

"Of course, Dad. Love ya," Julian said as he hung up.

George was on his way back to Los Angeles. He had been in touch with Crosby and Nash, and wanted to write some music with half of CSN&Y. So Harrison headed out to Crosby's home in Santa Ynez to meet with his two close friends. He would spend the next week with Crosby and Nash writing news songs and enjoying the California sunshine. They rarely left Crosby's mansion during that time, only going out for walks or the occasional lunch. Within a few short days, the three had written over ten songs together.

This was a direction Harrison had wanted to pursue ever since he became a fan of CSN's music in the early '70s. Having Crosby and Nash to sing with took Harrison to another level of writing. He had become so used to the Beatles' way of writing that this was new and refreshing. The songs reflected a new style and Harrison wanted to record them with his friends. Even though Harrison had completed more work for the Beatles' new records than what his contract required, he would still have to go through some legal hurdles if he were to think about releasing another solo album.

December 2, 1984—Back at home now, Harrison had decided he did want to go forward with recording a solo album. He contacted Geoff Emerick to engineer the new album and they began work at CBS Records. Since Harrison was not on contract at the time, the CBS executives were happy to have him record there. They assumed by having him record in their studios, they could be the label in which he would release the album. He recruited some of his music friends to help him record this new album. Crosby and Nash were already on board, so he called the other Beatles to see if they had interest in helping. Ringo was an easy recruit. He always played on George's solo albums. John and especially Paul would be much harder.

John didn't think it was proper for Harrison to go solo while the others were still under contract for two more albums. Paul was secretly jealous of the song output from George and felt a bit insecure about this. For many years, it was McCartney who brought most of the music to the band, and now his creative juices weren't flowing like before. Both John and Paul told George they would think about it and let him know.

Harrison expected this, so he continued recruiting others. After a few short hours of phone calls, George had secured Eric

Clapton, Tom Petty, Jeff Lynne (who would help produce the album), Stephen Stills, Neil Young, Jim Keltner, Leon Russell, Stevie Winwood, and Billy Preston. This would follow a trend for both Harrison and Starr where they would use many famous musicians on their records.

George had thought about having Phil Spector produce the album but did not trust that the eccentric music producer could stay sober during the recording. A drunken Spector had been kicked out of the *Living in the Material World* sessions for not showing up, and when he did show, he would do erratic things like pull a gun on the engineer. This was the kind of insanity Harrison had avoided his entire career, so Spector was out. Calling George Martin seemed to be his best option. So he phoned Martin about the new album.

"Hello, George. How are you?" said Martin. Harrison explained the group of songs and now musicians he had gathered for this record. Martin hesitated as he was aware that his inclusion may cause friction with the others if they weren't on board with this solo project. He asked Harrison if he could think about it for a night. When they got off the phone, Martin turned to call John.

"John, George just asked me to produce a solo album."

"Yeah, I know. He asked me to play on it but I'm not quite sure. I think we should bring as many good songs as possible to this band right now." Martin replied that while he agreed, Harrison was not legally bound to the band anymore, so he could do whatever he pleased. John's response was, "Fuck it. Let him do it. I've got at least four or five songs almost complete for our next album anyway. We might not even need 'im."

Martin then phoned McCartney and did not expect the response he received. "George, why in the world would you even consider working on his solo album when we still owe CBS two more records?" He felt helpless in protecting the Beatles' name and image. He thought, *If George releases some crazy album and it flops, it will look bad on all of us.*

Martin again explained that Harrison wasn't bound by any contract and thought that in the long run it would be best if they all supported him on this project. Paul thought about it and grudgingly agreed that if they were a part of it, they then might have some say as to how it would sound...especially if they had the Beatles' producer involved to make sure it sounded Beatle-ish. Within the next few days, George Martin, John, and Paul all called Harrison to say they would help out with the new record. Out of all of the Beatles, George was now writing the most songs and his output couldn't be suppressed...no matter what the others wanted.

December 7, 1984—This marked the first day in the studio for George's new album. They were to work on a song Harrison wrote with Crosby and Nash called "Let May Reign." Jeff Lynne had become the de facto producer until George Martin arrived a few days later for the sessions. Everyone respected Lynne's knowledge of producing as he had produced some of Harrison's last records and was also the main producer for the Traveling Wilburys' (the band with Harrison, Petty, Lynne, Bob Dylan, and Roy Orbison). Harrison liked Lynne as a producer—the friend and musician had lots of ideas. A lack of good ideas has left many songs on the cutting room floor. That wouldn't be the case with all these talents in one room.

After a long day that was approaching ten hours in the studio, Harrison was satisfied with the end result and offered to whomever was interested to come back to Friar Park for some drinks. Tomorrow was another day in the studio for Emerick, Harrison, and Lynne as they would bring in a small string section to complete the final buildup to this new song. George was elated at the progress of this first day and indulged in a bit too much alcohol afterward.

December 8, 1984—Harrison was supposed to be in the studio at 10 a.m. this morning but wouldn't roll in until shortly after 11 with tea in hand. He was a little wobbly on his feet so Emerick and Lynne suggested he just hang out while they worked on the song. He even still smelled like alcohol, so they knew he had drunk too much.

Emerick and Lynne positioned the five-man string ensemble to different parts of the studio as to not pick up overflow sounds from another instrument by the strategically placed microphones. While Emerick worked on setting up the mics, Lynne directed each one of the violin players about how the sound should start soft and light to build into a dramatic finish. The first few takes were good, but the producer urged them to dig deeper to achieve their very best performance for this track. Three hours into the recording, the song was ready to be mixed down when they noticed a commotion coming from the back left corner of the studio. One of the hired violinists had forgotten he had a lit cigarette and it rolled onto the carpet, igniting it and the back curtains that lined the studio walls. Within minutes, the flame was out of control and their fire extinguishers became useless.

Three fire trucks arrived at CBS Records in time to contain the fire to Studio 2, with minimal damage to Studio 4 and Studio 6 (the two adjoining studios to the fire). When Emerick realized how fast the fire was spreading, he quickly grabbed the tape of the new song and other tapes from recent recordings. He called for a studio assistant to help him grab whatever they could before the control room caught fire. This was crucial as the control room was completely ablaze within minutes of them exiting. The firemen finally got the fire under control but not before Studio 2 was completely destroyed.

Some studio instruments were also ruined in the fire, but they had saved all the valuable recordings. This rattled Harrison and Emerick mostly. In all the chaos, Harrison assumed the tape was ruined in the fire, so it was a huge relief to discover it was saved. It would have been a monumental task to have to re-record the whole song.

December 11, 1984—Harrison's phone rang this morning to the voice of an angry Paul McCartney. Paul had heard of the fire at CBS Records and claimed Harrison might have even put someone up to starting it. Paul assumed that George was bitter toward CBS because they didn't pursue his solo album with the same fervor they had with the Beatles. George laughed, which made the bass player even more upset. The two talked through the episode and Harrison explained what had happened in Studio 2. After Paul settled down, he suggested they all meet to see what the next steps for the band would be. Harrison reluctantly agreed to a meeting with the other Beatles but warned Paul that his main concern right now was his solo album. Paul did soften to let George know he would be there for his scheduled time in the studio for the new album in January. This was a relief to Harrison as he assumed Paul's motives were to stop his record and was prepared for the bassist to completely bow out of the project altogether.

December 15, 1984—This Beatles meeting took place at John's flat in Soho. Along with the band was Derek Taylor and George Martin. Yoko entered the large, white living room to offer them all tea and biscuits as they chatted amongst themselves. Derek was the first to address the issues at hand. "Boys, I think it's time to expand our product. I'd like to explore some requests we've been getting."

"Like what?" asked Lennon.

"Well, the one I really think we should do is another movie. We were offered by the CBS Records affiliate Columbia Pictures to do a film."

"Oh brother!" said George. "The first movie we made wasn't too bad, but the rest were drags!"

McCartney, who had previously written scores for movies, immediately started thinking this could be the opportunity to approach a new album to the rest of the group. But he just nodded his head as if to acknowledge the suggestion. Lennon said he wasn't sure at this point, but Ringo loved the movie industry, so he said he was up for it.

"What is the script about?" asked Starr.

"It's about a foreign student at the university who takes on the political institution." He informed them that the student would be played by actor John Cusack. "Your parts would vary," he continued. "They want John to be the boy's father, Paul to be his professor, George the diner owner where the boy frequents, and Ringo as the school dean. Then, all four of you play in the house band at the corner pub. Of course they're requesting a soundtrack of new material."

Paul smiled, but remained quiet. "In what ways does he take on the political institution?" asked John, always eager to fight an establishment.

"The lad seeks to become prime minister but refuses to mold to any one political party."

"Sounds like my kind of kid!" replied Lennon.

Paul finally chimed in. "Listen mates, I've got some songs that we can use for this film if we choose to do it. Lately the songs seem to be coming out quite easily—I don't know why."

The others didn't say a word. Derek hesitated, but then informed the band that the soundtrack they would create for the movie stood alone outside of the current four-record deal with CBS Records. The band had only given CBS two of the four albums they signed on for. The money they would be paid for this film would be upwards of £3.5 million per Beatle. This got their attention. They agreed to read the script and told their manager they would let him know if they wanted to pursue the film.

Paul then circled back around to recording another album. He explained how they could easily come up with enough material to do both a movie soundtrack and another new Beatles record. John and Ringo both had a couple songs in the works but were reluctant about committing to an album right now. Harrison was still on a roll writing songs and was maybe the best writer of the bunch at the time.

George Martin then interjected, "Gentlemen, I'm prepared to help if you do decide to pursue another record. I haven't been approached to produce a soundtrack for you, but I would request if you do go forward with another album, that you'd think about recording it at the EMI studios. Even if it were to be released by CBS Records."

John told the others that while he knew they still owed two albums, he wasn't sure if he was ready just yet. Ringo stated some reservations as well and was concerned about the tensions rising in a studio environment. As Harrison previously stated to the bassist, he wanted to finish his solo record before he would even think about another possible Beatles album. George told them that the work on his solo project would be complete by mid-March. So the band decided to put any talks of a new album on the back burner for a few months. Taylor asked them to place priority on deciding whether or not they wanted to do the film.

December 28, 1984—John woke this morning excited as he had read the script for the movie unofficially titled *The Unruly Candidate* that was being pitched to them. Derek had been pushing for all of them to read the script, but the Christmas holiday had put anything Beatles related on hold for the boys.

"Hey, Paul, did you get a chance to read that?"

"Oh the script?" replied McCartney, pretending to almost have forgotten about it. He didn't want to let John know how much he'd been thinking about the film since they first heard of it. Not only had he read the script the first night he got it, he had modified some of his current songs to fit the movie's theme. "No, not yet. Been doing stuff with the kids."

"It's fantastic!" said Lennon. "I thought it was really well written and it has a good message, ya know?" John urged Paul to read it and let him know what he thought, again secretly seeking his partner's approval.

Paul was smiling about John's excitement. Lennon then called the other two Beatles about the script. George had not yet read it, but Ringo had and also loved it. Harrison was still busy rehearsing songs at the mini studio in his home at Friar Park, but he told John he'd try to read it over the next few days.

December 31, 1984—On this last day of 1984, Derek Taylor received a call from Columbia Pictures executive Guy McElwaine to inform him of a change in movie personnel for the script the boys were given. They had now hired the services of famed Hollywood director Martin Scorsese to take over the directing of this movie. The film's initial director (Billy Wilder) had been in contract disputes with Columbia, and the aging director would not settle for anything less than the band was to make. This caused quite a stir in the Columbia Pictures offices and forced them to look elsewhere.

When they heard Scorsese was interested, they immediately wooed him in to fill the vacancy. Taylor knew this was a good change because the boys loved the Academy Award-winning director for his work on *Taxi Driver*, *The Last Waltz*, and more recently *Raging Bull*. Derek called each band member and was met with the same reaction—"Wow!! Martin Scorsese?"—followed by a short pause and then, "Okay, if he's directing, I'm in!" Even George was excited about working on a movie with the famous director. All steam ahead for the band to star in a new motion picture. They were still, by far, the hottest thing in the entertainment industry.

Chapter 15

January 14, 1985—George had moved to the EMI studios to finish recording his solo album. This day would include another star-studded group of musicians in the studio. Ringo, Crosby, Nash, Winwood, Petty, and Lynne would round out today's crew. The musicians would vary from day to day, and little was accomplished over the next three days. Harrison had allowed for a certain "looseness" in the studio that ended up being too loose. They had barely gotten a basic track for the song "Saving Grace" recorded over that three-day whirlwind. Even so, some EMI executives had gotten a sneak preview of Harrison's new song and were eager to hear the rest of the album. They had asked if Harrison would meet with them later that week to discuss the record. He agreed to meet with EMI and scheduled it for later in the week.

January 17, 1985—Harrison, his attorney, three EMI executives, and the EMI attorney were scheduled to meet this morning to discuss the new album. George and his attorney were both given a copy of the contract. George's attorney pointed out that this was an exclusive deal that locked him into EMI without an exit clause. The amount of money they would pay him for this album and a possible next one was £2 million per record, with a £250,000 signing bonus. This was an enormous amount and would cause Harrison to rethink being in the Beatles. The two sides hammered out details of this contract over the next three hours.

EMI had given in a bit to Harrison's request to be allowed to record or perform with the Beatles. The clause stated if Harrison did record another album with his other band, he would then forfeit his signing bonus. There was also a clause stating if he were to perform live with the Beatles, he would have to pay EMI 10% of his earnings from each show. This was an incredible amount of money for him to surrender for being with the Beatles. George requested a few days to think it over and said he would get back to them when he had made his decision.

Before the meeting adjourned, one of the EMI execs handed George the keys to a new Lamborghini Countach sports car. "Here, this is a little sweetener. You can keep it even if you don't sign with us. But of course, we're hoping you do!" Harrison loved sports cars and driving fast so this was a great gift for the guitarist. He was now being pursued by a record company in the same manner in which he had seen with the Beatles and it felt good. He had bargaining power because he was writing incredible songs and he still was a member of the most famous act in the land.

January 23, 1985—After a weekend break, it was another day back at the EMI studio. This day brought Crosby and Nash, John Lennon, Ringo, Harry Nilsson, and Eric Clapton together in the studio. It was a crazy bunch of musicians to gather for the next few days of recording. Whenever Nilsson was in the mix, everyone knew there would be insanity to the nth degree. This was absolutely the case over the next couple of days. John and Ringo were extremely close to Harry and would easily succumb to his desire to constantly be inebriated. So there was lots of drinking over a three-day period and little was recorded.

George, realizing this was a roadblock for the album, decided it best to not have Nilsson around for the remainder of the recording process. They had barely gotten a basic track for one song ("Don't Look Now") over that three-day whirlwind, so George asked the others back, only this time without Harry. Ringo pulled George aside to say he was appreciative that Harrison turned a blind eye to their antics while in Nilsson's company. George also had a fondness for the lovable Nilsson and let him know that. But since he wanted more focus from the musicians, Harry Nilsson was out.

January 25, 1985—It was Friday morning of a semi-productive week of recording for George's solo album. John and Paul were both scheduled to record that day. It would be the first time in the studio for these three specific Beatles to work on a solo project. George had played on many Lennon and Starr records; Ringo played for all the others on solo projects; and Paul assisted on the *Ringo* album. But John and Paul never played together on anything other than a Beatles record after their split in 1970. Ringo was not present for these recordings and all thought it best as to not make it a Beatles record on George's solo project. Crosby, Nash, Jim Keltner, Clapton, and Leon Russell rounded out the band over the next two days.

This would be a special day in the studio for all. They started work on another Harrison/Crosby/Nash composition called "Murky Creek." This song didn't start out sounding like a Beatles record but by the time it was recorded, it most definitely did. "Creek" went from a country-styled acoustic song to a semi-psychedelic rock dirge with John and Paul's handprints all over it. The song really did sound almost too Beatle-ee for George, but everyone else thought it was fabulous. There was a good feeling in this session and all the musicians played as if they had been together for years. The band for the track consisted of Clapton on lead guitar, Lennon on electric fuzz guitar, McCartney on his Rickenbacker bass, Keltner on drums, Leon playing keyboards, and Harrison, Crosby, and Nash all playing acoustic guitars.

The partly written song that Paul had brought for the album would be finished with John's help. The song had most of the chords, but only had one verse and the chorus of the lyrics. It was an upbeat song with another great melody. He showed the others the chord progression and then went off in a corner of the studio to finish the song with John.

Just like old times, the two sat nose to nose to hash out this new song. Everyone in the studio had one eye on the two as they knew this was a special moment. Mal tried not to make too much of it as he sneaked a couple of photographs of the two face-to-face writers. Within thirty minutes, John and Paul had completed writing the new song ("Apple Orchard") for George's album. It sounded like it could have been a song from the *Hard Day's Night* album. It was soft, but soaring; melodic, yet complex...it was as close to a "perfect" Lennon/McCartney composition as any song they'd ever written.

George and the others were thrilled at this creation. George had written a middle break, which would include his guitar solo. Now the song was ready to be recorded. The band spent that afternoon and most of the next day finishing the recording of the new gem.

George's new album, *Long Time*, would be released on March 1, 1985 and would sell 250,000 copies the first day. It would go to No. 1, where it stayed for three weeks. The album would go Platinum two times over and was considered Harrison's best work since *Living in the Material World* was released in 1973. The song "Apple Orchard," written by McCartney/Lennon/Harrison, held the No. 1 spot on the charts for an astonishing eleven weeks. George liked the album but thought that it was too much like a Beatles record. This would not sit well with him and he would never ask for his Beatle friends' help again on a solo project.

March 6, 1985—The band met with Derek Taylor and some Columbia Pictures executives (including President Guy McElwaine) regarding the movie they had been offered to do. They discussed the amount to be paid and the band negotiated a higher contract for the film. Each would be paid £5 million and they would own the publishing rights to their songs. This was an absurd amount for anyone to be paid for a movie and the boys were elated. So they proceeded to sign the movie contract. The movie execs were thrilled because they had just landed the most popular act in the world to star in a movie with one of the best directors in the industry. Filming was to begin in July at the studio in Burbank, California, so they set out to write music for the movie.

March 9, 1985—Back at the newly rebuilt Studio 2 at CBS Records, John, Paul, and Ringo were in the control room making a quick plan with George Martin and Geoff Emerick. George Harrison walked around the studio to find it was in decent shape, but not as good as before the fire. It seemed to him that they had cut corners to get the studio back up and running. Some walls had not been painted and only half the studio had soundproofing panels installed. There was also a not-so-pleasant odor that was a combination of fresh paint, smoldering ash, and mildew from the water used to put out the fire. As they would soon discover, the "new" equipment was also inferior to the equipment that had burned down. Emerick had difficulties setting up this refurbished mixing board. Turned out the studio had bought a used soundboard to get all of their recording studios back open.

Within two days, the band switched over to Studio 6, where the equipment was the same as the old Studio 2, but the room was much larger. This large room didn't have the nice sound they were used to from Studio 2 and it felt cold and damp. But having access to the better recording equipment made it worthwhile.

March 11, 1985—Now in Studio 6, both John and Paul had songs they wanted to work on for the movie. Paul had one specifically for the title track called "Own Way." The lyrics told of the young student and his desires to become elected while not conforming to any ideology. Lennon was surprised by how well the lyrics were written. He had always thought Paul could write a good lyric if he set his mind to it, and this was a dandy. The music wasn't complete so John and Paul, with a middle suggestion from Ringo, finished it up within an hour.

George didn't seem to be interested in being there. He felt they were forcing songs to come out in an uncomfortable environment. He sat fiddling with his guitar, talking to Mal. The others could sense Harrison's lack of interest and tried to continue despite the distraction. But this would not sit well—particularly with Paul—and a battle ensued. He yelled at Harrison to either "get your shit together or leave the studio! We can get much more done without you moping around here all day!" Harrison's response was to tell McCartney he would leave.

After they both calmed down, George did end up staying and later in the day helped contribute a fabulous guitar solo on Paul's song "Come Inside." This song would end up buried in the soundtrack and many would consider it to be the band's weakest effort. Skeptics would voice their affirmation of the band's rapid decline and that this was a belief they held since The Beatles reformed in 1982. The song had a similar sound as "Your Mother Should Know" from *Magical Mystery Tour* (which the others dreaded) but was slower and had strings throughout. Harrison's solo was his only real contribution to the whole soundtrack, but it was a doozy! One music critic would hail it as "...one of Harrison's best solos ever, almost never to be heard in the middle of this daft song."

The band would spend the next two days trying to get the sound right for "Own Way." Finally, they had completed recording the basic track and it sounded like nothing they had ever recorded. There were no guitars, and it was mostly keyboards, bass, and drums. Ringo had put a solid rock drumbeat behind this upbeat McCartney tune. John added some harmony vocals, and it was ready to be mixed. The rift between Paul and George would continue to simmer in the background while they tried to record this entire soundtrack.

March 17, 1985—The week had produced one complete song and part of another. The writing process had become more difficult because of looming deadlines and also because of expectations from the movie executives. Harrison was still not fully on board with a movie soundtrack. It wasn't an environment he was comfortable with and felt pressure to create music. That in itself caused all of them to withdraw a little and would lead to a stifling of the creative process.

George did have a new song but refused to give it to this movie. He thought it was too good for the movie and would not even offer it to a Beatles album. When Paul asked George if he had any songs to add to the soundtrack, Harrison responded with, "No. Sorry. I've got nothing." McCartney just looked at the guitarist. He knew better. Harrison was never very good at lying and McCartney was well aware of his lack of interest in this project.

Even George Martin would leave the sessions for a few days at one point due to the frustrations of not accomplishing much. This was the kind of recording session that mimicked the *White Album* sessions when no one was interested in the final product or assisting a band member with one of their songs. It had become toxic again to be in this band and the boys needed some time away from each other before finishing the soundtrack. They decided to take a month away from the studios.

April 15, 1985—Sitting at home in London, John was sipping tea and shaking his head thinking about how George's album had been so well received. It wasn't that John was mad or jealous at the quality of the songs on George's album or even how well it was selling; there was a burning sense of competition brewing in Lennon's belly and he couldn't wait to respond...musically.

He picked up his Gibson acoustic guitar and started playing the chords *A minor* to *D* to *C* to *F*... Out of him had begun the basic chord sequence to what would become his best-selling song ever, "Walking Down." This was another song that seemed to come easily and quickly. His guitar seemed to direct him where to put his fingers that day. The lyrics talked of bringing people together when faced with the adversity of difficult circumstances. (While this song was completed in April 1985, it would not be recorded until years later when finishing work on their third Phase 2 album.)

He called Paul and told him of the new song he had just written. Paul stated that he had recently written three more songs that he thought were really good. Paul had also felt the sting of Harrison's solo album going to No. 1 and the competition he had with Harrison wasn't so friendly. He was angry that George's album sold so well and assumed that would be detrimental to their next album and its sales. He told Lennon that he wanted to make Harrison "regret not saving those songs for a Beatles record!" and wanted their next album to be the best one they had ever done. Even Ringo was quietly not happy about George doing a solo project while the Beatles still owed CBS two more records.

April 16, 1985—After taking almost a month away from each other, the band was back in the studio to finalize the recordings for the movie soundtrack. They had finished two songs at this point and would spend the next month and a half rehearsing and then recording four more tracks for the movie.

Most of the songs were written by Paul, and the song "Own Way" would be the best-selling hit from the movie. The soundtrack would be released on June 6, 1985, where it would peak at No. 19 on the music charts. The song "Own Way" would go to No.

6 and would stay in the Top 10 for five weeks. Besides the tune "Come Inside" (which was panned by the critics), the other songs were good, but not quite the quality of what was expected of the Liverpudlians.

Unruly Candidate Soundtrack *(produced by George Martin)—CBS Records Music (1985)*

Own Way (McCartney/Lennon/Starkey)
Come Inside (McCartney)
Was It You? (Lennon/McCartney)
Election Day (McCartney)
Young Man (Lennon)
Equality (McCartney)

Chapter 16

July 15, 1985—The band was in Burbank, California, to work on the film *Unruly Candidate*. They were ready to be away from the sometimes restricting confines of the recording studio, and working on this film made them relax a bit toward each other. They were excited especially because they thought the script was superb and were eager to work with one of their favorite directors. It was starting to feel like the excitement generated from their first full-length movie, *A Hard Day's Night*. The energy exuding from the band was contagious, and all involved in the movie would feel that same energy to start the filming.

It was a glorious day in Southern Cal and the first shot was being filmed in the street outside of the studio's "City Hall." As the band gathered around to meet the actors and studio hands, they saw a stumbling Martin Scorsese approaching them.

"So this is the famous Beatles!" said Scorsese as he reached out his hand to greet them. They could immediately smell the alcohol on his breath and realized why he was stumbling around. The drunken director had fallen on hard times and was having quite a bit of trouble staying away from the bottle. It also was later discovered that Scorsese took less money to work with the Beatles. But when he found out how much the band would make, he became angry and held it against them. The boys knew this was a bad sign and it turned out to be the beginning of what would become a different kind of nightmare for them.

They had witnessed the ugliness from within, but now it appeared they would have to deal with it from an outside source over which they had no control. They had all hoped this was a one-off thing and that Scorsese would straighten up for the rest of the filming, but that was not the case. The director would end up being sloppy drunk throughout his entire time directing the movie. He rarely showed up and when he did, he was too drunk to do much more than goof off with the crew. He would spend hours with his arm on the shoulder of a cameraman telling jokes until he was in tears from laughing. It was the movie producers' worst nightmare—to have this wonderful director be so inebriated that they couldn't get a single good day's work out of him. It would change the direction of the film, and even some of the plot was changed to accommodate for Scorsese's absences.

The boys' interactions with Scorsese over the next few months were sparse. The band tried to be as cordial as possible although they were showing signs of frustration toward the man they used to admire. This would send them all reeling because they had put so much faith in the famed director and now only saw a shell of the man who had won Academy Awards.

This first day of filming was not at all what they had hoped for or expected. They tried to have fun with the crew and the bumbling director, but it was not the pleasant experience they had thought it would be. Ringo seemed to enjoy being on the set. He loved everything about the movies. He didn't even complain when there were some difficulties with the application of his makeup. The makeup artists initially had trouble making Ringo look older for the part of the dean of the university. It took them more than four hours with Ringo sitting still in a chair to get his look right. He never complained and joked the whole time through. The others were already wondering what they had gotten themselves into.

July 23, 1985—The band was to film the scene where they performed at the corner pub and played "Own Way" for the first time. It would be a memorable scene from the movie and ended up being the highlight of the film. They would perform this song at a fictional pub called The Flying Ivory. The pub was designed to mock the Cavern Club, and the band was playing downstairs to a smoked-filled room jam-packed with customers.

This day wound up being the last day they all had fun on the set. The boys reverted back to their slapstick style of humor. John stole a drumstick and smacked Ringo on the head with it. George danced his way right off the small stage area of the pub. It was pure Beatles' goofiness, and the entire set was electric during this scene. Their infectious personalities were a welcomed break from the chaos and seriousness that had dominated the filming to this point. The boys enjoyed each other's company that day for the first time in a long time. It would also be one of the last times all four would have this much fun together.

July 30, 1985—Again back at the Columbia Pictures studio, they were filming a scene that had John being intimate with his movie wife, Jessica Lange. After the cameras stopped rolling, the two were still embraced in a passionate kiss while the studio crew stood watching. This was another of many days Scorsese would not be present for filming, but everyone else involved was concerned. Most had seen the perils of actors falling for each other on a film set and were well aware of the dangers that it could cause a movie.

It turned out that Lennon was indeed smitten with his co-star. He spent the next two days in her trailer having drinks and trying to woo the actress. Lange had been charmed by the lead Beatle's wit and humor. The two had become inseparable and were in the glow of fresh love. Paul was the first to warn John of what could happen if he got caught cheating on his wife. Ringo confronted him next about it. But none of it seemed to matter to Lennon, who was infatuated with the beautiful Lange. Her soft sense of being was the exact opposite of Yoko, and Lennon craved that softness.

He found Lange irresistible, and from that point would almost always follow her around like a lost puppy on the movie set.

August 12, 1985—Filming had been going slow. Without Scorsese, there seemed to be less excitement and it was replaced by growing tension among the actors. This day would also cause the film's production to come to a halt. Yoko did in fact catch wind of her husband's misgivings and showed up at the studio set. It was a windy and rainy day on the set and most actors were in hiding. When Yoko saw Paul, she grabbed him by the sleeve and pleaded with him to tell her where John was. He claimed he had no idea where his writing partner was (even though he most definitely had an idea). Someone on the set mentioned they might be in Lange's trailer, so she frantically searched for it with tears mixing with the rain, streaming down her face.

When she did find the trailer, Yoko forced her way through the door. Inside the trailer, she found her husband and the actress naked on the floor. "What the...," Lange screamed before realizing who it was that had just burst through her door. Lange quickly escaped into the bathroom to avoid the mess that was about to take place.

"Get up! Get dressed and get out here NOW!!!" Yoko screamed at John.

He hurriedly got dressed while making up some excuse about how he and the actress were meditating together. Yoko and John would argue right outside of Lange's trailer for a good part of fifteen minutes, catching the attention of everyone within earshot. This would cause such a commotion among the crew that the filming would stop for two days after the event.

August 13, 1985—At the hotel with Yoko, John tried to smooth things over. Yoko had been understanding of John's promiscuity in the past, but as they had aged, she had hoped those habits would cease to continue. Her anger dissipated and was replaced by concern for their marriage and the effect on their nine-year-old son. John assured Yoko that this would never happen again and that he had a moment of weakness.

"Well, what's to stop you from being weak again...when I'm not around?" was Yoko's reply.

John sat with his head down and told Yoko, "I only have my word and that's it. If you don't believe me, there's really nothing I can do."

Yoko barked, "You're right! There's nothing you can do to make me believe your words. So I suggest you start acting more and talking less."

She was again fuming and walked off to the bedroom, slamming the door behind her. John spent the night on the hotel room couch contemplating his marriage, the band, and the woman he had secretly fallen in love with. He couldn't help but wonder what Jessica was doing at that moment. He wanted to call her but thought better. He was in enough trouble and didn't want to rock the boat any further.

August 15, 1985—Filming continued, and Scorsese showed up inebriated again. This time he was shouting all sorts of unusual requests at the actors. "Put a little mustard into that," "Be a garbage truck," and "Yell like a dying zebra!" were all heard to come from the drunken director. At this point of the movie, the actors would ignore him as he made no sense whatsoever most of the time.

Early that day, Scorsese went to get up on a stepladder to yell out more insane demands when he slipped and fell from the third step. He fell hard and stayed collapsed on the floor for quite some time. The medical team rushed in to examine the director. The doctor on staff determined that his left leg had been broken in the fall and he would most likely need surgery to repair it. He would be out of commission for almost two months, and that was a big problem for the movie producers. What started out as the dream movie set was turning into the exact opposite—an environment where no person would want to spend more time than absolutely necessary.

Guy McElwaine hurriedly got on the phone to Billy Wilder to see if the director could take over the reins for this movie. "I'm in the middle of filming a documentary on artificial intelligence for PBS and won't be done until next month" was Wilder's response. "Besides, you won't pay me enough to do this movie." McElwaine replied that they would pay him what they initially offered, and he would only have to direct a portion of the movie since some of the major scenes had already been filmed. Wilder told McElwaine he would think about the offer and let him know as soon as possible.

August 16, 1985—Wilder called Guy McElwaine to let him know he would join the film's set only if they would wait a month or more. He wasn't sure when the filming for the PBS special would end but assumed it would be done by September 16. So, they talked through the details and a desperate McElwaine agreed to all the demands of the eccentric director. The director knew he had bargaining power and took advantage of that. Wilder estimated he would show up on the set either at the end of September or the beginning of October. The Columbia Pictures president was ecstatic and thought that this hire would save the movie he had previously believed so much in. What he did not know at the time, though, was that it was most likely too late.

August 19, 1985—Another day on the movie set and this time without a director. The head of casting (Rebecca McKenzie) became the director's replacement. For the next month, most of the filming for the entire movie would be completed. McKenzie did a marvelous job with the little experience she had in directing. The set had become a dreadful place for them all to be as there was a stomach-wrenching acknowledgement among them that the film might not make it past the cutting room floor. But McKenzie brought new energy to the set and even the band felt her presence as the one positive so far for this movie. She battled her way through the mess that was left for her and got the most out of a bad situation. She was barely credited in the movie for her effort, but it was understood by everyone involved that anything good in it was most likely directed by Rebecca.

October 2, 1985—Billy Wilder made his debut as a director for the film on this day. He showed up with a fiery determination to get this movie back on track. But what he had not known was that there was little left of the primary filming. There were only a few scenes left to shoot. Besides those few scenes, all that was left was mostly editing and then fitting in a soundtrack for the movie. At first, the director became angry at what little influence he would have on the film but then realized he was in a good position. He was getting paid a lot of money to basically monitor the film's final touches.

This first day would find the lead actor (John Cusack) getting into a huge disagreement with the movie's new director. Cusack refused to say a line that Wilder added to the script. To Wilder, it was the perfect line for this scene. But for Cusack, he thought it was ridiculous and would not say the line: "I should kick your ass, but instead I'll take your vote!" He thought it was completely out of character for the passive candidate. He told Wilder to "Fuck off" and went back to his trailer, where he would stay for the better part of two days. The two would be at odds for the rest of the filming, and Cusack would later go on to say he would never again work with Wilder. He said in an interview that "even a drunken Scorsese was a much better option than a sober Wilder!"

The movie was destined to be a failure right from the start, and when it was released on the 20th of December, most involved knew it would not fare well at the box offices. The movie producers decided to spend an incredible amount of money on marketing and promoting the new movie. This was done in an effort to make it seem like the movie was better than it truly was. The movie would leave the Beatles with a bad taste in their mouths for any more films in the future.

December 20, 1985—The *Unruly Candidate* was released to little fanfare and would bring in a measly $300,000 on the first day. This would be a sign of things to come as word spread quickly of the Beatles' new movie flop. The initial screenings were met with horrible reviews and the critics did not let up. They trashed the movie as being disjointed, nonsensical, with horrible acting and having no real direction for the plot. "Miserable!" "Mess of a Movie!" "Beatles Flop!" "Scorsese's Last Hurrah?" were some of the headlines. The media was relentless in their attacks of anyone involved in this movie disaster.

Most of the actors had trouble doing their best for it because of the dysfunctional environment on the studio set. No one had taken the movie seriously and it was more than apparent. The one bright spot had been Ringo's acting performance as the dean of the university. He was brilliant and ended up being nominated for an Academy Award for Best Supporting Actor. Besides getting into the Top 10, the film's track "Own Way" went on to win a Grammy Award for Best Soundtrack Song. But this would be the only accolade given to the band aside from Ringo's acting. It would go on to become one of the worst-selling movies in Columbia Pictures history.

The film's critics gave praise to Ringo and the other Beatles for their performances and quickly placed the blame for its failure on the script and the directing. Ringo started getting offers to star in other movies and had become almost as known for his acting as his drumming. The boys were also given credit for breaking out of their Fab Four identity to venture into character roles on film.

The band, sullen by the film's failure, withdraw and stayed out of the public eye for almost a year. They refused any interviews about the movie and would never speak of it. Even the soundtrack was considered a flop besides the song "Own Way." This would go down as the Beatles' worst effort ever and would follow them for the rest of their careers. The future was unclear for this legendary band, and this film put them all on the run from anything that had to do with the entertainment industry.

Chapter 17

January 30, 1986—More than a month had passed since the release of the Beatles' new movie and the band was hidden from the public eye. Lennon was still head over heels in love with Jessica Lange and was having difficulties coming to terms with it. McCartney felt the bitter sting of the failed movie more than the rest. He believed that they had tainted the image of the band, and more than a few fans agreed. Paul met with the bands' attorneys to see if there was a legal recourse to be taken. The attorneys filed a defamation suit against Columbia Pictures. The rest of the band was named a party to this suit even though the others weren't as concerned as Paul was about their reputation. The suit was settled out of court and the band accepted a small settlement two years later. Guy McElwaine went public to verbally trash the Beatles and their lack of interest in the movie, which he claimed was the main reason for its failure. His time as Columbia Pictures president would come to a screeching halt after his public response to the movie.

It had been a few weeks since John had spoken with Jessica. The last time they had seen each other was at the movie premiere afterparty. That night had not gone well. Not many at the party were in good spirits because of the bad experiences surrounding the filming and also because of the overwhelming suspicion the movie would flop. Yoko caused another scene by lunging at Lange while the two stood near the ballroom's bar. John broke up the fracas but not before Yoko spat at Lange.

Though he was hesitant to call the actress, his desire for her overcame his concern for anything else. He called her and asked if she would like to get lunch the next week when he would be in New York. "Oh, John, I'm not so sure that's a good idea," she replied. She had recently started dating actor and playwright Sam Shepard. Even though she had feelings for John, she was confused. "John, you have no plans to divorce her and I've recently met someone myself," said Lange. Those words hit Lennon hard. He would plead with her to meet him, but she would continue to refuse. He hadn't felt the sting of rejection in a very long time and had no idea how to deal with it. So he took to drinking.

February 7, 1986—John had spiraled downward over the past week or so and was living on a steady diet of Brandy Alexanders. He was now in New York to help Harry Nilsson on an album and was devastated that Lange still wouldn't see him. She had told him to stop calling as she was getting more serious with Shepard. When he arrived at the studio, he was beyond drunk and would need help limping inside. Ringo was also invited to the recording sessions and was already there chatting with the band. Harry was excited to see John and gave him a big hug when he came in. The irony of John being completely annihilated while Harry was sober made the others laugh out loud. Even Nilsson thought it was comical, but he had no intention of staying sober. He had secretly been waiting for an opportunity to indulge himself, and his drunk Beatle friend was the perfect excuse.

After a few hours of goofing around playing old standards, Harry decided to order in for lunch. His idea of lunch was a bag of pretzels, some Oreo cookies, four cases of beer, and two cases of assorted liquor. Chances of them now getting something accomplished in the studio went downhill drastically. But they all had fun hanging out and jamming together. Harry would want to continue the festivities after the session, so they returned to his rented suite at the Waldorf-Astoria hotel. The band and some female companions were back at the hotel suite drinking and listening to music. Harry was dancing around with a top hat on (that he had found lying around the studio); Ringo was whooping it up with some of the women at the party; everyone was having a ball...except for John. He had turned back into a mean drunk and would bark at any woman that tried to approach him. The alcohol wasn't helping him forget Lange; it was making things worse. He was miserable...swearing at everyone and throwing bottles against the wall. He picked up an expensive lamp and smashed it on the floor.

His next move would come back to haunt him for years to come. In a drunken attempt to cause more hotel damage, Lennon picked up an end table and heaved it toward a wall. What he hadn't noticed was one of the female guests standing right in its path. The table hit her in the head, knocking her to the floor. Blood immediately trickled down her face. The hotel physician was contacted and he attended to the young woman, who was unconscious on the floor. At that moment, the police arrived and started asking questions of the guests. The band pleaded ignorant, claiming they didn't see anything. But one of the female guests said she saw the whole thing and placed the blame directly on Lennon. She claimed he had been out of control the whole evening and had been throwing things in the room all night.

The police arrested John and took him to the county jail for processing. The witness gave a sworn statement to the police and that pretty much sealed Lennon's fate. The New York police idolized the musician and put down the red carpet for him at the holding cell. They offered him tea and snacks. They put on music for him (of course, the Beatles, which he just grumbled at) and bent over backwards trying to keep the drunken Lennon pleased. He was being charged with assault and battery and would remain in jail overnight.

It was Harry and Ringo who came to get John the next day from his jail cell. Mal was in London and Yoko had not yet heard about the incident. The policemen gathered for a group photo with Lennon, Nilsson, and Starr. John, in turn, would send four baskets of fruit to the department for their fine treatment of the star.

February 13, 1986—John was back in London and Yoko wasn't speaking to him. He had tried for the past two days to smooth things over, but Yoko knew he still had feelings for Lange and that was probably the impetus behind what had gotten him into trouble with the law. She suggested they separate, but he begged her not to leave him. He told her he was struggling with the pressures of his life and needed her now more than ever. She said she would stay for Sean's sake and that things needed to change fast, or she would leave him for good. He felt he narrowly escaped one here, but he didn't realize that this was the last straw for Yoko. She thought that one more slip-up by John would cause her to leave him forever.

They slept in different beds for months to come. His only true friend (named Brandy Alexander) would come to his aid. John would spend the next year and a half living out of a glass of cognac, crème de cacao, and milk. This period would be referred to as John's "Lost Week." He would remain indoors mostly, not writing and essentially being a hermit. He wouldn't take calls and his only reprieve was having Sean there with him to take his mind off the misery that had become his life.

April 3, 1987—It had been more than a year since anyone had heard from John. The Beatles had been so far out of the limelight that the press assumed they had called it quits. Rumor spread that they had split up again. Some media outlets were interested in trying to determine if this was true, but most ignored the story.

Paul tried again to reach his friend. This time, John took the call. He had been in better spirits as of late but was still clinging to his fueled drunkenness.

"Hey, Paul, old buddy. How is Beatledom?"

McCartney could tell his partner was drunk again and was sad to see it was only 10:40 a.m. Paul felt he needed to help Lennon in whatever way he could and assumed getting them all back into the studio would be the remedy. "John, I've got a half a dozen songs that are ready to record. I know you had some you were working on. Let's get to recording a new album."

The happy drunk sprouted out, "Sure! Let's do it…" before realizing what he had just agreed to. The Beatles still owed CBS Records two more albums and Paul had been chomping at the bit to continue recording. Paul called the others and arranged a band meeting again at Friar Park.

April 19, 1987—The band met at George's house to discuss the possibility of another album. Derek Taylor was there, but George Martin had bowed out. He was still reeling from the movie soundtrack, which had turned out to be a disaster for everyone involved. John was the last to limp into the meeting and he looked like he hadn't slept in days.

"Jeez, John! What happened?" asked George.

"What do yer mean?" John replied while dead-falling onto an open couch.

Paul chimed in, "John, if you're not able to meet today, we can postpone the meeting."

"I'm fine. I'm fine. What's all the fuss about? I'm bloody here, aren't I?" spouted Lennon.

There was a time when Brian Epstein and even George Martin could get John back in line when needed. But those days were gone and not even Yoko could help him get his life back on track now.

They agreed to carry on with the meeting. Paul started by letting them know of the songs he had ready to record and suggested going into the studio. It seemed like the others knew John needed something to get him out of this alcohol-induced rut and felt this would be good for him. So they agreed to get studio time for the beginning of May at CBS.

May 1, 1987—The band was back in the CBS Records studios again in Studio 6, which had now become their preferred recording home. The boys were relaxed around each other. It had been long enough away from the studio walls for their memories of the last session (which was fraught with tension) to fade into obscurity. So they joked and fooled around, playing some of their Phase I memories like "Hold Me Tight" and "I Should Have Known Better." After playing about four warm-up songs, they gathered in the control room to discuss the plan. George Martin began the discussion.

"I've been approached by Phillips and Sony representatives who want to release all of your albums on compact disc. I think this would be a great thing and record sales will immediately skyrocket."

They all knew he was right. People would now go out and buy CDs of every album they had owned. The band agreed that Martin should spend the time and effort to remaster their previous albums to be released on CD.

Paul took the floor next. "I've got six songs that I think are really good. I'd like to present a couple of them to you all." John had been nodding in and out of sleep. He was in bad shape again.

"Hey, John! Are you okay?" Harrison called out.

"Huh, wha...yeah, I'm fine. What's happening?" He had not heard a word of the meeting. The others were more than frustrated with the ongoing antics. They spent the next three hours rehearsing a new Paul song when Lennon caused a scene. His guitar was not in tune, he was playing it overly loud, and he was screaming obscenities to anyone who tried to talk to him. The others realized it was time to get him home. So they asked big Mal to drive the drunken musician home.

When they got in the car, Lennon came to life. "Hey, Malcolm! Let's go play!" With quite a bit of conning and positioning, John had talked Mal into stopping for a few drinks. When the two entered a local pub called Queen's Row, the place was packed to the brim. They forced their way through the crowd to the bar. After Mal ordered their drinks, they stood waiting shoulder to shoulder with the wild crowd. In all of the chaos, a pub patron approached John with a half-drunken smile. He was looking for trouble and he was staring straight at Lennon.

The patron got right in John's face before shoving him into some bar stools. Mal had been reaching for their drinks and only caught part of what had happened. This infuriated him. He grabbed the patron, who was now standing over the fallen musician, picked him up from under his arms, and threw the troublemaker over the bar. This caused the man's head to be split wide open from smashing into the bottles of liquor on the bar.

It was almost midnight when the patrol car driving John got to his flat in Soho. The two officers escorted the still drunk Lennon to the door, where Yoko began screaming at her inebriated husband. She was fed up and again threatened to leave him if he didn't straighten up.

Mal wouldn't be going home that night and would be charged with "assault with intent to bodily harm." He would spend thirty days in jail and have to pay £50,000 to the troublemaking victim. John would end up paying this amount, but the incident changed Mal forever. He became more withdrawn and was not the happy-go-lucky fellow they had known all those years. It seemed to put an end to the everlasting smile on the big man's face. This had an adverse effect on them all. They didn't realize how much they'd relied on his smile and positive attitude. It was the one constant in a sea of changes surrounding the band. Unbeknownst to them at the time, it was Mal's glue that kept the band together. Without that, they were swimming in unchartered waters with no life preserver.

May 12, 1987—They had taken a week off to let things settle after the Mal and John incident. When John returned to the studio, they immediately noticed a change in him. He was alert and pleasant, but subdued. He knew how his drinking had affected the others and decided enough was enough. He had put down the bottle and was back to being the witty, sarcastic, and charming friend they had known their whole lives. He even presented the others with a new offering—a song he had written over the past week. The band indulged him and began working on the new tune, which seemed to be a little disjointed. It wasn't a song that would compete with John's best material, but they approached it with the same enthusiasm. After four hours they had completed a basic track for "Deeper Still" and had it sounding quite Beatle-ish. John was in fine form and even balked at lunch to keep working on more music.

So again they ordered lunch in and started work on one of Paul's new songs. George had been relatively quiet during these sessions. He wanted to have input but was unsure about how many songs he wanted to uncover for the band. He had as many as Paul and maybe even more laying around.

George felt that the most important issue surrounding these recordings was to help John stop drinking. Now that Lennon was sober, Harrison wondered what he was even doing in the studio with these three musicians he had spent more time with than anyone else in his life. He knew that this environment was not a good one for him. The others, try as they might, would never look at his songs with the same optimism they would for a John or a Paul song. So he sat pondering the best path for him and had for now decided to stick around the studio.

June 29, 1987—The band was back in the studio and had completed six tracks over the past month and a half. They were to work on George's new tune "Margie." It was a sort of protest song against British Prime Minister Margaret Thatcher, who had just been voted into office for a rare third term. Paul was uneasy about anything controversial and voiced that concern to the others. John told Paul to lighten up and encouraged George by saying, "We should make it the damned side A release!" This entitlement now felt by Harrison caused him to unleash on McCartney like he'd never had. Paul walked out of the studio instead of having this fight. The other three stayed and rehearsed the song, but their hearts weren't in it now.

Besides, whether they wanted to admit it or not, they needed Paul's playing, singing, and producing. They spent the next three hours fiddling around, talking, and sipping tea. They accomplished little and left the studio early that day. This would be the last day all four Beatles would be in the same studio at the same time.

July 18, 1987—Most of the Beatles' music catalog was released on this day on the new CD format. *Abbey Road* went back into the charts as CD sales went through the roof. Many of their Phase 1 records appeared again on the music charts, and even the two Phase 2 offerings would be back in the Top 20. George Martin was pleased with the response, and his hard work had most definitely paid off. The band decided to give Martin a bonus, so they bought him a red Ferrari 328 GTS sports car. The producer was not into flashy things or fast cars, but this was a treat. He would end up giving the sports car to his seventeen-year-old son, Giles, who had assisted him in the digital mastering process.

The band had been wrong about the new format of recording music. Compact discs were indeed taking over as the new recording medium, and vinyl albums were slowly being replaced. The musical trailblazers missed out on that trail.

Chapter 18

August 28, 1989—After over two years out of the public eye and six years since their last album was released (not including the movie soundtrack), the Beatles had a band meeting. Their third Phase 2 offering was not complete and had been sitting in wait for more than two years, as well.

John had spent fifty-nine days in the county jail after being prosecuted for his assault case and came out of jail with another perspective change. He had become leery of their fans and would keep his distance for quite some time. His stint in the county jail turned him into more of a recluse, and he would do all he could to avoid any encounters with fans.

Derek had been approached by one of the cable music channels, MTV, requesting the band play on their new acoustic-themed program. *MTV Unplugged* was being introduced as a new concept on the all-music channel. It would feature some of the most popular performers of the day and break down their sound in an acoustic environment. This was an idea that interested all four Beatles. They were on board with trying something different and new. Besides the ridiculous amount of money they would make, they would also be the first act to perform on this new show. Being the first show, MTV would license the performance to be broadcast around the globe.

At this meeting, there was no discussion of completing the unfinished album. It was a subject that only Paul wanted to pursue. The Beatles scheduled their performance on *Unplugged* for November 24 and set out to rehearse songs for the show. Even George was excited about this format and thought that his songs would be received in a new light. They sat down to write out the set list for the show and tensions rose immediately. They knew this would be telecast around the globe and wanted to put their best foot forward. So tempers flared about which songs to include while Ringo tried to act as the peacemaker. It would take three hours and an intervention from George Martin about which ones they should perform before they finally agreed to the list.

October 5, 1989—The band had been practicing at George's mansion for the past month or more. There was an air of frustration surrounding the group and it would not take much to ignite that simmering flame. After going through most of the songs they would play for the show, John showed the others his song "Walking Down." It was written over four years ago, but he never felt the right opportunity to introduce it to the band. The song caused the friction and frustration that had been brewing to immediately cease. It was a masterpiece and they knew it from the start. They spent the rest of the afternoon at Friar Park working on this incredible creation, drinking tea, and being pleasant with each other for a change.

"You know, I've got a bunch of others sittin' round," exclaimed John, who had been writing quite a bit since his heartbreak at the hands of Jessica Lange. Paul was always looking for a way to complete that third Phase 2 record. It was halfway recorded when they bailed on the project. "Yeah, we'll see" was George's response, not wanting to commit to anything.

November 22, 1989—Two days before the recording for the MTV *Unplugged* show, John came down with the flu. He had the cold sweats and was shivering like a jumping bean. Yoko had him wrapped up in his bed and was doing her best to keep her husband comfortable. John was supposed to fly out to New York the next morning, but Yoko called the airlines to cancel. Derek Taylor got on the phone to the others to let them know they might not perform on the show. The MTV producers were in a panic and started recruiting a backup band for the night. So they contacted the Rolling Stones to see if they could perform. The Stones were on tour and would be in Wisconsin the next night (November 23) but would be available to do the show on the 24th, if needed. They had not rehearsed anything for an acoustic set but were comfortable with their catalog of songs to choose from. When McCartney found out the Stones were going to replace them on the show, he became furious. He felt the MTV producers picked the Stones specifically to anger them.

Paul called John to see how he was doing and to discuss the show, but John wouldn't take the call. Yoko explained to Paul how bad he was feeling and that she didn't think he'd be able to play the next afternoon. Paul phoned the others to see if they could come up with an alternate plan. After a few hours of back and forth phone calls, John woke from his flu-induced fog to call McCartney. "Hey lithen, I'm going to make the show one way or another," Lennon told his mate. He said he would fly out to New York on the day of the filming and would be ready to play. The bassist was thrilled and let the others know the MTV gig was still going forward.

November 23, 1989—Mike Sampson was on the phone with the MTV producers to let them know the Beatles were still planning on playing the *Unplugged* show. He explained that John would arrive in New York the day of the show and would make it to the TV studio by their 4 p.m. start time. Sampson did end up chiding the producers for recruiting the Stones as a backup and told him the band was not pleased with that idea. He mildly suggested they throw in something to smooth things over with the band. Not only did the producers balk at giving them anything extra, they now invited the Rolling Stones to the recording. They were to be there at the request of the MTV producers in case the Beatles weren't able to perform.

November 24, 1989—It was the day of the MTV *Unplugged* recording and three of the Beatles were waiting in the TV studio for John. His plane had been held up and he was en route to the studio. It was a nervous time for them all. They had never played live acoustically besides the few songs John and Paul had done on Letterman. So this was nerve-wracking, for sure. It was 3:30 p.m. and John was still not there. Both Derek Taylor and Mike Sampson had been frantically trying to get in touch with the lead singer and had no updates as to John's whereabouts.

Just then, Lennon and Yoko walked into the studio. He looked miserable and had lost some weight from this bout with the flu. He grumbled at the others and shook hands with the MTV crew. The band met briefly prior to the taping and were ready to go. It was 4:15 p.m. when the Beatles walked onto the candlelit stage to a thunderous applause from the studio audience. Most of the audience had never even seen a Beatle, let alone witness this fabulous event from such close proximity.

"Hello, everyone!" Paul yelled into the mic as the others positioned themselves to get ready for this performance. John was wobbly from his illness and had trouble getting situated on his stool. He was barely functional that afternoon due to the illness. Immediately the band noticed Mick, Keith, Ron Wood, and Charlie Watts sitting in the first row. This caught them all off guard and Paul was easily the most irritated by it. It even angered George, who had become close friends with the Stones. He felt this was crossing the line and would later chastise the television studio manager about it. But they were determined to not be distracted for this worldwide event.

The four Beatles sat on stools with candles and incense burning, then started into "Good Day Sunshine." No one knew whether or not the band would play any Phase I Beatles songs and this first song answered that question. The band had put together a list of songs that mostly had either never been played live or were acoustic guitar type songs that they wouldn't typically play in a live setting. The song list they played that afternoon would be written about by many media outlets after the event and was even called "the set list of the century!" by one writer.

The sound mix was unbelievable and each note to these historic songs was heard like never before. After an amazing version of "Good Day Sunshine," the band went right into John's "All I've Got to Do." Even though John's voice was hoarse and scratchy sounding, he was able to sing this soft song with little difficulty. To hear a song from so early in their careers in this new acoustic format was a thing of beauty.

All four Beatles interacted with the crowd. John joked with them as much as possible for how miserable he felt. Paul was charming and asked some questions of the girls in the first few rows. Then, after playing McCartney's "Follow You," they fielded questions from the audience.

"How do you guys keep writing such amazing songs?" was the first question from a young man. Paul answered this one.

"We really don't know, to be honest. Most times the songs seem to be channeled through each one of us by an external source."

A young woman stood and asked, "John, you sound like you're sick. Are you feeling okay?" The audience howled in laughter.

"Yeah well, I've got me the flu or somethig and it's kickig my arse!"

Ringo intervened. "We weren't sure we'd be able to play today because of how sick he was. So let's hear it for our John for fighting through it!" The crowd stood and applauded.

The last question came from a woman who asked, "Are there plans for another album?"

The boys looked at each other and George responded, "Well, we have talked about it for some time but have not yet reached a conclusion about that." No one in the band wanted to let on that this had been a difficult subject to broach and that some music had already been recorded.

As the band continued, the audience went from being mesmerized through each song to complete elation afterward. Even the Stones were enjoying the event. The recording was going fabulously, and the MTV producers were glowing from the excitement of the new show. The band made its way through Phase 1 and 2 songs, and then some solo songs. Following Ringo's lead vocal performance on "See You There," it was George's turn at a Phase 1 tune.

Before they started, a producer had informed George of a young boy in the audience who had cancer and played guitar. The producer found out that the boy knew this George Harrison composition and asked the band if the boy could join them. A fourteen-year-old Dylan Faulkner walked onto the stage and was handed a guitar by Mal Evans. His parents were thrilled at the sight of their son playing with the Beatles and had tears of joy rolling down their faces. There sat Dylan in between George and Paul, as they went through an outstanding version of "Here Comes the Sun" to a standing ovation. The sight of the young cancer patient being given this once-in-a-lifetime opportunity caused many in the audience to become watery-eyed.

They made it through their set list and were about to play the last song of the day when Mick Jagger approached the stage. He grabbed the mic from Paul and told the audience the story of how the Rolling Stones learned to write songs from the two lead Beatles. "We were stuck in a rut and couldn't figure out the best songwriting process. John and Paul went off into a corner to complete the song they gave to us. When we saw them just come up with a song on the spot, it made us realize we could do the same. Now almost thirty years later, we wanted to thank them for helping us out and gettin' us going in the right direction. We wouldn't be where we are today if it wasn't for them! Thank you, BEATLES!!!" The crowd went wild to hear Mick acknowledge the band for assisting in their success.

The boys put down their guitars and Ringo pulled his hi-hat cymbals from the kit to the front of the stage to be next to the others. Paul, George, and John gathered around one microphone, with Ringo next to them playing only the hi-hat, to do a mostly a capella version of "Because." The three vocalists sounded superb together, and their harmonies were amazing. It was as if less was more.

The much stripped-down version of "Because" on MTV *Unplugged* would appear as one of the most popular music videos of the time. It was maybe their best live performance since their return to the public eye and would be played ad nauseum on the cable music channel. Media outlets all over the world gushed over this performance and the whole *Unplugged* show. It would go down as one of the most incredible recordings the Beatles had ever done. The CD and VHS video released from this event would go on to sell millions. *The Beatles Unplugged* would become one of their best-selling records ever, and the CD would go platinum nine times over.

The Beatles Unplugged *on MTV (with singer listed)—CBS Records Music (1989)*

Good Day Sunshine (Lennon/McCartney)—Paul
All I've Got to Do (Lennon/McCartney)—John
Solitude (Harrison/Lennon)—George
If I Fell (Lennon/McCartney)—John and Paul
I'm Looking Through You (Lennon/McCartney)—Paul
Old Brown Shoe (Harrison)—George
Given to Fly (Lennon)—John
And I Love Her (Lennon/McCartney)—Paul
Apple Scruffs (Harrison)—George
Follow You (McCartney/Lennon)—Paul
Working Class Hero (Lennon)—John
Mrs. Vanderbilt (McCartney)—Paul
For No One (Lennon/McCartney)—Paul
I'll Cry Instead (Lennon/McCartney)—John
Final Words (Harrison/McCartney)—George
Mother Nature's Son (Lennon/McCartney)—Paul
Intuition (Lennon)—John
Octopus' Garden (Starkey)—Ringo
Yes It Is (Lennon/McCartney)—John
Here Comes the Sun (Harrison)—George (with Dylan Faulkner)
Today's Road (McCartney)—Paul
She's Leaving Home (Lennon/McCartney)—Paul
Dear Prudence (Lennon/McCartney)—John
Because (Lennon/McCartney)—John, Paul, and George

Chapter 19

January 26, 1991—The band was on a media high throughout the first half of 1990. The CD from the MTV *Unplugged* show sat at the top spot on the charts for over two months. The band had not met since the end of October, when they signed some legal forms. Finally, after more than a year hiatus, they were scheduled to meet at CBS Studios to create a plan for their next steps.

This morning would find John, Paul, Ringo, Derek, and George Martin waiting for their lead guitarist. George Harrison had no intention of going to this meeting. He had had enough of the Beatles circus and refused to put himself through the headaches caused by being in this band again. The issue that pushed George over the edge was McCartney's insistence on finishing the third album for CBS while pushing his own songs to be spotlighted on the album. Harrison had dealt with Paul's constant aggression toward his songs and was not about to have another row regarding who's song was better. George was pleased with his output of songs and felt he needed to keep some distance between him and the others.

The meeting was scheduled for 10 a.m. and it was approaching 11:30. They now knew Harrison wasn't coming. This was a dagger to them, and Paul's brazen attitude was replaced with somber guilt. No one in the band wanted the Beatles to succeed and keep going as much as Paul did. This hit him hard and he backpedaled to try to be more agreeable to the others' suggestions. Paul would barely say a word through the meeting. John suggested calling "...Eric to see if he would help with the record." John got on the phone with the legendary guitarist.

"Hey, Eric, how are ya, mate? Look, we've got a problem and we need a guitarist. Can you help us out?" Clapton thought about it for a minute and expressed concerns about angering Harrison. In the end, though, Clapton knew this was a great opportunity, so he gladly accepted. They agreed to meet at the studio in the beginning of March.

March 4, 1991—Three Beatles plus Clapton met at the studio to work on finishing up their third Phase 2 album...this time without their original guitarist for the first time ever. John was interested in finally getting his song "Walking Down" recorded. He ran through the chords to show the others, and Clapton was the first to acknowledge this masterpiece.

"Wow, John! This is incredible!" The chord changes were similar to one of Clapton's best songs, "Let It Rain." They ran through the song a few times and it started to evolve into what some would call the pinnacle of the Beatles' recordings. Lennon played his Gibson acoustic guitar while Clapton played the Fender Stratocaster. The two guitars sounded fabulous together. They looked at each other with surprise at the way their sounds blended so perfectly. Paul, realizing that they could make this even better than it might have been with George, became excited about the new song.

Three hours into this new tune and the band had it ready to be recorded. There was some brief discussion about the arrangement and what to do during the one dramatic pause in the song. Some suggestions were tossed about but nothing was agreed upon. So they proceeded to track it. The band spent the next four hours recording basic tracks and decided to call it a day. They had been in the studio almost twelve hours and were exhausted. The song would have to wait until the next day to be completed.

March 5, 1991—This would be a monumental day for the band, but it didn't start out that way. Paul had been in the studio break room and cut his hand on a lid to a can of chickpeas. He would need to go to the hospital for stitches while the others continued to work on this new/old Lennon composition. The good news about Paul's cut was that it was on his left hand and would not be too detrimental to his playing.

The others started to again record a basic track to the song, but it was difficult without the bass. So they decided to play some rock standards to pass time. After versions of "Blue Suede Shoes," "Rock Around the Clock," "Johnny B. Goode," and "C'mon Everybody," they took a lunch break. At that point, Paul had returned to the studio. He had been given twelve stitches to close up the wound on his hand.

They now set out to complete the recording of John's "Walking Down." They had gone through eight different takes of the basic track, but something was missing from the song. So they took a short break to discuss what they should do about this. They were about to put the song on hold to work on a McCartney tune called "Make Waves" when George Martin walked in to announce that he had two musicians on their way to the studio. One was a celloist and the other a violinist—both classically trained. Martin explained how he heard in his head a violin being played through the verses of "Walking Down" and the cello to be the only instrument heard during the dramatic pause. The violinist was first to record, and it took him six takes to get what the producer had hoped to hear. The violin added depth and a certain mystique to the song. It also sounded a little darker with the added strings, and changed the entire dynamic of the song. They all agreed that was what was missing from the track.

Next, it was the cello player's turn to record. Martin had tracked down and hired the most famous cello player in the city, and possibly the world—Lynn Harrell. Harrell held the International Chair for Cello Studies at the Royal Academy of Music (RAM) in London. The band was not aware of the talent or the fame that followed their hired musician. It took Lynn one attempt to get the perfect take. It was so perfect that even Harrell himself was all smiles. They gathered in the control room to hear the track and it was obvious they had created a masterpiece. The middle dramatic pause that now included the cello playing of maybe the best celloist ever would soon become that of legends. Every critic from rock music to classical praised the song and especially the cello pause that elevated the song to a level they never thought possible.

After the cello recording, Clapton made some attempts at a guitar solo. The solo was to come directly after the cello pause. He grabbed his black Fender Stratocaster ("Blackie") and began recording takes. The first three takes were particularly good, but Eric knew he could do better. He asked if he could keep trying and the band was all for it. After almost thirty minutes, he played a solo that was so incredible that he kept playing longer than the spot on the track dedicated to it. This was an easy fix for Geoff Emerick. He took the music behind it, then copied and pasted to create another whole section to house Clapton's historic solo. Music critics would praise this solo as being even better than his legendary "Crossroads" solo when he was with Cream.

This Lennon composition would not only become the Beatles' best-selling song ever, it would also be copied by other artists more than any song in history—even surpassing "Yesterday" in that category. The song would be described as "...Beatle-rock", "... intensely interesting", "...mix of rock, pop, classical and jazz", "... best Beatles song ever!!" It would be included on their third Phase 2 album.

March 26, 1991—The band had discussed bringing in some other musicians to help finish the record. They had contacted a slew of other celebrity musicians. The list included Elton John, Billy Preston, Stevie Wonder, Bruce Springsteen, Ray Davies, Paul Simon, Stephen Stills, Barry Gibb, Bob Dylan, Leon Russell, Stevie Nicks, David Bowie, Jimmy Page, Jeff Beck, and Michael Jackson. Today there would be Billy Preston, Jimmy Page, Stephen Stills, and Stevie Nicks together in the studio. This day was highlighted by a change of direction inspired by Billy Preston. Paul had wanted to rehearse and record his new song "One Last Time" when Preston (who was warming up and played some chords on the organ) turned all of their heads. The band quickly caught onto what Billy was playing and joined in. Lennon had suggested a middle break and McCartney added an introduction to the beginning of the song. Since Clapton could not attend this session, Jimmy Page took over as the lead guitarist. Page added a Zeppelin-sounding solo into a bridge section that he wrote for the song. Within an hour, the song was finished.

The song they ended up collaborating on was called "Paper Town," which was based on the lyrics Stills had begun to sing during their first run-through of it. There was an excitement in the CBS studios that day as they all enjoyed the spontaneity of the song creation process. It was what they would call "organic" as the song appeared from nowhere and blossomed to completion within minutes. The new song would include elements of each player's style and spotlighted Nicks' mesmerizing vocal that floated around the others to create a visual carnival effect. This was a suggestion from George Martin, and it turned out to be another fabulous idea.

Everyone was amazed at the sound now coming through this new tune. The song went from a warm-up idea on Preston's organ to being recorded in less than eight hours. It was an incredible performance that contained some of the best harmony vocals any of them had ever done. "Paper Town" would go on to become one of the most popular tracks on the album and would rise to No. 1 on the music charts. The writing credits would go to Lennon/McCartney/Preston/Stills/Nicks/Page. It was an amazing list of writers for this one song on the Beatles' new album.

April 30, 1991—Back in Maryland, Marsha Boucha had been in contact with the editors of the *New York Post* and was lambasting them for an inaccurate story on the Beatles. The story had claimed that the Beatles had broken up and that they were trying to keep it hidden from the public. Marsha didn't pull any punches and explained in no uncertain terms that they were still together. She went on to threaten them with a lawsuit if they did not retract the story. Her job had been relatively easy since the band hired her almost eight years ago. She had previously dealt with some smaller publications that would report incorrectly about the band, but this was a big deal.

Marsha got on the phone to Mike Sampson and explained the situation. Mike told her she'd handled it perfectly and that they would indeed bring a lawsuit to the newspaper if they didn't correct their error. Mike sat back after that phone call and smiled at how this had all worked out for both him and Marsha. Neither one of them ever dreamed of working with the most popular act in the world, but here they were. The boys were a delight to work with, he thought, and Derek Taylor gave Mike enough freedom to make his own decisions without guidance. So it had been an amazing job and he felt a sense of gratitude now toward the band. His humble nature had been on display after John's shooting, and while he had thanked the band on several occasions, he still felt the need to thank John on a more personal level. He got up the nerve and dialed the lead singer's number.

"John, hello, it's Mike," he said into the receiver.

"Mr. Mike Sampson?" was John's reply.

"John, you know you thanked me for what I did and I know I thanked you for what you did in return, but...I don't think I really thanked you properly."

"What do ya mean, mate?"

"Well, I'd like to take you and Yoko out for a nice dinner."

"That would be fantastic, Mike! We would love that."

They also spoke about Marsha, and Mike explained what a marvelous job she had been doing. John suggested they invite her and her husband as well.

May 18, 1991—Mike and Trish Sampson arrived at Heathrow Airport on this morning and were scheduled to have dinner the next night with the Lennons. Hank and Marsha Boucha would arrive late that night as their flight had been canceled due to poor weather conditions. This was an exciting time for both Mike and Marsha. Their lives had completely changed after crossing paths with the band. The Sampsons had bought a new house on Long Island and were living in a gated community. His life had again become kind of an anomaly to fans and media. It was a fairy tale type story of rags to riches at the hands of the most famous band in the land.

Even though George Harrison was not currently in the picture with the Beatles, he showed up at the hotel when he heard of the Sampsons being in town. George came with bottles of champagne for Mike and flowers for Trish. They sat for two hours in the hotel lobby laughing at the guitarist's jokes and wit. He truly was the funny one out of them all. Mike had been touched by Harrison making an effort to come see him and asked if he would like to join them for dinner the next evening. George politely declined. Even though he wasn't at odds with Lennon, it would surely have been an uncomfortable situation. Harrison left the hotel and Mike just smiled. He was not only their assistant manager, but he was also their friend and that was pleasing to him.

May 19, 1991—The Sampsons, the Bouchas, and the Lennons gather at the Rose Garden in London for a nice dinner. John had been staying away from alcohol, but he would drink this evening. His marriage to Yoko was still hanging by a thread. The six of them spent the evening drinking, laughing, and eating. Three hours passed, and they were all having too much fun to go home. So they headed to John and Yoko's flat in Soho.

John was in rare form that night. His recent quiet demeanor toward his fans was loosening up. He realized he couldn't pretend to be something other than who he was, no matter the danger. John would often claim that "you can't be born round and die square." He was not an introvert. He enjoyed the interactions with the public. That night, he joked with the wait staff and any customer who approached the famous musician. He not only gave of his time to all he came in contact with, he started handing out cash to people. He tipped the waiter £1,000, and when a little boy came to ask for an autograph, John put the boy on his lap.

"What's yer name, little man?"

"Eddie," replied the four-year-old. Lennon asked more questions until he found out the boy's favorite Beatles song was "Why Don't We Do It in the Road?"

"What, don't you like any of my songs?" Lennon joked as he handed the boy £500. Mike couldn't help but see John in a new light. He was almost angelic. His renewed love for humanity was contagious, and everyone around him would feel this.

They arrived back at the Lennons' flat and continued having drinks. John sauntered over to the white baby grand piano and started playing some chords of a song he had just written. *C...D* *sharp...F...Am...*were the opening chords to this new song. The others gathered around the piano to listen. The Sampsons and the Bouchas were elated that they were witnessing a new song creation right before their eyes. As John decided what chord changes he wanted for the middle, a half-drunk, slightly nervous Trish Sampson spilled her almost full mimosa on top of the beautiful white piano. That didn't faze John and he continued to create the chords to this new tune. As Yoko and Trish cleaned up the mess, with Trish apologizing profusely, Mike asked John if the song had lyrics. "Not yet, my boy. But soon!"

Sampson grabbed a pen and paper and started writing words to this new creation. Within ten minutes, he had almost completely written the lyrics. John changed a few lines but for the most part, they were written right there by Mike Sampson. The lyrics spoke of a young man on hard times who had run into a messenger from the Gods. The messenger then enlightened the young man and changed his life to become the new messenger for the Gods.

John smiled and said, "What a fantastic story!" The story rang true to both the Sampsons and the Bouchas. Their lives had been changed for the better after meeting a "messenger from the Gods." After two hours, it was approaching midnight and the song John had presented to the others was complete. Mike had given the song the title "Chrysalis" to reflect how it was a new beginning for them all. The Sampsons and Bouchas left the Lennon flat at around 2 a.m. It was pure magic that night and the Bouchas were congratulating Mike on the way back to their hotel. They knew he had just made history for himself. He just smiled and slowly shook his head in disbelief.

June 13, 1991—John had been in contact with Bob Dylan and they had worked out a time for Bob to come in and record with the band. Bob was a little insecure about his playing and singing, so he requested that he be the only other musician in the studio that day.

Dylan already had lyrics to a song completed and would only need some help for the music. John and Bob sat down to go over some chords. At first, Dylan didn't like the suggestions and thought it was becoming too much of a rock song. He wanted to stay loyal to his folk roots. John grabbed his acoustic guitar and Dylan nodded in approval. That was what Dylan had wanted from the beginning, but it was John's nature to rock things up a bit.

After almost five hours, the song was ready to be recorded. The new track was titled "Hope" and was archetypal Dylan. He was a lyrical genius and Lennon had always secretly been jealous of that. Ironically, Dylan was always jealous of Lennon's ability to write incredible music to go along with some pretty amazing lyrics, as well. "Hope" would be John's favorite tune from this record. He liked it even more than his own massive hit, "Walking Down."

June 25, 1991—The band was in the studio today with Elton John, Ray Davies, David Bowie, and Jeff Beck. They were to rehearse and record the last track for the album, which was just written by John and Mike Sampson. "Chrysalis" was undeniably a Lennon composition in that it was melodic, and the chord changes were a little dark. McCartney usually wrote the light and fluffy type of songs, while Lennon leaned toward the darker music...the kind with an edge.

The song was highlighted by a dynamic sax solo by Bowie and duo guitar solos by Beck and Clapton. The two guitar legends had fun with the many takes of their solos. They had a long history together and had come full circle to play on this Beatles' track. After seven years, losing a guitarist and piecemealing a band together, the Beatles' third Phase 2 offering was complete. It was Elton who suggested the CD title *Dark Skies*, and the album would go straight to No. 1, where it would stay for seven weeks. John's "Walking Down" topped the charts for an amazing twenty-two weeks. This would also be the last Beatles record of new material to be released while they were all still alive.

Dark Skies *(produced by George Martin)—CBS Records Music (1991)*

Deeper Still (Lennon)
Flight (McCartney)
Thunderstorms (Harrison)
Hidden Gem (McCartney)
Meaningless (Lennon)
Speed Demon (Harrison)
One Last Time (McCartney/Lennon)
Walking Down (Lennon)
Paper Town (Lennon/McCartney/Preston/Stills/Nicks/Page)
Make Waves (McCartney)
Hope (Dylan/Lennon)
Chrysalis (Lennon/Sampson)

Billboard Charts – Week of June 29, 1991

THIS WEEK	LAST WEEK	2 WKS AGO	WEEKS ON CHART	ARTIST LABEL	TITLE	PEAK POSITION
1	NEW ▶		1	THE BEATLES ★ ★ No. 1 ★ ★	WALKING DOWN	1
2	1	1	8	PAULA ABDUL	RUSH RUSH	1
3	2	2	13	COLOR ME BAD	I WANNA SEX YOU UP	2
4	6	12	11	EMF	UNBELIEVABLE	3
5	7	4	6	LUTHER VANDROSS	POWER OF LOVE/LOVE POWER	4
6	4	5	13	R.E.M.	LOSING MY RELIGION	4
7	3	3	15	EXTREME	MORE THAN WORDS	1
8	10	7	10	JESUS JONES	RIGHT HERE, RIGHT NOW	7
9	5	6	11	MICHAEL BOLTON	LOVE IS A WONDERFUL THING	4
10	8	8	13	BLACK BOX	STRIKE IT UP	8
11	7	9	17	ANOTHER BAD CREATION	PLAYGROUND	7
12	15	10	11	CHRYSTAL WATERS	GYPSY WOMAN (SHE'S HOMELESS)	9
13	NEW ▶		1	THE BEATLES	PAPER TOWN	13
14	13	13	15	UB40	HERE I AM (COME AND TAKE ME)	12
15	19	20	9	MICHAEL W. SMITH	PLACE IN THIS WORLD	13
16	18	18	12	LAURA FISCHER	HOW CAN I EASE THE PAIN	14
17	NEW ▶		1	MARC COHN	WALKING IN MEMPHIS	17
18	9	11	13	MARIAH CAREY	I DON'T WANNA CRY	1
19	NEW ▶		1	THE BEATLES	CHRYSALIS	19
20	17	17	8	TARA KEMP	PIECE OF MY HEART	17

Chapter 20

September 13, 1991—The band minus George met at Paul's house in Peasmarsh East Sussex. Derek and George Martin were also present for this band meeting. "Well, boys, we have a few options now and I'll go over some of them...," said Taylor. He then went on to explain the offers they had received. There were offers to be game show hosts; to host a television special; to do another tour; to play the halftime show of the Super Bowl. But the one thing they agreed to do was *The Tonight Show starring Johnny Carson*. They all loved Carson and thought it would be a fun event. Carson was about to retire and wanted the Beatles on his second from last show. It would be the last show he had with guests as his last show would have none.

The band had not invited Clapton to this meeting, but he was definitely their new guitarist. They wanted Eric in the band, but he still carried a lot of weight with his stardom, so they didn't want to be unduly influenced by his desires or suggestions. Besides, they all knew Eric was pleased as punch to be in the Beatles. The show would be recorded in May 1992, so they had some time to get ready.

Paul suggested looking into another tour but both John and Ringo declined. They still had a bad taste in their mouths from the last one. Paul was the only one interested in all of the offers. He would have done them all if he didn't have the others saying "no." This made him think about going solo again. He had an innate need to be in charge, and being in the Beatles had not offered him that opportunity. There were too many egos and ideas of what each thought was right for the band.

"Maybe we should call it quits," McCartney said to no one in particular. Both John and Ringo looked down but didn't say a word. They knew things were going in that direction, but no one wanted to pull the plug just yet. George had quit the band numerous times. Ringo had walked out a few times. Even John had been fed up to the point of leaving. Paul officially broke up the band in 1970 but that was only because he knew John was about to quit. He never wanted the show to end. So for him to suggest a split showed how frustrated he was with their current situation.

The band left the meeting, which had accomplished nothing except to agree on playing *The Tonight Show*. This would be a new low for the band. The three remaining members were all secretly thinking about life without the Beatles. The misery that caused their split in 1970 had resurfaced. John now longed for "Beatle-less" days and was second-guessing being in this band. He left the meeting and called George.

"Hello, George!" he yelled into the phone.

"Well hello, John. How are you and your friends doing?"

John laughed and explained that not much was happening in Harrison's former band. They spent the next twenty minutes catching up on what was going on in each other's lives and discussing everything but music. John still felt a certain connection with George. Harrison's calm demeanor was something that Lennon was drawn to like a bug to a light. After they hung up, John sat and thought about his friend and former bandmate. He felt good knowing how close they had become.

September 16, 1991—This day George would call John. "John, what are you doing now?"

Lennon replied he was just waking up and hanging out with Sean.

"No, that's not what I mean. What are you doing musically? Do you have any plans to record?" George asked.

"Well, I have a few songs, but things aren't going well in Beatle land," John replied.

Harrison continued. "I've got about six or seven songs I'd like to record. Want to put something together, you and I?"

John had not thought about a solo album at all, let alone one with George, and was caught off guard. "I don't know, mate. I guess I'll have to think about that," said John. They hung up and John pondered the idea of recording with his former bandmate on a solo (or semi-solo) project. It made sense to him. Their musical styles were much more similar than that of his and Paul's.

But John's mind wasn't on his former bandmate or even his current world-famous band. He was thinking about Stevie Nicks. They had met in New York before their two shows at Madison Square Garden in 1983. Their paths crossed again in the studio during the recording of "Paper Town." That was when John became interested in the beautiful musician and songwriter. They chatted for almost two hours that day in the studio. John had been thinking about her again now as things were going bad with Yoko. It had been almost six months since they were in the studio together and John phoned Nicks.

"Hello, Ms. Nicks!" he said into the phone, trying to maintain the aura of coolness.

"Well hello, Mr. Lennon!" was her response. Nicks had also been thinking about John and was pleasantly surprised to hear from him. "When are you coming to Los Angeles to take me out for a night on the town?" Those words were like a drug to John and he was now more intrigued by Nicks than before their call.

"I'll check into it and let you know, my sweets!"

Lennon was ecstatic about his conversation with Nicks and started making arrangements to get out to L.A. as soon as possible. Again he would use Harry Nilsson as an excuse to pursue a love interest. He told Yoko they were going to record more music. So two days later, John was on a plane to Los Angeles.

September 18, 1991—Arriving at LAX, John exited the airplane to see airport security escorting two passengers away in handcuffs. He had just caught the tail end of an episode from another flight. The two drunken passengers caused such a ruckus that the plane had to return to the gate. The two then threatened the pilot before being put into submission by police. This rattled Lennon, and he didn't seem to pay much attention to the group of fans that circled him and followed him through the airport. There were some reporters that caught wind of Lennon's arrival and flocked to him for information on his band.

"Have the Beatles broken up?"

"Where are the other Beatles? Especially George?"

"Will you be recording any new music? Or do a tour?"

The musician was barraged with questions but ignored them all and made his way to the waiting limo, which Nicks had arranged for him.

John called Nilsson and explained that he was supposedly in L.A. to work with Harry. He didn't elaborate, but Nilsson knew the plan and wouldn't let on to anything different. John had secured a hotel room, but Stevie had other plans. She had the limo driver bring him right to her mansion in Bell Canyon. When John arrived at her house late that morning, the limo driver carried his luggage while Nicks met him at the door...half naked. She didn't hesitate to pull John up to her bedroom, where the two spent the next three hours making love and talking. It was the first time the two slept together, but Nicks had been thinking about it for some time and couldn't wait any longer when John arrived.

John got up to get something to drink and Stevie offered one of her robes for him to wear. He put it on and pretended to model it for her. This felt so comfortable to him. Things had been so miserable lately with Yoko that his own home didn't even feel like home. This did. He had no reservation with helping himself to whatever was available in her kitchen. She hadn't told John, but she had plans for the two to stay indoors the entire time he was in L.A. As the evening approached, Nicks had her butler make them a nice candlelit dinner. The two spent the night drinking wine, listening to music, and having sex.

September 23, 1991—John did in fact spend five days inside of Nick's mansion and the two ended up writing some songs together. John felt like he was walking on air. He had an extra bounce in his step and a smile permanently etched on his face. About halfway through the flight back to London, John became anxious at the thought of returning to the toxic environment of home. When he arrived at Heathrow, he decided to go right to George's house. It was raining hard. John stood at the door getting drenched. *Knock, knock...ringgggggg...* Olivia Harrison answered the door and warmly greeted John. She didn't question why he was carrying his luggage into their house at Friar Park but sensed there was trouble.

George waltzed down the stairway to see a soaking-wet Lennon drying off in his foyer. "Hello, John!" They shook hands and George invited John into the kitchen for some tea. John let George know that he wasn't sure about going back to his flat in Soho because of how bad things were with Yoko. George offered a room on the third floor for his friend and John took him up on it. It was a perfect room with a full bathroom and a small refrigerator close by. It was like an apartment and felt comfortable to John. He thought about calling Yoko to let her know he was back in town but decided against it. He couldn't face her wrath now and was in too good of a mood thinking about Nicks to deal with that.

October 3, 1991—It had been more than a week since John returned to London and he still had not called his wife.

"Hello?" answered Yoko.

"Hello, how are you?" he replied.

Yoko was reserved and knew their marriage was hanging by threads. She suggested that he come home but he voiced his concerns about how they had been behaving toward each other. Yoko then told John she would set up separate spaces for them both so they would barely cross paths. John wanted an assurance that she wouldn't go back to the verbal bashing that had become commonplace at the Lennon residence. Yoko only assured John that she would stay away from him. He decided to give it a shot and go back home. When he arrived, he was greeted by Sean and the nanny. Yoko made sure that she was not at home when he got there.

October 6, 1991—John had only been home three days when he woke to find Yoko had not come home the previous night. Part of him was upset by this, but another part was secretly happy about it. He wanted nothing more than to be back in Nicks' arms. But when Yoko sauntered in a few hours later arm in arm with Elliot Mintz, John was rattled. It was one thing to know Yoko was cheating on him, but with their friend?! This was unacceptable to John. He quickly grabbed a bag of clothes and called Mal for a ride back to Friar Park. Mal drove John to George's but no one was at home. They drove around for about an hour and then waited for another hour in the driveway. George arrived at about 2 p.m. and invited them in.

George, John, and Mal drank hard for the next four hours and ended up causing such a disturbance that police were called. It wasn't so much the loud music, explained the bobbies, but some not-so-near neighbors heard gunshots. Mal had an affinity for guns and always carried one. He brought it out after a joke about hunting in the jungle and pretended to be shooting at a rhino. He shot right through Harrison's front window...multiple times. The shots rang out so loudly that they could be clearly heard by the nearest neighbor (almost three kilometers away).

Luckily, no charges were brought, and Mal explained it was an accidental discharge. It was also lucky the police didn't investigate because they would have found four bullet holes in George's front window, not just the one shot they claimed had discharged. John sent for his personal items and set out to live with the Harrisons for a short period.

February 28, 1992—The new year started with the Beatles falling off the radar. Their last album had wandered out of the music charts; the radio stations were playing them less and less; the world had kept moving while the Beatles rollercoaster was slowing down. John had moved back in with Yoko into a separate bedroom, but things were still uneasy in the Lennon residence.

The current lineup for the Beatles (Lennon, McCartney, Clapton, and Starr) would be in CBS Studios this morning to work on new material and rehearse for *The Tonight Show*. John had become extremely close to Harrison in the months he spent at Friar Park. So Lennon was starting to have little patience for anything Clapton might do. Eric had been drinking that morning. The pressures of being a "Beatle" were taking its toll on him. John snapped at him, "Come on, ya sod! Stop fumblin' around and let's get going!"

Eric was caught by surprise and didn't expect to be chastised by the feisty Lennon. He had attained a status where no one would question his behavior. But this was the Beatles and no band or act had attained that level of success.

Clapton retreated into a shell and barely spoke over the next few weeks in the studio. There was a new air of tension in the group that John brought due to his closeness with the ex-Beatle. John made his way through the three weeks of rehearsals and immediately flew out to Los Angeles when they were complete. His relationship with Nicks was on a fast track to becoming a full-blown partnership. They had spent the holidays together as Nicks came out to London for a few weeks. She was madly in love with John and would do whatever she could to be with him.

Their time in London was wonderful for them both. They went to art museums and historical sites, and visited many of the different cultural restaurants the city had to offer. Lennon found himself at times taking a back seat to Nicks as she was quite the celebrity herself and had multiple requests for her time. This wasn't something Lennon was familiar with, but he enjoyed it immensely. He would much rather be in the background and see his love interest getting the attention. Their love story was now tabloid fodder and would be discussed daily.

May 22, 1992—The band was in Los Angeles getting ready to record Johnny Carson's second from last episode of *The Tonight Show*. It had again become an impossible environment to be in the Beatles. Even Clapton was now thinking about leaving the group. Most of the tension still stemmed from Lennon's close friendship with Harrison. John either wanted George back in the band or he was planning on leaving. He had not yet told this to the others, but his demeanor screamed his displeasure of the situation.

As they readied themselves for the show, John confronted Eric to say, "You'd better not be too loud out there or try to steal too much of the spotlight. This is still my fucking band!!" Clapton was shocked to hear Lennon berate him like that. Eric had known of the troubles within the band but now felt he was being blamed for those problems. This caused Clapton to shut down to any conversation with the others. His time with the greatest band on earth was coming to an end and he knew it.

About twenty minutes into the ninety-minute show, the Beatles were introduced, to the roar of the crowd. Even though they were not the draw they used to be and were slowly fading from the public eye, this was still an incredible event for every audience member. John, Paul, Eric, and Ringo sat down on chairs besides Carson. He started with the usual questions about how they were doing, what was new, etc. Johnny was not one to ask controversial or confrontational questions, so he stayed away from asking about Harrison. He did, though, ask Clapton how he liked being in the Beatles. Clapton gave a two-word response, which was more telling than anything. "It's great!" The others looked away from the uncomfortable moment and pretended they didn't hear the response. To them, Clapton had just about let out of the bag how bad things were with the band.

After ten minutes of conversation, Carson asked the band if they would play some music. They grabbed their instruments and started into "Follow You," the McCartney Phase 2 gem. After that they played the relatively new "Walking Down." Both songs sounded fabulous and the audience stood with approval. This was another unbelievable spectacle. Clapton with the Beatles would go down as one of the most interesting periods of the band.

After another half hour of talking with Carson, they were asked to perform again. This time they would pull out a couple Phase 1 goodies. The band started into "Can't Buy Me Love" and the crowd went wild. It was another fine performance. Next up was John's immortal "Come Together." This song would contain a pivotal moment for the band. As the middle part of the song approached, John backed off the mic and got behind Clapton, so they were back to back while Eric played the solo. It appeared that John was showing some stage presence and was having fun with their guitarist. As the solo was about to end, John pulled away from the back-to-back position with Clapton, but not before giving the guitarist a hard elbow to the ribs. Eric's knees buckled at the sharp pain he felt from his rib cage. John waltzed back to the mic to finish the song.

The producers and camera people did not see the incident because Lennon was directly behind Clapton when he did it. Clapton glared at Lennon while John finished singing the song. The song ended to another standing ovation from the studio audience.

Backstage after the taping of the show, Clapton got in Lennon's face and shoved the legend. Lennon lashed out at Clapton, telling him things like, "You're useless and overrated," "You're lucky to have even been in this band!" and "Why don't you go find your own fucking band!"

Eric had had enough. *BAM!!!* One punch from Clapton put Lennon on the floor. As blood trickled from John's nose, he started laughing. The range of emotions he had gone through in that short period confused his senses and all he could do was laugh. Clapton left and would never come back to the greatest band in the land.

Chapter 21

January 7, 1993—There had been no Beatles activity newsworthy enough for the general public to take notice. Months had gone by since their last public appearance on *The Tonight Show*. That show had been well received and did not add fuel to the rumor mill fire about the band breaking up. The irony was that they were indeed falling apart right in front of their adoring fans. If one were to analyze the remarks from those last interviews, they would clearly hear signs of them moving on without each other. Clapton was already through with the band. Besides, they weren't boys anymore. They were all in their early fifties now and their priorities had changed. Well, all of them except Paul. He wanted to keep it going and he tried to figure out a way to do that. But after many unsuccessful attempts at a solution, he too gave up.

So, on this cold, winter day in early 1993, Paul held a press conference at CBS Studios. There were almost two dozen reporters and some camera people filming the event (which was not deemed important enough by any network to be televised).

"Hello," Paul started. "This is an unfortunate day for the Beatles as we're calling it quits."

Cameras flashed. People scrambled. The entire room was now in a raised level of awareness at the shock of what was being said. Paul didn't elaborate much about why. He only stated that they were all still friends and wanted to pursue other interests. One reporter got his attention to ask about rumors of the tension between Clapton and Lennon.

"Look, we've all had our battles with each other and then we'd get along famously. It's the nature of bein' in a band. But at the end of the day, we all care about each other and feel like we're family."

Reporters were yelling, "Paul"..."Paul" to try to get his attention for their question, and the musician recognized one.

"Go ahead," he said to the reporter.

"There has been talk about how difficult it can be to work with you in the studio. Is that true?"

McCartney stared the reporter down and before saying what was on his mind, he stood up and walked out. The cameras were still clicking away. The reporters were still shouting out their final questions. But McCartney had vanished.

The news spread like wildfire. Reporters couldn't get their stories to the editors fast enough. The few cameras that were rolling during this news conference now had the best opportunity to advance their operators' careers.

The *CBS Evening News* was the first to break the news. Dan Rather started this evening's broadcast with, "Good evening. Our headline story...the Beatles are history!"

The newscast spent the first ten minutes on the story. Every other news program was doing the same thing. The Beatles had again become front-page news and the news was not good for their fans. Once again, there was a multitude of fans who would now only see film footage of the band and not be able to see them perform live. Just like when they broke up in 1970, this was the issue that most Beatles fans struggled with.

January 8, 1993—John woke to the news of the band breaking up. He was livid. Again, Paul had pulled the plug on the band without letting him know. "What the fuck is wrong with you?" Lennon screamed into the phone at Paul. "This is the kind of shit I don't need in my life. If we had all decided to announce this, it would be different. You're an asshole!" and he hung up the phone.

John remained angry with McCartney for years after this episode. He had dealt in the past with Paul acting like a prima donna and then pulling the plug on the band. This was even worse. The boys had grown into men and he had expected more of the others. He felt that, at this point in their lives, they should act a little more professionally.

When George Harrison heard the news this morning, a smile came to his face. He knew this was coming and was happy to not be a part of the fallout. George grabbed the phone and called Ringo.

"Hey, Ring, how's it going?"

"Hey, George, how are you? Yeah Beatle living is through! None of us knew it but Paul. He decided he'd had enough, I guess."

"Well, we'll have to go write and record some music now that you're out of prison!"

Ringo laughed and suggested they get together soon for some tea. When Clapton heard the news, he was relieved that he didn't have to actually tell the group he was leaving. The band blew up around him and he was pleased to have had the chance to be a part of it for a short time.

January 19, 1993—John had been in contact with the producers from the Howard Stern radio show on WXRK in New York. They wanted to have him on their show, but he was hesitant because of how candid Stern had always been. But one cocktail-fueled afternoon a few days after McCartney announced the breakup, Lennon contacted the show's producers to agree to an interview. Today was the day of that interview.

The station had been advertising for a solid week about the former Beatle's appearance. So when John limped into the radio station, a crowd of over a hundred people were waiting outside the studio. Inside, the studio was abuzz. Most of the station's other disc jockeys were present that morning and wanted to witness the event.

"So, John," Stern began, "thanks for coming on the show."

"You're welcome Howard. It's a pleasure."

"Tell me why Paul was alone at the press conference to announce the Beatles split."

"Well, Howard, we all do ridiculous things once in a while, don't we?" The room erupted in laughter.

"But seriously, why weren't you the one who announced it? It was your band, right?"

"You see, I only heard about it when you did, otherwise I would have been there. That's how bad things had gotten again in this band. No one talked much to each other. It wasn't even arguments. It was just that we were tired of it all. Tired of playing the whole game. When Paul announced it, I had already emotionally left the band."

"Were you pissed at Paul? There was rumor of a phone call you made after the news conference."

"Haha.... Yeah it got me socks in a wad for a day or two. But that's only because the chickenshit did it behind my back again."

John went on to discuss everything in Stern's arsenal of questions. The topics ranged from John's claims of Paul's inability to be a leader to Ringo's sloppy playing to Clapton's false bravado. When Stern asked about Harrison, John went on for some time talking about his friend. He explained how they had gotten closer through all of this and even hinted about doing something with the guitarist in the future. The questioning then turned to John's love life.

"So, rumor has it you're spending time with the beautiful and talented Stevie Nicks. Is that true?"

"What? No, no, no...I'm a married man," Lennon said with a sly smile. Before the interview ended, Stern asked Lennon to do an impromptu song.

"John, would you do our audience a favor and play them a song? I have to hear 'Cold Turkey' because that's my favorite song ever."

"Sure, Howie! We'll play ya a song. Not sure if I'll remember that un, though." They handed him an acoustic guitar. "Hmmmm...let me see...it's in *A*, I know that. Okay, the change is *C* to *G*." He went into a rough but outstanding version of his hit single and ended to a huge round of applause from the studio employees. "There ya go!" John said as he handed the guitar back.

Stern again thanked Lennon and ended the interview with, "You're better off without those other bums!"

That night, John met up with Stevie Nicks, who had flown in to meet her lover. The two had gotten so close, in fact, that John had kept a full set of personal belongings at her home in Bell Canyon, California. They decided to go out for a nice dinner at The Four Seasons restaurant in midtown Manhattan. The restaurant goers were in awe to see John Lennon back in New York and out to dinner with Stevie Nicks. This was an establishment used to celebrities, but Lennon was on another stratosphere compared to the others.

As they sat for dinner, they were approached multiple times by curious onlookers until Lennon pulled aside the manager to ask if they could be left alone. The two were left alone the rest of the evening but not before pictures of them were taken and then released on television and in the newspapers. Tabloids read "Lennon Cheating on Yoko?" and "Ex-Beatle Has Affair!" This news bothered John slightly, but he had been thinking of leaving Yoko for some time. He figured the news would eventually get out, so this was not much of an issue to him.

January 20, 1993—Marsha Boucha had been frantically trying to do damage control after Paul announced the band's split. But now she had to try to quench the fire of this latest report. She found the hotel where John was staying and phoned him.

"Hello," said the soft voice.

"Yes, I'm looking for John Lennon," was Marsha's reply.

"Oh, hold on..." Nicks handed the phone to John.

"John, I was about to ask if the rumors were true but no need to ask now," she said in the kindest way possible.

"Well, Marsh, can you calm down the wolves until I decide it's time to let on about it?" he said, referring to his imminent split with Yoko. She said she would do her best but also explained this was a difficult situation to keep under wraps. "Oh come on, sweets, I know you can handle this. You're a tiger and they're all lambs!"

John thought about the news breaking of his romance and did not want Yoko to hear it from someone else. So he phoned her in London.

"Hello there," he said. "Look, I'm done. Can't do it anymore. We had a good run and now it's time to do our own thing. Good luck to ya!" and he hung up. Yoko had been trying to get in a word during that twenty-second conversation and could not. She hung up, stunned. She knew their relationship was going sour and was still having an affair with Elliot Mintz, but she didn't want her marriage to the famous musician to end. Deep inside, she knew John was her meal ticket and was more than hesitant to lose that perk.

Back in the New York hotel, John threw a pillow into the air in celebratory fashion. Nicks had not expected to witness this and threw her arms around John. She kissed him hard and long. They spent the next four hours naked and drinking.

"John, I can't believe you just dumped Yoko!" said a startled Nicks.

"Yeah, well...she had it coming!" was his comical retort.

Now there was nothing stopping the two from sharing their lives together...and that's exactly what they did. John called for all of his personal items to be removed from his Soho flat and moved into the Nicks' mansion in Bell Canyon, California. John loved the new freedom of not having to sneak around with Stevie. They now found themselves walking public streets, hand in hand; being seen at events and gatherings; and even doing some interviews together. The two were now headline news, and both musical icons were too much in love to care.

February 14, 1993—John received a call this evening from Mike Sampson, who had been in contact with Harry Nilsson's camp. Lennon's friend and fellow musician had suffered a heart attack. John knew that Harry's ticker had always been suspect as he was born with congenital heart problems. But this hit John hard. He phoned Harry's wife, Una, but she was at her husband's side and would not take any calls. John got a ride over to the hospital where Harry was in the Intensive Care Unit. He stayed overnight in the hospital waiting room. The next morning, Una came into the waiting room to tell John (and some other friends and family) that Harry was recovering. While his heart was still weak, he was going to make it.

John was tired and wanted to see Harry before he left, but the doctor said no visitors. As he was walking out of the hospital, he noticed a limo pulling up to the front door. Out of it came Ringo. The drummer and Nilsson had also become extremely close. The two former Beatles embraced when they saw each other. There was no bad blood between the two, even if Lennon wasn't interested in playing with Ringo going forward.

April 25, 1993—The music scene had changed quite a bit, and the style of music being played on the radio was called "Grunge" music. Bands like Nirvana, Alice in Chains, Pearl Jam, Stone Temple Pilots, and Soundgarden inundated the airwaves. It was a different kind of rock and not typically the kind of music the former Fabs would write. But John was drawn to this music and especially loved the lyrical genius of Kurt Cobain. John could hear

Beatles harmonies and melodies in the dark, crunchy rock Cobain was writing. So he decided to call up Nirvana's leader.

"Hi, Kurt, it's John Lennon." Cobain sat in quiet for a moment.

"Who the fuck is this?" he said.

"It's Lennon, really. I've heard 'Teen Spirit' and loved that fuckin' song."

"Really? That's fucking cool," replied Cobain.

As the two talked, John could tell Kurt was high on heroin. That made John hesitate because of his experiences with the drug. He wanted no part of that scene anymore. But he could sense a warm and caring individual underneath the heroin mask.

"Kurt, I think you and I should write a tune or two."

Cobain was shocked but excited. He had indeed been influenced by the Beatles and jumped at the chance to write with their former leader. They decided to meet at John's place in May to see if they could put something together.

May 6, 1993—Kurt Cobain arrived at the Nicks/Lennon estate that morning to share tea and conversation with the two hosts. John and Kurt went off into the small home studio to write. They both grabbed pens and paper. These two musicians were both extremely lyric-minded in the same vein as Bob Dylan...considered masters at the craft of writing good lyrics. They talked about some current events and at first wanted to write about the new U.S./Russia arms reduction treaty. Then the conversation turned toward the mass murder in Waco, Texas, that had happened a few months prior. They felt it was too soon after the tragedy to write about it.

So, they decided on a theme that would bring people with different ideas and beliefs together through music—in particular, this song: "*Wanted only to lead, with it hung to my knees...,*" started Kurt. John came back with, "*It's what I have to give, to help us all live..."* The two spent well over an hour crafting the lyrics to their new song and had not yet picked up an instrument. They both so enjoyed the lyrical aspect that the music was most definitely secondary.

When they finally did pick up their guitars, Kurt's sound was so raw and rough that it made Lennon light up. John grabbed his guitar and tweaked it to get as dirty a sound as possible. Within minutes, they had come up with a brilliant combination of chords. They started in *E* and went to *B flat*, then *A* to *C*. It was loud and distorted and sounded every bit like the Seattle sound with Beatles influences.

Their new song, "Dreams," would be recorded and released in less than two weeks. The name they chose for this project was "The Fools." The band for the recording session included John and Kurt on guitars and vocals, Robert DeLeo (from Stone Temple Pilots) on bass/vocals, and Dave Grohl (from Nirvana) on drums/vocals. The song was everything Lennon had wanted from the start. It went immediately to Number 1 on the charts, where it stayed for seven weeks.

July 13, 1993—The Fools played their only song live in front of a television studio audience for the *Today Show* on NBC. Katie Couric was the host and introduced the band without an interview. Neither Lennon nor Cobain was interested in that. They only agreed to do the show to promote their song. They played a rousing extended version of "Dreams" with John and Kurt sharing vocals and Grohl smashing the drums to pieces. It was the most powerful performance of Lennon's career and the media loved it. There were offers for ridiculous amounts of money to do a whole album and tour. But The Fools' longevity would last exactly one song.

January 5, 1994—There had been little news in the Beatles' camp heading into 1994. John and Yoko had finalized their divorce in October of '93. Lennon had moved in full-time with Nicks and as far as he knew, Yoko was living with Mintz. The other ex-Beatles (including Clapton) were keeping a low profile and had not been in the public eye for months.

John received a call this morning from Una Nilsson. Harry was in bad shape again. So, John rushed over to see his friend. When he arrived, Harry was in his bed and looked horrible. He hadn't shaved in weeks; he had put on weight; he looked as pale as could be; and his medication made him slur while speaking.

"Hey, Harry Houdini!" said Lennon as he made his way into the bedroom where Harry lay. They spent more than two hours together before Harry became too tired to converse anymore. John left with a tear in his eye. He somehow knew it would be the last time he would see his friend.

January 15, 1994—John happened to be watching the morning news when he heard his friend, Harry Nilsson, had died of heart failure. This rocked him to the core, and he grabbed onto a kitchen counter to steady himself. The next days into weeks were especially difficult for John and Ringo, who were the closest ex-Beatles to Harry. John phoned George to tell him the news. Harrison had not heard and was shocked, as well.

"Hey, George, I think we should do a song for him. I've got the beginning of something we can make really good."

"You know what, John? I'd really like that!" was Harrison's response. They agreed to meet in a few weeks to see if they could complete the song.

January 31, 1994—George arrived in Los Angeles to get together with John at his residence at the Nicks' mansion. John's song had gone from a working title of "Midnight" to the now more appropriate "Harry." The lyrics were only partially complete, and the music only had a chorus. Harrison came in and immediately added key changes and a middle bridge and even created a beautiful ending. The music they were writing soared into a crescendo before coming back down to a quiet, dramatic end. The end part of the song would go on to be analyzed by music critics for years to come. It was praised as "complex," "beautiful," "dramatic," and "melancholy." It was a fitting end to a sad song. The two former Beatles completed the song in less than an hour and John realized just how easy it was to write with George. They decided to record it as soon as possible to keep Nilsson's name on the minds of music fans.

February 4, 1994—It was John who suggested bringing Ringo in to play drums for this new track. Harrison always enjoyed having Starr behind the kit when recording. But John's reason was different—he knew how close Starr and Nilsson were and felt Ringo needed to be part of this song. It was a thoughtful move and Ringo was elated to be included. There was a somber mood floating throughout the studio that day while recording this sad song. It took twelve takes for the three ex-Beatles and Klaus Voorman to complete the basic track to "Harry."

When "Harry" had been mixed and mastered, the song sounded nothing like a Beatles tune—it was unusual in the sense that Harry would have written it that way. John had done a vocal scat part during the middle break—the kind of ad lib vocal Harry had become famous for. Ringo closed his eyes and put down his best effort possible. It was indeed hailed as "one of Ringo's finest performances" by the press.

When the song was released a week later under a band name of Watch Tower, not many knew the artists behind the name. Even so, the song went to No. 1 on the charts. By the time the general public caught on that this was a Lennon/Harrison composition, the song had attained a new level of success. It was being played constantly on radio stations around the world. "Harry" remained at the No. 1 spot for eight weeks and fans were chomping at the bit to see them form a proper band.

Chapter 22

March 21, 1994—John and Stevie were having some morning tea when John suggested an idea that had been bouncing around in his head. "Hey Steph," he said to her, "want to do an album together?"

Nicks' eyes lit up at the thought. She had been writing songs in hopes of recording with her musician lover. "John, I think that would be incredible!"

He smiled at her and finished his tea. His mind was racing around ideas for an album. But he also spent some time contemplating his life and how happy he had been with Nicks. In Yoko, John had found a pillar of strength that was missing from his life. He could lean hard on her. With Nicks, however, he found a soft and vulnerable side that mirrored his own psyche. He now craved to be the "man" to support Stevie when she was down in the dumps. He was the one who wanted to be the pillar of strength for her. This was now his life's pleasure—to make her feel safe and loved. He never thought he could love like this. He truly adored her and would watch her every move that morning.

His mind went back to the shooting. His leg and hip still caused him daily pain. The limp he acquired from that incident was sometimes hardly noticeable. He was in amazement at how his life had become the kind of life many people dream about. It was a life he had always hoped for but never thought was possible. He couldn't be happier.

John picked up an acoustic guitar that was hanging on the wall next to the couch in their living room. Out came the chords *F...E minor...G...C....* "*Me and you are wandering through this special life we have...*" Stevie sat on the ottoman across from the couch John was on, facing him. Their faces were less than two feet apart as she added to the verse... *"You and me can always see the way to move ahead..."* The two sat face to face, with Nicks occasionally giving Lennon a kiss on the cheek between verses. John continued to create a chorus on the guitar and felt this may have been the happiest writing session he'd ever had.

He had never felt this much of a sense of gratitude and happiness while writing music. He was writing a song with someone he was in love with and that had never happened in his fifty-three years on the planet. John had come up with chords for the chorus and Stevie jumped right in with lyrics... *"Falling..."* John jumped in immediately to echo her powerful cry. *"Falling,"* he sang, and she finished with *"Falling for you..."* In less than two hours, the new song "Me and You" was complete. It was the perfect song to start their new project together.

March 30, 1994—Lennon and Nicks were in Studio 6 at CBS Studios to record "Me and You." John had recruited Geoff Emerick for his services again. Emerick had not been working for some time. He had been dealing with some health issues that took him away from engineering. His last project was the Beatles release "Dark Skies" in 1991. He was excited about these recording sessions and knew Lennon would be on his best behavior around his girlfriend. John had decided to have unknown studio musicians as their band, to keep the sessions drama-free. Besides, he didn't want any attention to be taken away from Nicks. He had discovered that not only did she have an angelic voice, she was a fine musician and could write as well as he could.

The song did not change much during the recording session. The studio musicians weren't comfortable enough with the music icon to suggest any changes to it. After eleven takes, the song was ready to be mixed. John had been in a wonderful mood all day and it showed as he constantly joked with the musicians in the band. He even paid for catering to be brought in for them all. John was proud of Stevie and how she handled herself like the rock star she was. He loved that she was getting more attention (well, almost more) than himself. There was a sense of freedom he felt to not have to be the leader. He had always felt that extra pressure in the Beatles. Now, with Nicks by his side, everything was 50-50. That's why they chose the name of their project to be simply Lennon/Nicks.

John, Stevie, Geoff Emerick, and the band spent the next three months recording the new album. John would later state in an interview that these months were some of the best of his life. He was over the moon in love and his lover was now his writing partner. Things couldn't get better. He had also just found out that his two sons (Julian, now thirty, and Sean, nineteen) were coming to California to spend a month with him. The boys had met Nicks once briefly and were looking forward to spending time with their dad and his girlfriend.

Sean was a little uncomfortable at first and wouldn't come around to Stevie for a few days. The four would spend the next month exploring California. They went to the beach, to the mountains, to Hollywood, and they even took a drive down to San Diego for a few days. Julian and Sean were getting the "dad" out of their famous father and it felt good to them both. They would both later treasure this month as the best time they had spent with their father.

September 26, 1994—The album, simply titled *Lennon/Nicks* by the band Lennon/Nicks was released on this day. The other ex-Beatles had not been heard from in some time. Rumor had it that Paul was in the studio recording a solo album. George had been working on some side projects. Ringo would take an odd sit-in job as drummer here and there but had no regular band or gig. Clapton had put his own band together and released an album. His band was currently on tour in the U.S.

The only news from Beatle World was that CBS Studios was pressuring Derek Taylor to get the band back together to record their fourth (and final) album of the contract they signed. All Taylor could do was assure the record executives that he would pass along their message. He had no control in getting them back together. Frankly, he thought that was an impossible task. Too many things needed to be fixed in order for them to think about the possibility of reuniting.

Lennon/Nicks *(produced by John Lennon & Stevie Nicks)—CBS Records Music (1994). All tracks written by Lennon/Nicks except Track 12, written by Willie Nelson.*

Me and You
Finding Today
You Won't Get Away
I Feel You
Waiting in Peace(s)
Low Tide
Hopeful Ground
Red Star
Can You See It?
Only Once
Lone Wolf (No More)
Crazy

October 17, 1994—The Lennon/Nicks album entered the music charts at No. 21 and would go as high as No. 3. It went on to become platinum with three songs getting substantial airplay—"Me and

You," "Hopeful Ground," and "Crazy." Their version of the Willie Nelson hit featured only Nicks and Lennon, both on acoustic guitar. In the studio, they had sung this literally inches from each other's face. This feeling translated through the song and many felt it was their most powerful and dynamic effort on the record.

"Me and You" rose to No. 5 on the charts while "Crazy" held the top spot for two weeks. They had numerous offers to play live, for interviews, and even to host talk shows. But one offer caught their attention. It was to do a television series of their own—à la Sonny and Cher. The two agreed that it would be fun to do a show with musicians, comedians, artists and entertainers of all sorts. So they decided to pursue this offer.

February 22, 1995—After months of negotiating with the National Broadcast Corporation in America, John and Stevie (and their attorneys) agreed to do ten episodes of their new show. The show would be called *Open Doors* in reference to John's invitation for all entertainers to submit work when Apple Studios first opened in 1969. This show would have two main writers—Steve Martin and Martin Short. The two Martins were not only hilariously funny comedians, they were both musicians, as well. So having them as writers almost guaranteed the show's success. The two comedians would also make cameo appearances in the show. Their scheduled guests included all the ex-Beatles (and Eric Clapton), Mick Jagger, Keith Richards, Richard Pryor, Robin Williams, Eddie Murphy, Stevie Wonder, Paul Simon, Brian Wilson, John Sebastian, Pete Townsend, Lyndsey Buckingham, Mick Fleetwood, David Bowie, Billy Preston, John Cleese, Eric Idle, Rodney Dangerfield, and Elton John.

May 13, 1995—The first episode of *Open Doors* would start off with the two Martins on stage saying there had been a problem and the show was canceled. The studio audience burst into laughter, but both comedians pushed their hands downward to try to quell the laughter.

"No, seriously," continued Steve Martin, "John has a bad case of diarrhea!" Now, the audience laughed hysterically.

"Wait, wait," said Short. "I hear the toilet flushing! Maybe...."

Just then a curtain rose to see John and Stevie sitting on stools starting into the hit song "Me and You" from their debut album. The two sung beautifully and the studio audience was electric with excitement at the idea of seeing a variety show with these two musical icons. The guests on their first show included George Harrison, Paul Simon, and Rodney Dangerfield. After the opening monologue of current-event jokes, the two hosts invited Harrison onto the set. They gathered in stage props designed to look like the living room at their mansion in Bell Canyon. The lighting was low with lava lamps scattered about, and candles and incense burning. George sat on the couch in between John and Stevie, drinking tea and chatting with the couple. They talked about everything from the Beatles to solo work to George's interest in fast cars.

They asked George to play a few songs. So George grabbed an acoustic guitar and went into "Dark Horse." After a brilliant version of that, he dove right into "Solitude" (the Beatles' Phase 2 hit written by George and John). John immediately requested a guitar to play along. The three sat on the studio couch singing this haunting Harrison/Lennon composition. After the song ended, they talked for a few more minutes before George asked to have a friend come out to help play a few more songs. The audience applauded as George introduced Paul Simon.

Simon came out with a guitar in hand. The four exchanged pleasantries and chatted for a few minutes. Then the two musical guests of the show put capos on their guitars and went into the Beatles' song "Here Comes the Sun." It was another standout performance. George told John and Stevie that they had one more song they would like to do. With that, they went into "Homeward Bound," the Simon and Garfunkel hit tune. It was a mesmerizing performance and again the crowd went berserk.

They talked a bit more and then introduced Rodney Dangerfield. The standup comedian was at his best that night. Before the show, Rodney had busted open Lennon's dressing room door. John was first shocked and then laughed at seeing the larger-than-life comedian. Rodney slammed the door shut behind him and pulled out the biggest joint Lennon had ever seen. The two sat backstage smoking pot, telling stories, and just having fun. Dangerfield would go on to say that "....John Lennon is one of the finest people I've ever met...and it doesn't hurt that he has the hottest girlfriend in rock!" Dangerfield walked out to a thunderous round of applause and immediately ripped into the Beatles. "Those Beatles, I tell ya. Are they still around? I tell ya, you guys are relics! They're so old they put in a new wing at the Natural History Museum dedicated to you guys! They re-released your first album on cave rocks!" Rodney's act was a highlight of the night.

John and Stevie then performed "Crazy" to end the show. The two would end every show with this song. As Lennon and Nicks were about to say their goodnights to the viewing audience, they were interrupted by two older people who had wandered onto the stage. The two elderly people looked lost and confused. John slowly approached them and asked if he could help them find their way. Just as the couple started to respond, they both threw off their wigs and costumes. It was Sonny and Cher! They were making a cameo appearance in support of the new show. The audience again roared with laughter. It was a funny and ironic twist to end the night. The first episode of the show would be an enormous success. The media loved the writing, the guests, and the performances. It was written that the new show "...had roots that go all the way back to Lennon's introduction to America—*The Ed Sullivan Show*."

It was the highest rated television program that evening and would continue to garner the highest ratings as the season progressed.

June 17, 1995—*Open Doors* had been a huge television sensation and millions of fans would schedule their Saturday nights around this entertaining show. This week's show would include Paul McCartney, Stevie Wonder, a band called Kings X, and Richard Pryor. Paul and John opened the show on acoustic guitars playing a slower, more soulful version of the Beatles' "I'll Be Back." It was an amazing performance to one of their most incredible songs. The lights were low, and the burning candles provided most of the illumination. This would be one of the best episodes of the season with John and Paul sharing stories from the past and playing some of the Beatles' all-time classics. The two former bandmates and Nicks spent thirty minutes telling stories and discussing world events. Next, Stevie Wonder came out and played "Isn't She Lovely?" before doing "Ebony and Ivory" with McCartney.

After a short commercial break, Lennon and Nicks introduced Kings X. Lennon had heard the band when Mike Sampson sent over a copy of their album *Faith, Love, Hope*. Lennon was shocked to hear such hard rock with harmonies that were definitely influenced by his own work. The song "It's Love" was so Beatle-esque that the middle vocal break could have easily ended up in a Beatles' song. Paul and John had heard the tune multiple times and wanted to join the band and sing the harmonies. So, Kings X performed an outstanding version of "It's Love" with John and Paul helping on the vocal harmonies. It was a brilliant performance and one that would become a season highlight.

After Richard Pryor tore up the audience with his outrageously hilarious set, Kings X came back out to play "Black the Sky" from their new *Dogman* album. It was a hard rock song and Lennon loved it. His rock roots and the sometimes dark edge of his writing were in alignment with this heavy sound. The song would become one of Lennon's all-time favorites. To again end the show, John and Stevie started into "Crazy." Suddenly, Lennon stopped and waved McCartney over to join them. Lennon, Nicks, and McCartney sat on stools with John playing the only guitar. The three did a wonderful version of the Willie Nelson song, and Episode 6 was in the books.

July 15, 1995—The final episode of *Open Doors* had Lyndsey Buckingham, Mick Fleetwood, and Robin Williams as the show's guests. After the usual opening song (this night it would be "Hopeful Ground"), the two hosts invited Buckingham and Fleetwood out to join them. The former bandmates of Nicks while in Fleetwood Mac came out to a big round of applause. Buckingham stumbled onto his spot on the couch, while almost knocking John over in the process. He was rip-roaring drunk and his love for Nicks was still haunting him. Every question John asked was answered with a slurred, nasty response from Buckingham. He was mad at Lennon for what he believed was stealing his woman.

After the show backstage, Buckingham approached Lennon and grabbed him by the shirt. Lennon pushed Buckingham hard and the drunken musician fell easily to the floor. John had pity on his girlfriend's ex beau, so he had security help him back to his dressing room. Stevie apologized to John for Buckingham's behavior, but Lennon was already laughing about it. He wouldn't be the first or last man to try to gain the attention of one of the prettiest women in the entertainment industry.

July 22, 1995—The NBC executives were scrambling, trying to find a way to secure Lennon and Nicks to at least one more season of the top-ranked television show of the summer. But the two musician lovers were not up for it. There was too much work involved with a television series, and while the first season was fun, it was borderline beginning to feel like a job (which they both abhorred). *Open Doors* would go down in history as one of the all-time memorable television shows and would be that of legends because it was such a success that only lasted one season.

John phoned George this day to ask about writing more songs. They had previously released the song "Harry" and had gone over a few others together. John was now on board with doing a full album with George, so the two former Mop Tops agreed to meet at John's place in California in two weeks. Both were excited at the thought of creating a record together for the first time.

John walked into the kitchen, where Stevie had been reading a book at the table with her feet propped up on a chair, drinking tea. "Hey, Steph, George is coming to stay with us for a few weeks. We're gonna do an album."

"That's great news, John!" She felt the desire to ask if she could participate but held back to allow her lover to proceed how he wished.

"Do you think you could sing on a track or two?" John asked.

"Well of course, darling! It would be my pleasure," she said. She was thrilled with her relationship with John. He treated her like gold and was so protective of her that she thought it was a sweet way for him to show his love. She felt this had been the perfect relationship for her. The two were so like-minded that it would only take a quick look from one to know what the other was thinking. Stevie thought of asking him to marry her. She had been married once, but only briefly. Instead, she threw her arms around him, kissed him, and said, "I love you, baby." She sat back, stared, and smiled at him while he made phone calls to other musicians to assist in the record.

Chapter 23

August 3, 1995—George was again in Los Angeles and John sent a limo to retrieve him. The two would spend the next week writing songs. They found themselves writing just like John and Paul did in the early days—face to face. George would come up with a guitar part and John would follow it with some lyrics. They started to develop their own writing style. It was like musical brainstorming. One would throw out an idea and the other would either go with it or go in a different direction. They were volleying up ideas and having a blast doing it. The two felt limitless in this environment. Ideas weren't laughed or scowled at—it was either a good idea and was included or it was not, and they moved on. Between alternating rounds of tea and liquor, they were truly having fun with this project.

"George, I've been thinking of who we should have record with us and I think we should go with just two others—a drummer and bassist," John suggested. He didn't want celebrity musicians and they both agreed that they didn't want Paul or Ringo involved. The goal was to not have this record be associated in any way with the Beatles. They both wanted to put space between their current writing and the historical content of their amazing catalog of music.

So, the two musicians they both agreed on were Carol Kaye on bass and Alan White on drums. Kaye had a long history as a session musician with jazz roots. Her playing was found on some of the most popular songs of the '60s and they loved her style. She had worked on many hit records including many of the Beach Boys' hits. White had played on both Lennon and Harrison solo albums. He was currently the drummer for Yes, but they were hoping they could borrow him for a month or two. After a few phone calls, the two musicians were on board to help John and George record this album.

August 24, 1995—John, George, Carol, and Alan were in EMI Studios to begin recording their new album. The four first played some rock standards like "Heartbreak Hotel" and "Mustang Sally" to warm up. Instantly, they felt a bond in their playing. Each musician was talented enough to be solo artists, but when playing together, the sum became better than the individual parts. Alan White was the drummer they needed. His solid drumming, intricate drum rolls and fills, and easygoing personality were a perfect fit for this group. Kaye may have been the most talented musician either had ever played with. She could play multiple instruments, learned songs almost instantaneously, was the only one that knew how to read music, and was a joy to have in the studio.

George started into a steady-paced distorted guitar chord... driving the beat for White to catch on. White and Kaye both jumped in and after Lennon finally got past a guitar cord problem, he also joined in. They spent the next twenty minutes on this jam but were having trouble coming up with changes. The guitars and bass were droning on an *E* chord and they couldn't think of anything suitable for a key change.

Just then, Stevie Nicks walked into the studio. She had shown up unexpectedly and had been in the control room talking with Geoff Emerick. "Hello, everyone!" she said. "John, why not jump from that *E* to a *C*, then to a *G*."

The band looked at each other and George said, "Sure. Let's give it a try."

They went through the new change and Stevie said, "That sounded nice, but I think you should hit a *D* chord for two counts before going back to the *E*." They all smiled at how she was becoming a producer. Her ideas were openly welcomed, and the band was amazed at her ability to see the entire picture of how the song could sound. She would be given producing credits for the entire album.

John started singing some words and Stevie joined in. Within twenty minutes, they had completed the lyrics to their new song, "In the Wind." Even though John and George had written eight songs that were ready to be recorded, they all wanted to record this new tune immediately. So they spent the rest of the day and into evening working on it. At about 7 p.m., they all gathered in the control room to hear how it sounded. It was amazing as Geoff Emerick came up with more studio tricks to make the song similar to the Wall of Sound, made famous by Phil Spector. It was full and rich and had layer upon layer of overdubbed instruments. Emerick had asked them all to do separate takes of their original and to make that take slightly different from the previous one. With that, Emerick had created a background to the song that felt like an entire orchestra had recorded it.

November 30, 1995—After more than three months in the studio, the new album by the Inner Demons was to be released. Nicks would offer up a title for the album, *Greedy Seeds*. There was much fanfare for this album and band. Marsha Boucha had gotten involved and marketed the album and band all over the country. So, by the time the record was released, there was a back order of more than 250,000 copies. It was the most anticipated album of the decade. Radio stations had heard the pre-release song, "In the Wind," and were eagerly anticipating the entire record release. The album entered the charts at No. 6 and would go up to No. 1, where it would remain for three weeks. The songs "In the Wind" and "Assist" would go to No. 1 while two others ("Free Spirit" and "Get It Right") cracked the Top 20.

Greedy Seeds *by the Inner Demons (produced by Stevie Nicks)—EMI Music (1995). All songs written by (Harrison/Lennon) except where noted.*

In the Wind (Harrison/Lennon/Nicks)
Greed
Kingdom Come
Get It Right
Imagination
Assist
My Scene
Final Frame
Something or Nothing
Apple Garden
Free Spirit

December 13, 1995—At the same time John and George were recording their album, Paul was also recording one. He had invited other celebrity musicians to join him and had Billy Joel, Michael Jackson, Stevie Wonder, and Neil Diamond help with it. He also asked Ringo to play drums on two tracks. Paul's solo album, *Crosshairs*, would be released on this day and would also enter the charts in the Top 10 at No. 8. Even though there wasn't a lot of friction between John and Paul, they made a point of purposely not asking the other for help on their solo projects. As of now, it was a friendly competition and both ex-Beatles were still at the top of their game.

Paul called John to say hello and the two talked briefly as John was about to go to the doctor to have his hip/leg examined. "Hey, congrats on your album going to No. 1," said Paul into the phone.

"Yeah, well it looks like you've done okay yourself," was Lennon's reply.

They talked about things other than music when John finally

said he had to leave. Paul hung up and had a strange feeling that he wouldn't speak to John for some time after that call...and he was right.

January 15, 1998—More than two years had passed, and the Beatles were becoming a distant memory. John and Stevie were still madly in love. Paul had done a six-month tour of America in '96. George and Ringo were barely heard from, and Clapton was still touring the world. John heard news that Paul's wife, Linda, was battling breast cancer. That was a shock to John, and he called Paul that morning.

"How's it going, mate?" asked Lennon. The two talked for almost an hour and McCartney thanked his former writing partner for the call. Before the call ended, John threw out a suggestion. "Ya know, I'm wonderin' what would happen if we got back together for one big final show..." Paul had always hoped to resurrect the Beatles and this proposition made him smile.

April 17, 1998—Linda McCartney died this morning after a long battle with breast cancer. She was the love of Paul's life and the other Beatles knew this. It was John who came to aid Paul in his time of need. Lennon had adored Linda and respected that she never took advantage of her connection with the band. Lennon and McCartney would not be seen without each other for the next week and a half. Stevie watched Paul's kids while the small funeral was held. Paul was wrecked by the loss of his longtime wife and friend. He could barely function, so John became Paul's mouthpiece. It was a completely different side of Lennon that no one had seen. He was now the protector and coordinator.

Paul would go weeks without coming out of his house. He was shattered. But this was one of the wonderful things about the Beatles—it didn't matter how much tension there was between them, if one of them needed help, the others were there to assist. The next few weeks would find all of the former Beatles spending time with McCartney to help him get through this.

December 31, 1999—It was New Year's Eve, 1999, and the new millennium was about to begin. That evening began with appetizers and cocktails at the Harrison residence. At about 10 p.m., an intruder had broken into Friar Park. In the struggle, George had been stabbed with a knife in the chest. Olivia was able to knock the attacker off of her husband with a fire poker she grabbed from the fireplace. By the time the police arrived, George had subdued the knife-wielding maniac. For the extremely private ex-Beatle, this event had rocked him. He was already certain he would die at the hands of a crazed fan and this seemed to be confirmation of that premonition. Again, the other three Beatles came to George's aid. Ringo stayed at Friar Park for a few days. John flew in from California to spend a week with George. Paul found himself coming and going for the next couple of weeks. The band always came together during rough times and this was definitely one of them.

January 7, 2000—John, Ringo, George, and Olivia were sitting around the table that morning, drinking tea and eating biscuits. It was George who brought up doing a live performance. "What do you think about putting the Fabs back together for one show?"

John smiled as this was something he had recently suggested to Paul. Ringo lit up. "Yeah, that sounds like a wonderful idea, George!" said Ringo. John agreed that it would be fun. They were all approaching sixty years old and there was no time like the present to do something so grandiose.

When Paul arrived that morning, George mentioned his idea to McCartney. Surprisingly, Paul was hesitant. He was worried about them doing a show while not having fulfilled their record contract with CBS. It was his way to try to get them back into the recording studio. But Paul could not pass the opportunity to play with his former bandmates one more time. They discussed options and the one they thought would be best was to do a daytime show similar to that of Woodstock, but with only one band.

January 12, 2000—Mike Sampson had been on the phone after receiving many suggestions of places for the band to play this ultimate concert. After hours of phone calls, the area that seemed like a good possibility for the show was in Livingston, California, on a six hundred-acre vineyard. The owner of the vineyard, Tom Marino, had been guaranteed $100,000 or 1% of the door, whichever was the higher amount of the two. When all was said and done, Marino would be pulling from the percentage of the door as that number would be much higher than the $100,000 guarantee.

The idea of the concert would be for the band to play four sets of music, broken up by three hour-long breaks. The band would start at 2 p.m. and play into the night, most likely ending around 9 p.m. or so. The concert would be held on May 20, 2000. Marsha Boucha got on the phone to start promoting the show.

Mike Sampson had come up with an idea that changed the way businesses work together. He had struck a deal with American Airlines to offer free roundtrip airline tickets to anyone who had a verified ticket to the Beatles' final concert. The promoters of the show, the vendors, and even the airports chipped in to cover the airline expense. This kind of cooperation between so many unrelated companies would become a template for business deals in the future. This new method of doing business was being referred to as doing it "Sampson Style."

May 17, 2000—The four Beatles plus Nicky Hopkins began rehearsing for the show at George's Friar Park residence. They would rehearse here for the next two months in preparation for the concert.

During that time, four new songs were written with the makings of another four that were started, but not completed. Because they all knew this would be their last concert, spirits were high. Everyone wanted to make this final show a pleasant experience for all involved. They would pull pranks on each other and generally stir up as much trouble as possible with Lennon being the pranking leader. He reversed George's guitar cords one morning and Harrison spent an hour trying to figure out why his guitar wasn't working. The whole time, the other three tried to contain their laughter at the sight of their guitarist struggling with his equipment.

Today they would put the set list for the final show together. With four hours of music to play, they were delighted to be able to play so much of their catalog. They decided not to play any solo songs for this show. It would be all Beatles songs. Derek Taylor had put together a comprehensive list of all their songs and handed a copy to each band member. Then, each one took turns suggesting a song to play. If any of the others disagreed with a choice, they would simply choose another. Once a song was chosen, it was crossed off the list. This process took a good part of the afternoon and when it was completed, the set list was mind-numbing. It was difficult to imagine any one band having so many incredible songs to choose from.

The band rehearsed about six songs before they decided to call it quits. They had spent almost ten hours at George's house and were ready to be done for the day. The set list was ready, and the band was starting to prepare for this final chapter of their historic run at the top of the music industry. There was an enormous amount of excitement throughout the rehearsals for this show. Hopkins was like a kid in a candy store knowing the magnitude of this event.

Paul had been extremely happy during these months. He had gained a new excitement that was also accompanied by a calming sense of closure. Even George felt some excitement. As much as he dreaded the dangers involved in public appearances, he seemed at ease about this concert. He, too, appreciated the finality of doing one last show.

The show would end up going down as one of the greatest music festivals since Woodstock in 1969. The ideas of playing on a farm (or vineyard, in this case) and playing for hours were stolen directly from the historic '69 event. But there would only be one band—one immensely popular band. And that band would play all day long. Beatles fan or not, this was a musical event to behold.

May 20, 2000—The band plus Hopkins readied themselves to play the event. It was the morning of the show and the band met with the vineyard owner, Tom Marino, to thank him and have a quick chat. "Hey, you guys better not mess up my property!" said Marino, half-joking. He knew it would be trashed by the end and didn't mind. He would be getting paid enough money to buy another vineyard if he wanted. They spent an hour with the winemaker and had some good laughs with him. Marino was later quoted as saying that he was "...pleasantly surprised at how welcoming they were. We sat in a circle and made fun of each other's outfits. They were good guys!"

The crowd had been building up for the past week. People had arrived on the vineyard and set up tents to camp out. The ticket cost was $100 apiece and from the early morning turnout, it appeared Marsha Boucha did a fine job of marketing this event. More than 850,000 people were on hand that morning and by the time the show started at 2 p.m. (2:10, to be exact), there were more than 1.5 million people on the vineyard.

The sponsors of the event (Coca-Cola, Microsoft, and Verizon Wireless) had together helped create a more interactive concert. Having an idea of the size of the crowd, they had decided to build four different stages surrounding the entire area. The band would play one one-hour set on each stage. This way the audience would have turns at seeing the larger than life band's final show upfront and personal.

A line of celebrities waited to greet the band backstage, but they decided it was better to wait until after the show was over to hang out. The stage was set. The band was ready. The final concert from the greatest band in music history was about to begin.

Chapter 24

May 20, 2000, 2:10 p.m.—At 2:10 on this hot Saturday afternoon in northern California, John Lennon (now fifty-nine years old), Paul McCartney (fifty-seven), George Harrison (fifty-seven), and Ringo Starr (fifty-nine) walked onto a stage for the very last time. It was a hot day and temperatures were expected to reach ninety-three degrees. The crowd was hysterical at the sight of the four musicians from Liverpool. This was a Beatles fan's dream—to see them play live, especially for a four-hour show.

The opening chords to "Magical Mystery Tour" sent the audience into a euphoric frenzy. The massive P.A. speakers surrounded the crowd and large video screens were positioned around the vineyard for all to see the band up close. The energy the band felt from playing in front of the largest audience ever assembled for a musical event caused a little nervousness for them. They played their first song at a breakneck pace.

There was a minor problem during "Tour." The stage monitors were not on and the band could not hear themselves singing. They had been so used to playing live and running into unexpected issues that they blazed right through this without missing a beat. The volume of the screams from such an enormous amount of people almost startled the band.

After "Tour" ended, Paul stepped to the microphone. "Hello, everyone!" He paused for the cheers to slow. "We are happy to be here with you all today and want you to know how much we appreciate the support you've given to us over all these years."

Ringo had told the others before the show that he had come

up with a new intro to "Come Together," which was next on the set list. Instead of the whole band coming in at the same time like it does on the album, Ringo played the opening beat to the song alone for four measures. *Tickita tickita, boo ba da boo, ba ba da ba ba da ba ba da ba....* The others pretended as if they had rehearsed this many times and joined in after his four-measure intro. In reality, John, Paul, and George were blown away by what Ringo had just done. It had dramatically changed the familiar song and gave it a new life. This was the first of many surprises that night. Reporters wrote about Ringo's intro to "Come Together" and it would go down as his signature drumbeat.

With each song the band played, the crowd became wilder at the amazing spectacle. This all-day event was being broadcast live on the cable music channels MTV and VH1, and even the news channel CNN was constantly showing footage of the concert.

May 20, 2000, 3:17 p.m.—The last notes of "I Am the Walrus" rang out with Hopkins playing the studio sounds from the record. The audience was stunned at how much the song sounded like the original recording. It would be one of the highlights of the concert. With the first set complete, the band went back to relax for a short time. As they entered the backstage area, they noticed a group of men wearing dark suits surrounding a figure they couldn't at first recognize. As they got closer, they saw it was Ronald Reagan, the former U.S. president. Reagan walked over to the band and shook all their hands.

"Great show so far! Truly amazing! And I won't hold it against you that you turned down my offer to play at the White House!" The room erupted in laughter. The band indeed had turned down an offer to play for the president in 1985, as they were filming a movie. Besides, Lennon was not a Republican and his political views were vastly different from the former president's views.

They all had laughs with Reagan and found him to be the most charming and personable politician they had ever met.

The band relaxed, ate some snacks, and had some cocktails. They were getting along famously and even Harrison was joking with McCartney. "I'm not so sure 'Getting Better' was actually getting better!" Paul laughed and put George in a loose headlock. The two would finally put their differences aside and become close friends in their "retirement."

May 20, 2000, 4:24 p.m.—The band readied themselves to head to the East Stage for the second set. But prior to that, George again produced a large joint for the band to smoke. They did and happily strode onto the East Stage, high as kites. The opening guitar riff to "I Feel Fine" sent the crowd into a frenzy. That guitar lick was so powerful and the band played it twice as long to let it sink in. It was an amazing addition to an already incredible song.

John had always thought the song "Why Don't We Do It in the Road?" was more suited for his raunchy style of vocals. So this day he talked Paul into letting him sing it. Lennon's version of "Why Don't We Do It in the Road?" became a legendary performance that cable music channels would play for years. Paul got a kick out of watching Lennon scream this tune at the tops of his lungs.

After a fabulous version of "It Won't Be Long," a song they had never played live, the band put down the electric guitars for some acoustic songs. The stage was set up now similar to that of the MTV *Unplugged* show. There were candles lit as the band sat on stools in a semicircle. John started the opening chords to "This Boy" and the audience roared in approval. The three-part harmony in this song was brilliantly sung by John, Paul, and George. It was again proof that no other group in pop history could sing together as well as the Beatles. Paul ended the acoustic portion singing "Yesterday" alone on his guitar. This song brought tears to many of the paying customers in attendance. It was beautifully performed, and the standing ovation lasted almost four full minutes.

This set would cause the band some minor problems as there were songs they had never played live before. During "Don't Bother Me," George forgot the second verse and mumbled some nonsensical words through it, which caused John and Paul to laugh hysterically. Then on "Not a Second Time," John started the song by singing the second verse first and then stopped the band altogether. This caused the audience to laugh as John cracked a joke about his memory going. But they pulled it all together for the last song of the set. George approached the microphone and thanked everyone for coming.

He then talked about how Eric Clapton inspired this next song with his sweet tooth. The song started with Ringo and Nicky, mostly. When George sang the first line of "Savoy Truffle," *"Cream tangerine....and montelimar...,"* accompanied by his screaming guitar lick, the audience again roared in approval. It was one of the best performances of the concert and, so far, the band was as tight as they had ever been.

May 20, 2000, 5:32 p.m.—The band ended Set 2 with a bang and everyone in attendance could feel the excitement building as the show went on. This time backstage John went off to be alone with Stevie. The two found an empty trailer and locked themselves inside for an hour. "Hey, Steph, do you want to come up and sing one with us?" John asked.

"No, no....I couldn't do that. This is your last hurrah and I would never take that away from you." Stevie adored him for offering but she was sincere about it. Even though California was her home and the crowd would have loved to hear her perform, she knew it was not the right thing to do.

The others were entertaining the swarms of celebrities and

politicians who refused to wait until after the show to hang with the band. George found himself in a conversation with Dennis Hopper. "Man, you don't know how fucking crazy it is that you guys are playing on a vineyard owned by a guy who supports the KKK!" Hopper ranted. George had heard the rumblings of this rumor and had Derek do some research before the show. It turned out Marino's brother-in-law had been involved in some Klan activity some twenty-five years ago and it was still being attributed to the winemaker. Harrison approached Marino about it. Tom laughed when George brought it up and said it was complete bullshit.

"Yeah, that rumor has been following me around for some time now!" he stated calmly. "The fact is, and no one seems to mention this, I was married to a black woman for twelve years. So, how on earth can I be racist?" They both laughed at that claim.

May 20, 2000, 6:38 PM—The band walked out onto the South Stage to the most raucous ovation of the day. It appeared the craziest (and most drunk) fans were in this section of the vineyard. *"Can't buy me love, love...,"* started Paul, as the band went right into this Phase I treasure. The four band members could see immediately that the crowd by this stage was different. They were louder, wilder, and definitely more aggressive than the previous two crowds they played in front of that day. This put George on high alert, and he tried to keep away from the front of the stage as much as possible. But his vocal responsibility kept pushing him upfront to where the microphone stood. This was the kind of thing he dreaded. The security team that was hired had been positioned all around the perimeter of the stage, so that eased the band for the time being.

After "Can't Buy Me Love," they went right into "I'll Cry Instead." This song would be the most dramatically altered tune they would play. John had the idea of playing it much slower, much harder (with louder and more distorted guitars), and with Ringo playing only on the drum toms to mimic a Native American beat. The sound of the song was what would be called "groove-oriented rock." The entire audience now swayed in unison to this raw, funky sound...a sound very unlike the Beatles, yet very much the Beatles. This performance would be talked about and analyzed for years to come. It would be written about in many articles that covered the show and appear endlessly on MTV. Within the span of two songs in this third set, the Beatles had brought this audience to the edge of insanity.

During an added middle break, which included a guitar solo on "Another Girl," two teenaged girls broke through the security and raced onto the stage. Before Paul knew it, the girls threw their arms around him, almost toppling him to the floor. John and Ringo laughed, but George was visibly shaken that anyone got past security. Then toward the end of "Nowhere Man," as John and Paul were repeating the ending phrase "...*Making all his nowhere plans for nobody*...," someone had thrown a lit joint directly in between the two singers. John noticed it and smiled while finishing up the song. He then picked it up, took a puff, and handed it to McCartney, who turned away from the audience before taking his own drag. The South Stage would prove to have the wildest fans they had ever played before (with the Detroit show as an exception).

Before the final song of the set ("Helter Skelter"), Paul asked John if he thought they should play this tune because the crowd had become so wild. John said, "Fuck it! Let's play it extra raunchy!" With that, the opening guitar and Paul's vocal began the song. "*When I get to the bottom I go back to the top of the slide...*" The song introduction was all that was needed to tip the scales of the frenzied crowd. It had become all-out chaos in the first thirty feet from the stage. People were bashing into each other, pieces of sod were being ripped out and thrown, and a fight broke out right up front. The whole time, Lennon stood there smiling at the outbreak. It was pleasing to him that they had stirred the audience into this music-induced chaos. George was panic-stricken at this sight. He felt vulnerable to an attack and almost walked off the stage. The security team was quick to calm things down, but not before the stage was littered with sod and dirt, even getting into the electronics of the band's equipment.

May 20, 2000, 7:41 p.m.—This time in the backstage area, there was an immediate crisis. George refused to go back on stage for the fourth and final set. Paul was more understanding than usual. "You know, I'm half thinkin' of not going back myself," Paul stated. "I saw that fight out front and then when security got involved, I knew it left a gap in our protection. So I was just as worried as you, mate."

The band talked with Mike Sampson about having security sweep the area around the West Stage. They were all a little rattled by the rowdiness of the South Stage crowd. Sampson spoke with the head of security and demanded they pull all of their personnel to the West Stage or the band would not perform the final set.

Since the band had to wait to hear the results of the security sweep and also for the team to get in place, they relaxed for what would be their last break between sets ever. They were all aware of this and decided to open up a couple bottles of Dom Perignon champagne. John started the champagne toast with the band.

"It's been a long road, hasn't it, men? We've had plenty of ups and downs, but there ain't three other chaps I would have rather done this with. Well, you too, Nick, of course. Cheers!!"

They clinked glasses and sipped the expensive drink. George Martin had also showed up for the final show and enjoyed the celebratory toast with the band. There sat John and Stevie, Paul and his new girlfriend Heather Mills, George and Olivia, Ringo and Barbara, Nicky Hopkins, George Martin, Derek Taylor, Mike

Sampson, and Mal Evans enjoying what would be one of the last times they were all together. A somewhat sentimental Paul had let in a few photographers to capture the scene backstage. The cameras clicked as they sat and talked for almost an hour. They had almost forgotten they had one more set to play.

The security sweep found the area around the West Stage to be much more relaxed than the South Stage. Their security team now surrounded the stage and in front they were two deep. There was an impenetrable wall in front of the band. They were shown pictures of the area and some footage from the television crews. They agreed it was safe enough to proceed.

The champagne had taken its effect on George and he stood up to announce it was time to go "rock this fucking place!" The others stood, did one final toast, and headed toward the stage. Before getting there, Ringo stopped them all.

"Look, men, I have to say that you are all my brothers and I'll love you forever." With that, they all embraced each other as one and jumped upon the stage.

May 20, 2000, 9:03 p.m.—The West Stage looked like a military zone with so much protection surrounding them. The crowd was not quite as hysterical as the South had been, but were still beyond enthusiastic and erupted at the sight of these legends. From the opening notes of "Sgt. Pepper" and throughout every song in the fourth set, the band energy was at max power. They joked with each other and with the crowd in between and even during songs.

Ringo's drumming especially in this last set was a thing to behold. His heavy beats and near-perfect timing almost stole the show from the other three outstanding musicians. That night, he once and for all proved to the critics that his drumming was what made this band go from good to fantastic.

By the time the band got to the last song of the set ("Tomorrow Never Knows"), they were exhausted. It had been a long day and they had not played live for this many hours since playing at the Star Club in Hamburg. The final notes of Lennon's Phase I classic were met with a collective scream from the audience that had now swelled to a record 1.7 million people. It appeared the vineyard owner (Tom Marino) was in line to be a millionaire after this concert. His measly 1% of the proceeds from the door came to a whopping $1.7 million.

May 20, 2000, 10:08 p.m.—The band again went backstage to relax for a few minutes and have another drink. They were prepared to play an encore and knew the fans would want one. So after letting the crowd chant "One more!! One more!!" and "Beatles! Beatles! Beatles!" for almost ten minutes, they appeared on the West Stage...for the very last time anywhere as the Beatles.

The encore from this final concert would go down as the most spectacular section of music ever played live. They would start the encore with two songs from *Pepper* and had decided to play the entire Side Two of *Abbey Road* (excluding "Here Comes the Sun"). The viewing audience around the world was in for a real treat.

They started the encore with the last two songs on *Sgt. Pepper*—the "Pepper (Reprise)" right into "A Day in the Life." This was another song that the band had never played live, and the performance was more mesmerizing than the album version. The audience seemed to be in a trance as the song created musical images in their heads. It was hard to imagine 1.7 million people being so quiet that a dropped pin could be heard, but that's exactly what happened on this immortal Lennon composition.

The final piano chord of "A Day in the Life" rang out on Hopkins' keys—the chord that lasts almost a minute on the record. While still holding that chord with his left hand, Hopkins started right into the piano intro of "You Never Give Me Your Money." It was the most sublime song transition of the show and the crowd screamed in delight. The last songs the Beatles were to play live were considered to be their best performances ever.

The entirety of Side Two from *Abbey Road* was in the books except for one special gem. They decided to do an a cappella version of "Because" to close the show. Some would think this song was too mellow and slow for an ending to such an unbelievable concert, but the intricate harmonies made the hairs on necks stand straight up. It turned out to be the perfect song to end the show with, and when it ended with all four Beatles up front, they performed one final "Beatles bow" before exiting a stage for the last time together.

May 20, 2000, 10:56 p.m.—The band that constantly made history was now history. It was a joyous moment for them. They had just successfully completed the final show of their illustrious careers to a record-breaking audience. They were excited at what the future would bring, but Paul was a bit more reserved. He wanted to enjoy the last moments together as a band but was saddened that it was over. The Beatles meant everything to Paul. He had spent his entire adult life dedicated to the product and now that it was over, he felt lost.

Set list: *Final Concert, Marino Vineyard (May 20, 2000) with the singer listed next to each song:*

Set 1—(North Stage)
Magical Mystery Tour—Paul with John
Come Together—John
Get Back—Paul
Given to Fly—John

Boys—Ringo
Think for Yourself—George
Getting Better—Paul
Rain—John
Lady Madonna—Paul
Glass Onion—John
I Want to Tell You—George
The Night Before—Paul
No Reply—John
Hey Bulldog—John
Fool on the Hill—Paul
Solitude—George with John
Day Tripper—John
Follow You—Paul
Hard Day's Night—John
Penny Lane—Paul
I Am the Walrus—John

Set 2—(East Stage)

I Feel Fine—John
Why Don't We Do It in the Road?—John
Most Days—George and John
Please, Please Me—John and Paul
Fixing a Hole—Paul
Ticket to Ride—John
Old Brown Shoe—George
It Won't Be Long—John

Acoustic portion

This Boy—John, Paul and George
Blackbird—Paul
Dear Prudence—John
Final Words—George

I'll Follow the Sun—Paul
Julia—John
Yesterday—Paul

Acoustic portion ends

I've Got a Feeling—Paul
Don't Bother Me—George
Dr. Robert—John
Seeds of Love—Paul
Not a Second Time—John
Savoy Truffle—George

Set 3—(South Stage)

Can't Buy Me Love—Paul
I'll Cry Instead—John
I Me Mine—George
You Can't Do That—John
Today's Road—Paul
I'll Be Back—John
Good Morning, Good Morning—John
Another Girl—Paul
Dig a Pony—John
Intuition—John
You Won't See Me—Paul
Being for the Benefit of Mr. Kite—John
For You Blue—George
Chrysalis—John
Wait—John
Hey Jude—Paul
And Your Bird Can Sing—John
Nowhere Man—John
Helter Skelter—Paul

Set 4—(West Stage)

Sgt. Pepper's Lonely Heart's Club Band—Paul

With A Little Help from My Friends—Ringo

Don't Let Me Down—John

Hold Me Tight—Paul

I Want to Hold Your Hand—John

The Word—John

If I Needed Someone—George

Happiness is a Warm Gun—John

Taxman—George

I'm Only Sleeping—John

Yellow Submarine—Ringo

Walking Down—John

Something—George

Sexy Sadie—John

She Said, She Said—John

Oh Darling—Paul

Mr. Sampson—Paul with John

Strawberry Fields Forever—John

Paperback Writer—Paul

Tomorrow Never Knows—John

Encore

Sgt. Pepper's Lonely Heart's Club Band (Reprise)—Paul

A Day in the Life—John

You Never Give Me Your Money—Paul

Sun King/Mean Mr. Mustard/Polythene Pam—John

She Came in Through the Bathroom Window—Paul

Golden Slumbers/Carry That Weight/The End—Paul

Because—John, Paul, and George (a capella)

Chapter 25

November 29, 2001—George Harrison died this day after a short battle with lung cancer. He was fifty-eight years old and passed at Paul's property in Beverly Hills, California. The other three ex-Beatles were in attendance at the funeral.

John seemed to take his death the hardest. He had recently become so close with Harrison that Lennon felt like he'd lost a brother. The usually stoic Lennon bawled like a baby at the funeral, and all Stevie could do was put her arms around him. Ringo was equally distraught. He had joined the band in 1962 and had been close to George the entire time in the Beatles and afterwards. The first Beatle to die caused the realization that the band would never create more music or play live again. This was a tough pill to swallow for every Beatles fan.

November 29, 2002—Exactly one year after Harrison's death, Clapton and Lennon put together a concert dedicated to their fallen friend. "The Concert for George" would be a huge success and make millions of dollars through the CD and DVD sales. They played all Harrison songs and the stars came out by the dozens to offer their services. The band of famous musicians would play a spectacular three-hour show, highlighting some of George's best works of his career.

December 14, 2004—Another Beatles album was released by CBS Records. This record contained previously released Phase 2 songs in their early stages and demos.

Phase II *(produced by George Martin)—CBS Records Music (2004)*

Walking Down—Take 1 (Lennon)
Walking Down—Take 7 (Lennon)
Given to Fly—(demo) (Lennon)
Given to Fly—Take 6 (Lennon)
Given to Fly—(alternate version) (Lennon)
Deeper—Take 4 (McCartney)
Free as a Bird—Takes 1 & 2 (Lennon/McCartney)
Free as a Bird—(alternate version) (Lennon/McCartney)
Solitude—(demo) (Harrison/Lennon)
Real Love—(alternate version) (Lennon)
Seeds of Love—Take 2 (McCartney)
Mr. Sampson—(initial run-through) (McCartney)
Most Days—Take 5 (Harrison/Lennon)
Today's Road (demo) (McCartney)
Follow You—(alternate version) (McCartney/Lennon)
Wallows of Sound—Take 1 (Harrison)
One Last Time—Takes 6 & 7 (McCartney/Lennon)
Existential—Take 1 (Lennon/McCartney/Wilson)
Walking Down—(demo) (Lennon)
Walking Down—Take 3 (Lennon)
Paper Town—Take 6 (Lennon/McCartney/Preston/Stills/Nicks/
Page)
Paper Town—(alternate version of Jimmy Page solo) (Lennon/
McCartney/Preston/Stills/Nicks/Page)

December 19, 2006—CBS Records again decided to release more Beatles material. This time it was of songs they had started to record but never released. This album, titled *Once More*, would be the band's last album ever released and would have the Beatles topping the musical charts also for the very last time. *Once More* would go to No. 1 on the music charts and stay there for nine weeks. The song "Aim High" (a Lennon/McCartney composition) would also top the charts and stay at No. 1 for 14 weeks. It was an amazing way to put a cherry on top of their already legendary careers.

Once More *(produced by George Martin)—CBS Records Music (2006)*

    Sell it Elsewhere—(Lennon)
    Mod Man—(McCartney)
    Bad Intent—(Harrison/Starkey)
    Aim High—(Lennon/McCartney)
    It's True—(McCartney)
    Dark Skies—(Lennon)
    10.9—(Lennon)
    Just Makin' It—(Harrison)

March 31, 2008—John had not been feeling well and assumed he had a cold. His throat was sore, and it seemed like he had caught a bug of some sort. Stevie took John to the doctor, where he was examined by the attending physician. Not much was said at first and then they took scans and x-rays of John's throat.

"Mr. Lennon," the physician started, "I regret to tell you that you have acquired throat cancer."

Stevie burst into tears and became almost hysterical. She had never loved someone like she loved the former Beatle and had felt their time was only beginning. The doctor prescribed radiation and chemotherapy, but John just shook his head. He had witnessed others go through cancer treatment and wanted no part of that.

April 1, 2008—Stevie woke this morning and could not contain herself at the idea she had thought about all night. "John, will you marry me?" Lennon had indeed thought about tying the knot with his beautiful girlfriend.

"Well, of course, my dear! I would love to be Mr. Nicks!" he joked as they hugged long and hard.

April 26, 2008—The small exclusive wedding of John Lennon and Stevie Nicks was held at their mansion in Bell Canyon, California. Only three dozen people were there including Paul and Ringo and their wives. George Martin, Nicky Hopkins, Derek Taylor, Mike Sampson, Marsha Boucha, and Mal Evans were also in attendance. The backyard where the ceremony took place was decorated as if they were still in the psychedelic '60s. Tie-dye and floral paintings surrounded the yard. John had requested all '50s and early '60s music to be played at the wedding. These were the songs that had influenced John and the other Beatles.

After the ceremony, Paul approached John. They talked and walked to the back of the property to have some alone time. Paul sensed John was dying and the thought of that almost wrecked him inside.

"John, I want to say that I appreciate your leadership of the band over all those years. I don't think we could have done it without your guidance. It means a lot to me that you've been my only writing partner. I'm proud of that."

John had not said a word but had listened intently. With what he believed was now limited time left to live, Lennon would live in the moment and be present for every conversation. He was moved by McCartney's sentiment and put his arm around his former writing partner. Paul continued, "Where we grew up was one of the toughest towns I've ever been to...and that came with a certain toughness that we all carry. I guess what I'm tryin' to say is...I

know it's not something us Liverpudlians are supposed to do...
show our emotions...but...you've always been my best mate and I
just wanted to say that I love you."

With that, Lennon came to tears. He knew this wasn't a topic
ever discussed by them. It was so obvious, yet so obscured by the
fast-paced lives they led. No one ever thought to tell the other they
loved them. It just wasn't on the radar.

Everyone in attendance watched intently as the two former
Beatles stood alone in the back of the yard, hugging for more than
a minute. It appeared they would never let go. John backed up for
a minute to say, "You know, I never told you that either, but I love
you too, mate. You made me a better musician and person over the
years, and I have always respected you more than you knew."

This brought McCartney to tears as they spent what would
be their last moments together. Stevie wanted to come over and
make sure that her husband was okay, but she thought better of
it. She knew the history between the two songwriters and felt they
needed that alone time.

October 9, 2008—John Lennon died on his 68th birthday at
his home in Bell Canyon, California, with his wife, Stevie Len-
non-Nicks, and his two sons (Julian, now forty-five, and Sean, on
this his thirty-third birthday) by his side. Stevie thought it fitting
that he had died on his and Sean's birthday. He had always known
the number nine was special to him and now he died on that same
day. The person who went through life like a tornado had now
succumbed to this dreadful disease.

News spread quickly about John's death, and the world
mourned the loss of another music icon. The most famous band in
history would not be forgotten. Their music would be considered
as important as Bach and Beethoven. No band would ever achieve
the heights of stardom that the Beatles had. It had been the most

amazing run for any band or entertainer, and their timeless music would influence generations to come. *"And in the end....the love you take is equal to the love...you make."*

If only...

About the Author

ED DAVID loves sports and music. He has been a musician for over 45 years and worked in IT most of his career. His music is available on iTunes, Amazon, Spotify, and YouTube. Born and raised in a suburb of Detroit, MI, he now lives in Raleigh, NC. His current job is to raise three children.

Ed had worked as a programmer for a publishing company in Michigan. In 2001, he came up with an idea to put all of their publications on a small electronic device to save money (and trees.) So he created a proposal to pitch his idea to the publishing company, which rejected it. If he would have pursued this idea, he could have invented the Kindle. He learned from that experience to take action on his creative ideas.

When the pandemic hit America in March 2020, Ed decided to put his spare time to good use by writing a novel. His gift of storytelling came from telling his children stories before bedtime. If you ask his kids now, they'll probably roll their eyes, but they truly did enjoy these stories growing up. He's not losing hair, he's growing skin. *The Beatles Come Together Again* is his debut novel.

Learn more at www.eddavidauthor.com.